THE PREDATOR

Book **Three** of the
Munro Family Series

CHRIS TAYLOR

LCT Productions Pty Ltd
18364 Kamilaroi Highway, Narrabri NSW 2390

ISBN. 978-1-925119-03-9

The Predator is a work of fiction. Names, characters, places, brands, media and incidents either are the product of the author's imagination or are used fictitiously. Any resemblance to actual persons, living or dead, events, or locales, is entirely coincidental.

Published in the United States of America

DEDICATION

This book is dedicated to
Detective Superintendent Michael Kilfoyle
and as always to my husband Linden,
who has made it all possible.

ACKNOWLEDGMENTS

As usual, no book comes into being without a lot of help and support from my friends and family. A world of thanks must go to my friend and fellow author Angela Bissell, critique partner extraordinaire, and a girl who loves the Munro family as much as I do.

To Detective Superintendent Michael Kilfoyle, thank you for your enthusiasm and willingness to answer my endless questions. It was wonderful working with you.

To my editor, Pat Thomas, the best editor in the world. To Damon Za for my fantastic cover. My sister, Nicole Guihot, for her excellent editorial comments and suggestions. Nic, I hope you like the final result.

To the fantastic writer organizations such as Romance Writers of Australia, Romance Writers of America and Romance Writers of New Zealand for all the help, support and encouragement they offer new and aspiring writers, including me.

To my readers, thank you for your support and love for the Munro family. Your encouragement and enjoyment make this journey all worthwhile.

And lastly, to my friends and family, especially my husband and children. Thank you for putting up with late dinners and even later conversations as I've emerged day after day from the sometimes scary but always enthralling world I've created on my computer.

Everything comes at a price…

When Australian Federal Agent Brandon Munro walked out on his wife without a word of explanation, he had no idea the price would be so high.

Alex Cavanaugh's world fell apart the night Brandon told her their marriage was over. Devastated over his refusal to tell her why and unwilling to keep him by her side out of a sense of duty, she conceals from him her pregnancy.

Four years later, Alex has rebuilt her life and has found success as an Australian Federal Agent working in a High Tech Operations team hunting online predators. In conjunction with INTERPOL and the FBI, her team is in pursuit of a pedophile ring that has its origins in Belgium.

When Brandon transfers to her Unit, Alex's life is thrown into turmoil once again. Pitted together in a race to uncover a global ring of online pedophiles, Alex and Brandon are forced to confront each other…and their past.

As the pressure mounts, Brandon struggles to deal with his guilt and reconnect with the woman he still loves. Alex lives on tenterhooks that Brandon may discover he has a son. Despite her sound reasons for keeping the child a secret, she fears he will never forgive her once he discovers the extent of her treachery.

While both struggle with guilt and forgiveness and the resurgence of love, they are unaware of the predator who stalks close to home…

THE
PREDATOR

PROLOGUE

The tomb-like darkness of the room was broken only by the light from his brightly backlit computer screen. The murmur of late-night traffic passing outside the window of his cramped ground-floor unit, squeezed between two similarly ugly apartment blocks in the northern Sydney suburb of Hornsby, barely registered.

He opened his email and waited for new messages to appear. He chewed on his fingernail, nervous, excited, hopeful... And there it was. The email he'd been waiting for. His heart stuttered with excitement.

He moved the mouse and clicked on the file, his hand quivering. The thirty-inch screen filled with images. He clicked on a photo and his breathing quickened. His belly clenched at the beauty of the image before him. She was everything he dreamed of: dark curly hair, alabaster skin, guileless eyes. Young...oh, so young. Just how he liked them. She stared up at him from the tangled sheets, a dazed expression on her innocent, heart-shaped face.

His gaze drifted over the screen, across her unblemished, near-naked body that showed the first blush of womanhood. The picture was flawless, taken by a high quality camera and a photographer with a talent for lighting. The international supplier had boasted to him that the pictures were perfect and worth every dollar he'd paid for them. He was relieved and ecstatic the supplier hadn't exaggerated. He'd be able to offer them to his own clients for a hefty price. The profit would be more than pleasing.

But first, he'd take his own pleasure...

His body tightened and he embraced the surge of desire that rushed through him, tingling his nerve endings. The tip of his cock twitched and hardened, pressing against the fabric of his clothes. He released his hold on the mouse and jerked at his zipper.

Her dark, vulnerable eyes held him captive.

Succumbing to his body's urgent demands, he started to stroke.

CHAPTER 1

Federal Agent Alexandra Cavanaugh stared at the flickering computer screen in front of her and willed a message to appear. She'd been logged in since the beginning of her shift, nearly twelve hours earlier, and hadn't received a single bite.

Her gaze drifted around the squad room of the Australian Federal Police High Tech Operations Team and paused at the window on the far side. It was only a little after five-thirty, but night was already closing in. Darkness came earlier this time of year.

Alex had always loved winter, although a typical Sydney winter was so much milder than one in her native hometown of Canberra. A slight smile tugged at her lips. There was no chance she'd see snow in Sydney's beachside suburb of Bondi.

With a sigh, she turned back to the screen and picked up the pen that lay idle beside her keyboard. Today she'd logged in as Casey, a thirteen-year-old schoolgirl who liked to visit chat rooms during her free periods and in the hours after school, before her mother called her to dinner.

But no one had been interested today. At least, not during Alex's shift. The night shift usually fared better. There was something about the anonymity of darkness that brought out the worst in the men they hunted.

"Got any plans for the weekend?"

Alex glanced across at Ryan Boland, who'd turned away

from his own computer screen and now faced her.

Ryan was a good agent. He'd been an Australian Federal Police Officer and a member of the online Child Protection Unit almost as long as she had and he was just as committed to seeing the cyber pedophiles locked up for a very long time.

Alex shook her head. "*Nup.* I'm staying home with Sam. It's been too long since we had some quality time together." She leaned back in her chair and stretched. "What about you? What are you doing with your weekend off?"

"Ah. Two whole days away from this place…" He sighed. "I can barely contain myself."

"What are your plans?"

Ryan pushed his chair backwards and stretched his long legs out over his desk, crossing his ankles and stacking his hands behind his head. "I'm going to take my boat out."

Alex raised one dark eyebrow. "You bought a boat?"

"I bought a boat."

A grin threatened. "Do you even know how to drive a boat?"

A look of mock-outrage crossed his handsome features. "Of course I do. What kind of question is that? I went down to the Roads and Maritime Services and sat for their test. Passed with flying colors."

"Okay, so you can read a handbook. Have you actually ever been *in* a boat—like, at the *wheel*?"

Ryan rolled his eyes. "It's called the helm, for your information, and of course I've steered one before. It's not like I just strolled into a boat shop one afternoon, picked out a vessel and drove away with it."

She looked at him, askance.

"*What?*" he protested at her doubtful look. "I had a few lessons. The boat shop owner took me down to the river and showed me a few things. How to get it on and off the trailer, how to get it started—you know, that kind of thing."

Alex threw back her head and laughed. "Only you would get away with something like that, Boland. I don't know how you do it. What was her name?"

He grinned, ignoring her last comment, and rose from his chair, closing the short distance between them. Propping a hip against her desk and crossing his arms, he spoke again, his face sober.

"I live up north of Avalon, not far from the Hawkesbury River. I leave here after a long shift with the world on my shoulders, wondering how there can be so many sick fucks out there and I pass one pickup truck after another—all towing boats. Heading out for some recreation time. Heading out for some *fun*." His expression became earnest. "And you know what? Every one of those blokes has a smile on his face. They're *happy*. They're boat owners and they're happy."

Alex's smile faded. She reached out and squeezed his arm, her voice gentling. "Okay, Boland. I get it. I really do. Have a break. Go and have some fun."

Ryan looked away and let out a breath. "You ought to come out with me some day, Alex. Who knows? You might even enjoy it."

Memories from an earlier time, a time when she'd been high on love and life, snuck up on her, stealing her breath. Her stomach knotted with a pang of regret. "No, I don't think so, Ryan. But thanks."

"I promise I won't drown you."

She shook her head. "It's not that. It's... I-I just don't do boats."

His gaze lingered on her face, curiosity lighting the dark depths of his eyes, but he said nothing. With a slight shrug, he returned to his seat. Reaching for his mouse, he turned his attention back to the screen in front of him.

Alex let her breath out in slow increments and willed herself to relax.

"Nearly time to log off," Ryan said.

"Today it can't come soon enough," she murmured and tried to concentrate on her screen.

"Alex. Ryan."

They both looked up as Superintendent Patrick Manahan approached them from the direction of his office.

"What is it, boss?" Alex asked.

Patrick ran a hand through his thick, closely cropped gray hair. "I've been meaning to tell you all week. I've got some good news, for a change. We have a recruit. An AFP officer who's worked for ten years in counter terrorism. He's transferring to the CPU."

Ryan whistled. "Wow, that's a coup—getting someone with that much experience. Has he worked in Child Protection Operations before?"

Patrick shook his head. "No, but he's the one who requested the transfer, so I'm guessing he has some idea what he's getting into. I expect the two of you to help him settle in and bring him up to speed."

"When does he start?" Alex asked.

Patrick glanced at his watch. "In about five minutes. He opted to start on the late shift."

Alex pulled back in surprise. "He wants to kick off on the night shift? On the *Friday* night shift? Does he have any idea how busy it can get?"

Patrick shrugged. "What can I say? Must be a glutton for punishment."

Alex sat back in her chair. The new guy was either dedicated to the cause or just plain green. Most recruits to the unit chose to start on a morning shift—preferably a Monday morning when the cyber predators tended to be at their quietest: sleeping off the effects of a couple of late nights or attending to their day jobs. She could only guess at the reasons, but it was a fact the fake profiles set up by the unit's team members in the various online chat rooms received much less attention from the cyber predators during weekdays.

The squad room door opened, snagging her attention.

"Ah, there he is now." Patrick turned and met the newcomer halfway across the room.

Alex looked up and froze. It couldn't be...

Patrick turned toward them and smiled. "Everyone, I'd like you to meet Federal Agent Brandon Munro. Brandon, welcome to the Child Protection Unit."

The rest of what was said was drowned out by the pounding of blood in her ears. *Brandon Munro*. It *was* him. And he was striding toward her... Greeting Ryan with a polite handshake. Nodding toward the other team members who had gathered nearby.

Then, he directed his attention to her.

Her legs were concrete pylons, holding her to the chair. Her throat was desert dry. He was now close enough that she could see time had treated him well, although a myriad of fine lines crowded the corners of his eyes. Lines that hadn't been there the last time she'd seen him.

Then, his hand came out. Her heart beat an erratic staccato against her chest. She hesitated, a rush of nerves paralyzing her.

A familiar flash of mocking humor lit the deep blue of his eyes. Lips that had once driven her wild with need now curved into a taunting smile.

Patrick filled the silence. "Brandon, this is our senior online investigator, Alex Cavanaugh."

The smile turned feral. "Cavanaugh, is it? Funny, I seem to remember it was Munro."

Anger erupted through Alex's veins and fueled the heat that seared her cheeks. She was pleased to see he'd withdrawn his hand. She sure as hell wasn't in the mood to offer him even the most basic of pleasantries.

The lines marring Patrick's forehead deepened. "Oh, I'm sorry. I didn't realize the two of you had already met."

"Met?" Brandon replied. "I guess you could say that."

The tension in his stance belied the casualness of his tone. The weight of his gaze burned into her, but she refused to look at him.

From out of the corner of her eye, she saw him take a step toward her and she stiffened.

"I can't believe you never told them, sweetheart." He spoke with casual inflection, glancing around at her co-workers.

Her eyes closed reflexively. She fought off a wave of panic. Surely he wouldn't? Not here, in front of everyone?

"Tell us what?" asked Ryan, curiosity plain on his face.

Brandon looked across at him and then over to Patrick. He gave a nonchalant shrug, but his voice rang with challenge.

"Alex is my wife."

———

Alex was still fuming twenty minutes later when she braked sharply to avoid missing the turn into the parking lot of Bondi's Sunny Smiles Long Daycare Center. The large, yellow sun with its wide, white grin gracing the billboard outside the Center usually brought a smile to her face, but the unexpected return of Brandon Munro into her life had left her tense and edgy, and she could barely think.

It had been a lifetime since she'd seen him. So much had happened. So much had changed. *She* had changed.

He looked as good as ever. Apart from the tiny lines around his eyes, he'd barely aged a day. His dark-blond hair was still thick and free from gray. His golden-toned skin, inherited from his Caucasian mother and aboriginal father, glowed with vitality and good health. From the way he filled out his tailored suit, she could tell his tall frame housed not an ounce of fat and it looked as though he still hit the gym as often as she used to.

Way back when.

Way back when she was married to him.

What do you mean, was? You're still married.

The thought intruded, harsh and entirely unwelcome. She pounded the steering wheel with her fists and tried to deny the silent truth, biting her lip in frustration.

It was true. She was still married. *They* were still married. She'd never taken the time to analyze why she hadn't filed for divorce. Hadn't wanted to analyze that. And until about half an hour ago, it hadn't been an issue. Apart from the fact memories of his proposal on a forty-foot yacht meant she was reluctant to step on board a boat. And she'd long since gotten over the night he came home and told her they were over. *Hadn't* she?

Some tiny part of her wondered from time to time why Brandon hadn't filed either, but those thoughts had intruded only on the rarest of occasions and usually late at night when she'd indulged in too much merlot. In the morning, she'd wake and push the lingering memories back into the farthest corner of her mind and go about her day.

Why the hell had he chosen *her* unit to work in? He could have gone anywhere. The last time she'd seen him, he'd been up to his neck trying to infiltrate Indonesian terrorist cells—as far removed from online child pornography rings as she could imagine.

Perhaps he hadn't known? After all, she'd had made three transfers since their split. Maybe she was flattering herself that he'd kept track of her movements. She certainly hadn't kept track of his. Not really.

Who was she kidding?

Alex sighed and opened the car door. Retrieving her handbag and keys, she headed toward the front gate of the Center.

The sound of late-afternoon shouts, cries and laughter greeted her as she entered the preschool room. She looked around and spotted Sam. He was playing in Home Corner, as usual, dwarfed in dress-up clothes—a man's shirt and belt—and nursing a doll that looked so lifelike, it could be mistaken for a real baby.

"Hey, Sam!" she called out to him.

He looked up and saw her and his face filled with sunshine. Swallowing the lump in her throat, Alex bent down on one knee and braced herself against the impact of the small, warm body that launched itself against her.

"Mommy! Mommy! Mommy! You came!"

"Of course I came, Sammy," she murmured, wrapping her arms around him and nuzzling her lips against the softness of his dark, curly hair. "I told you I would."

"I know, but you took so *long*. Look at my baby, Mommy! Her name's Isabelle. She's my little sister."

Alex's heart clenched, but as she gazed into his earnest brown eyes—eyes that looked nothing like his father's—she forced a smile.

Her heart hammered at the thought of what Brandon would do if he discovered he had a son. She pulled slightly away, cupping her hands around Sam's much-loved face, searching a little frantically for signs of his father.

There were none. She was sure of it. He had none of Brandon's blond coloring. He was a male version of her. Everyone commented on it, even her mother.

A wave of relief rushed through her and she pulled him tightly against her.

"Mom, you can let me go now. You're crushing me and you're hurting Isabelle."

With reluctance, Alex released him and stood a little shakily, trying to catch her breath. Busying herself by signing him out, she waited while he tugged off the dress-ups, laid the doll gently into a cradle and went to collect his bag.

She took another steadying breath. It was okay. Everything was going to be all right. So, her husband had stepped back into her life. A husband she hadn't seen or heard from for more than four years. It didn't mean he was looking for a reunion. He'd probably been as surprised as she when he'd discovered she worked in the same department.

Really, what was she worrying about? The likelihood of him wanting to take up where they'd left off was ludicrous. Besides, she could always have a word with the boss and minimize the number of shifts they shared. With a little manoeuvring, she could probably manage to forget all about him.

As long as he didn't find out about Sam.

CHAPTER 2

Cassie Munro twirled a piece of ash-blond hair around her finger and read the message on her computer screen. A smile broke across her face. It was him. Justin. He was online.

Her pulse skipped a beat and she willed her fingers to type faster, wishing she'd agreed to take the touch typing course with her mother at the local TAFE college when she'd asked her last summer.

It was nearly time for lunch and she had so much to tell him, starting with the nasty Mr Purvis who'd given them two whole pages of algebra to finish by Monday morning. School was the pits. She knew he'd understand. He was only a couple of grades ahead of her.

Of course, his real name probably wasn't Justin, just like she wasn't Lady G, but it was fun to pretend and much more glamorous than using her real name. Besides, she had listened to all those lectures her parents had given her about online safety, even if they thought she hadn't. She knew better than to give out her real name.

A response flashed on her screen and she smiled. Justin knew exactly what she meant about Mr Purvis. His science teacher was exactly the same. He called him 'Homework Hitler.' She loved it.

"Cassie, come downstairs and get ready for lunch, please. Uncle Brandon's going to be here soon."

Cassie grimaced. Not that she didn't love seeing Uncle

Brandon. Out of all her uncles, he was her favorite. It helped that he was cute. He was getting a bit old, but not as old as her dad. Her father had already turned thirty-five.

"Cassie."

Her mother's voice held a note of warning and Cassie shot off a quick response to Justin, her fingers moving quickly over the keyboard.

"Mom's calling me for lunch. Gotta go."

The reply was just as quick.

"Come back as soon as you've finished, gorgeous. I'll be waiting."

Cassie blushed and her stomach flip-flopped. She loved it when he called her that. It made her feel like a woman—grown-up, sexy, cool. Even with her braces.

Snatching a quick breath, she darted into the adjoining bathroom and splashed water across her cheeks. It wouldn't do for her parents to wonder about her high color.

She walked back into her bedroom, closed her laptop and headed down the stairs.

CHAPTER 3

Brandon Munro gave a perfunctory knock and turned the knob of the stained glass paneled wooden door that graced the entryway of his brother's two storey 1950's bungalow, perched on the corner of one of Chatswood's quiet, leafy streets.

"Hello?" he called out, glancing around. "Tom? Lily?" He hung his coat on the hatstand that stood in the corner and brushed off the fine droplets of mist that clung to its folds. Winter was closing in and there was a definite chill in the air.

A noise above him captured his attention. Looking up, he smiled and watched his niece bound down the stairs toward him with the natural athleticism inherited from her Aboriginal grandfather. Her long blond hair hung loose around her shoulders. At twelve, she was still all arms and legs, but it was already obvious she'd be a stunner.

Brandon grinned back at her and enveloped her in a warm hug. "How's my favorite niece? You're getting prettier by the minute. I'll have to make sure that brother of mine has his shotgun at the ready. It won't be long and the boys will be queuing at the door."

Cassie ducked her head and her cheeks turned scarlet. "Uncle Brandon, you're so silly. Daddy doesn't even own a shotgun."

"Aha, so you're not denying the boys will be lining up?"

Cassie blushed again and shook her head. Brandon took

pity on her. He wasn't that old that he couldn't remember what it was like to be in that in-between stage—not an adult, but no longer a child—and feeling uncomfortable in both worlds.

"So," he said, draping his arm around her shoulders as they headed toward the kitchen. "Where's that brother of yours?"

Cassie grinned. "Joe's gone to Billy's house for a sleepover." Her eyes sparkled with triumph. "I get the TV remote for the *whole* weekend."

Brandon chuckled. "How's school going?"

"It's okay, I guess," Cassie replied. "I can't wait for next term. We're going on an excursion to the Blue Mountains. We're going *camping*. In tents with sleeping bags and everything. It's going to be so cool. I'm going to share with Madeleine and Lucy. We're already planning what clothes we're going to take."

"Wow, school excursions have come a long way since my day. I remember the most excitement I ever had was visiting a dairy farm on the north coast."

Cassie's eyes gleamed with interest. "Really?"

"Yep. We traveled a few hours on a bus, up around the mountain range and over the other side. Stopped for Stanley Woods to be sick on the way there *and* back and that's about it. Oh, and the smell of the dairy. *That* was unforgettable."

She giggled. "You went to school in Grafton, didn't you? Like Daddy?"

"I sure did. Your dad's a few years older than I am, but we went to the same school. I think he did the dairy farm excursion, too. You should ask him about it one day. I'm sure that was the time he managed to sneak a kiss with Donna Burton."

Cassie's eyes went wide, twinkling with mischief. "Daddy kissed a girl? Really? Does Mom know?"

"Does Mom know what?" Tom Munro asked, walking into the kitchen.

Brandon closed the distance and gave his brother's hand

a shake, grinning. "Hey, big brother, how's it going? We were talking about you, not to you."

The twinkle in Tom's eyes, eyes the exact same shade as his daughter's, belied the frown that creased his forehead.

"Uncle Brandon was telling me about your school excursion. The one where you went to a dairy farm and kissed Donna Burton."

Tom smiled and met Brandon's gaze in shared confidence. "Donna Burton. Well, that's a blast from the past. She was fourteen and built in all the right places. I was a year younger. I thought I'd died and gone to heaven when she said I could kiss her." He shook his head in reminiscence. "I wonder what happened to her?"

"What happened to who?"

The brothers turned. Lily Munro came toward them. Her simple, chocolate-brown dress emphasized her blond coloring and clung to her soft curves before falling away in an elegant swathe just below her knees. A scarf made from some kind of soft fabric in red and cream and orange hues hung around her neck. Brandon stepped forward and greeted his sister-in-law with a warm hug.

"Hey, Lily. You look lovely. Thanks for inviting me over. Something smells great."

Lily held him at arm's length and looked him up and down. She shook her head. "You're looking way too scrawny, Brandon. It's been far too long since you've been here. I intend to stuff you full of garlic-and-herb bread fresh from the breadmaker, sweet potato bake, fresh green beans in a honey and mustard glaze and a choice cut of rump steak."

"And afterwards?" he asked, widening his eyes innocently.

She slapped him lightly on his arm. "Cheeky as ever, I see. It just happens I've baked your favorite triple-chocolate cheesecake with freshly whipped cream and strawberries straight from the garden."

Brandon groaned in appreciation. "If you ever get sick of

living with this brother of mine, you know where to come."

"You're on." Lily gave him a smile, but they both knew it was said in jest. Tom and his wife were nearly joined at the hip.

A pang of envy went through him and he immediately squelched it. He'd forfeited a happy home life more than four years ago. Single-handedly, he'd destroyed his marriage and no amount of looking for excuses would change that fact.

He'd screwed up. Pure and simple. And in the process, he'd lost the only woman he ever loved.

———————

Thoughts of Alex still crowded Brandon's mind a few hours later when he took his second bottle of beer out of the fridge and followed his brother outside. The meal was over and the plates had been cleared. He was relaxed and sated with good food and even better company.

Between Lily entertaining them with amusing anecdotes from her work as a primary school teacher and Cassie groaning about her younger brother and the irritations he caused her on a daily basis, the tension that had held him in its grip ever since he'd walked through the doors of the CPU had eased.

His thoughts wandered to his swag of brothers and sisters. Tom was the oldest. Then came Declan. Brandon was third in line and after him came the twins, Clayton and Riley. Then came the babies of the family, his two younger sisters, Josie and Chanel. With Clayton and Tom both now married with children and Riley newly engaged, the family was quickly expanding.

He drew in a deep breath, filling his lungs to capacity. The early afternoon air was pleasantly crisp and the earlier mist had lifted. Pulling out a deck chair, he sat down at the rectangular-shaped outdoor table across from his brother and stared up at the mid-afternoon sky littered with puffy, white clouds.

Tom took a swig of his beer and exhaled. "Okay, spill it, bro. What's up?"

Brandon started in surprise, but he should have known he couldn't hide anything from Tom. Despite the three-year age gap, they'd always been close.

He debated about lying, but couldn't bring himself to do it. Tom had only asked because he cared. Besides, it would be good to tell someone. It had been eating him up inside since he'd seen her again.

"It's about Alex. I saw her again."

Tom's eyes went wide in the dimness. "Wow. Really? That's a blast from the past. Where was she?"

Brandon drew in another deep breath and exhaled slowly. "I ran into her at work. She's a senior investigator in the Child Protection Unit. I started there last night."

"Last night? You started on a night shift? Who does that?"

Brandon offered a wry grin. "Me, I guess. I volunteered for a string of them, including tonight."

A frown creased Tom's forehead. "Did you know Alex works there?"

Unable to meet his brother's worried gaze, Brandon picked up his beer and looked away. Taking a mouthful, he let the yeasty liquid slide down his throat and tried to come up with the words to explain.

Brandon hadn't told Tom or anyone else in his family why his marriage had fallen apart. No one knew. No one, but him.

He decided on the truth. "Yes, but we're both adults. I'm sure we can work together without drawing blood."

The concern in Tom's gaze didn't waver, but he reached over and took another sip from his beer. "How was she?"

Brandon closed his eyes. A kaleidoscope of images bombarded him.

Alex.

Her hair, still curly and dark, was longer than she used to wear it, and now hung well below her shoulders. Her compact, athletic figure looked much as it always had, still slim in the white silk blouse and navy pencil skirt she'd worn when he'd seen her.

It was only her eyes that had changed.

The hurt and anger and bewilderment that had torn at his guts the last time he'd seen her were gone—replaced by a coldness that was totally foreign and seemed utterly impenetrable. Funny how that scared him even more.

He looked across at Tom and offered a casual shrug. "She looked good, I guess. Much as she's always looked."

"Of all the people for you to run into. Christ, it must be four years or so since it happened?"

"Yep. Four years and three months." He gave Tom a desultory grin that didn't fool either of them. "The night of my twenty-eighth birthday, remember?"

"Shit, yes, of course I remember. How could I forget? I'd never seen you so lost. For months I had no idea what to say to you."

Brandon clamped his teeth together to ward off the memories and stared unseeingly across the backyard to the in-ground swimming pool that was now covered in anticipation of the upcoming winter.

"She never even tried to stay in touch with us, you know," Tom murmured. "I don't know how many times Lily called her and invited her over. I mean, they were good friends. She was family. Just because it hadn't worked out between the two of you, didn't mean we all had to fall out." Tom shook his head, his voice reflecting the puzzlement in his face. "It was like she didn't want to know us anymore. She wouldn't return any of Lily's calls. She literally dropped out of sight."

Tom's lips pursed. "Eventually, we gave up. Lily told me we had to respect Alex's right to privacy and let her deal with the breakup in her own way, even if that meant shutting us out. By then I was angry. Her behavior, ignoring us, ignoring Lily—it all seemed plain rude to me."

Brandon heard the hurt in his brother's voice and familiar guilt stirred inside him. He was the one who'd walked out on his marriage. It was his fault Alex had cut off his family. It was him and him alone who'd caused the hurt and confusion in his brother's eyes. Despite the fact at the time he'd had good reasons to end his marriage, he'd regret for the rest of his life the pain he'd caused the people he loved.

It was time to make things right. He couldn't stand by a minute longer and watch the anguish in Tom's face and know that he had put it there. Finishing his beer quickly, he sat the empty bottle on the table and dug deep for the courage to do what had to be done.

"There's something I need to tell you."

Tom stared at him, Brandon's sober tone catching his attention. "What is it?"

"My marriage breakdown wasn't because of Alex. Well, not really. We'd been having problems for awhile, but that's not what broke us."

Tom leaned forward, his face serious. "You've never told us what happened."

Brandon blew out his breath on a heavy sigh and nodded. "You're right."

Tom waited a few moments. When Brandon remained silent, he prodded, "So? Are you going to tell me?"

With a grimace, Brandon nodded again. "It's more than time."

CHAPTER 4

Alex sucked in a deep breath and let it out slowly in an effort to release the tension in her belly. Little puffs of air clouded on the winter-crisp interior of her secondhand Toyota.

The squad room lights shone palely through the drawn venetians and leaked down the scarred concrete walls below. Walls that housed her husband.

Her ex-husband.

She'd spent a restless weekend at home doing her best not to think about the fact he now worked in her unit. For the most part, she'd failed and despite two days' respite, she was tired and irritable and on edge at the thought of facing him again.

Another car pulled in behind her and she recognized Ryan's pickup. The morning shift was gathering. A renewed flood of nervousness surged through her and she quickly pushed it away.

Brandon had just completed another night shift. It had been two days since she'd seen him. She'd barely have to acknowledge him. She'd be in his company a few minutes, at the most. Just like his first evening.

There would be a hand-over of the night's activities, the usual banter between work mates clocking on and those clocking off and that would be it. He'd be gone. And she could get on with her job. Just like that. Easy. *Yeah, right.*

Setting her jaw with determination, Alex collected her

handbag and keys and climbed out of her vehicle, praying she could get this over with quickly. Squinting against the brighter light of the fluorescents after the dimness of the dawn outside, Alex kept her head down and made a beeline for her desk. It was located on the far side of the squad room. Reaching it took a lifetime.

She arrived at her destination without incident and heaved a sigh of relief. After setting her handbag on the floor near her chair, she squatted to switch on her computer.

"How was your weekend?"

Jerking upwards, Alex narrowly missed hitting her head on the desk and she cursed under her breath. Pointedly ignoring Brandon's outstretched hand, she took a couple of paces backwards and braced herself for the impact of his eyes.

Even knowing what was coming, she wasn't prepared for the intensity of those sexy blue orbs, or for the barrage of memories they evoked.

Her belly somersaulted. He looked tired and rumpled, but it was a sexy I-just-climbed-out-of-bed rumpled. Not at all how *she* usually looked after a twelve-hour night shift.

Irritation surged through her. He had no right looking that good. It wasn't fair. And it wasn't fair that she had to see him looking like that. This was *her* turf. She'd been here for years. He was the interloper, the one who didn't belong. And he had no right smiling at her in that manner. Like they were friends.

She narrowed her eyes at him. "What are you doing here, Brandon?"

His eyebrows rose a notch at the steel in her voice. The smile faded. "Working, Alex. Same as you."

She gritted her teeth. "That's not what I meant and you know it. What are you doing *here*?"

He shrugged. "I've been knee-deep in terrorist cells for years. Decided I needed a change." He lifted his arms in a sign of surrender and smiled disarmingly. "So, here I am."

She wasn't buying it and eyed him with distrust. "Why the CPU? You've been part of the High Tech Operations Team for years. You could have gone to any number of other departments. Children never interested you in the past."

The barb was intentional. A shadow crossed his face. It was gone so quickly, she wondered if she'd imagined it.

"We all change. Who's to say why we do, but it happens." His attention moved to her desk, zeroing in on the framed photo of Sam that took pride of place near her phone. Her heart hammered.

"Cute kid. Is he yours?"

Alex swallowed and forced a reply. "Yes."

Brandon leaned over and picked up the picture frame, studying it closely. "How old is he?"

Panic clawed at her belly, tightening her throat. *Oh, God. She'd forgotten all about the photo. What could she say?* Frantic thoughts batted the inside of her brain.

Thirty seconds passed. It felt like a lifetime. "Umm... Er..." She cleared her throat.

Brandon frowned, causing lines to mar the smooth, tanned skin of his forehead. "You don't know?"

"Of course I know," she snapped, finding her voice at last. "I was just wondering what the hell business it was of yours."

His gaze hardened and his tone was dismissive. "You're right. It's none of my business. I was merely curious. I guess I didn't realize the age of your son was a state secret."

Heat seared her cheeks. "Don't be ridiculous! Of course it's not a state secret." She looked away. "He's two," she muttered, slicing more than twelve months off his age. She almost choked on the lie.

Pain flashed across Brandon's handsome features. Just as quickly, it was gone.

Guilt assailed her, but she brushed that aside. Surely she no longer had the power to hurt him? He was the one who'd done the hurting. And he'd never wanted kids. That had been the problem. Well, one of them.

"Funny, he looks older than that."

Alex clenched her teeth together and willed Brandon to leave. She didn't know how much more of this she could take. She'd never been a good liar and Brandon knew her better than anyone.

He shrugged at her silence, a sardonic curve to his lips. "I guess you got what you wanted, after all." His gaze fell to her ringless fingers. "So, where's his father?"

"We—we're not together anymore."

He cocked an eyebrow, a mocking glint in his eye. "I see. Well, it doesn't look like you wasted much time."

"Hey, Brandon? Are you coming, mate?"

Brandon's attention was snagged by the other officer and a surge of relief weakened Alex's knees. She caught hold of the chair in front of her.

"Yeah, thanks. I'll be right there." Throwing her an inscrutable look, he strode away without a backward glance.

The rhythmic sound of his feet as they pounded the pavement helped to ease some of the tension in Brandon's shoulders as he jogged the final mile home. He pushed himself harder. His breath came in harsh pants. Sweat dripped off his forehead and soaked the front of his faded Dire Straits T-shirt.

Fatigue had sapped his energy after a long night shift, but he'd been too wired to sleep. Arriving home, he'd changed out of his work clothes and into some running gear. Ignoring the protests of his body, he'd headed back through the door and into the fresh crispness of the morning.

Opening up to Tom had been cathartic and Brandon had left his brother's house feeling better about himself than he had in years. And more determined than ever to make things right with Alex... But ever since he'd left the squad room, anger and confusion had warred with an underlying sense of betrayal. The shock of discovering Alex had a son still hadn't worn off. The boy looked just like her. All curly dark hair, bright, dark eyes and an impish smile.

Irritation surged through him. What the hell did he care who the boy's father was? There was no way the child could be his. Why should he care that Alex had jumped into the cot with another man before his side of the bed had even cooled?

They were over. Had been for more than four years. The discovery that she had a son shouldn't have affected him. He'd known she'd wanted kids—it had been a serious bone of contention between them during the last couple of years of their marriage.

Memories crowded his mind. Early on, it had been perfect—they'd been perfect. They even shared the same birthday. They'd been two young kids drunk on love with a wide open future.

But then, they'd slid over the other side of twenty-six and all of a sudden, Alex had worried about her biological clock. They'd never discussed kids. Before they married, he'd assumed she didn't want them. She'd assumed he did. Even now, the irony wasn't lost on him. Both of them had received a high standard of training in communications and yet their lack of that had been the reason their marriage hadn't made the distance.

They'd both been devoted to their careers—risky, dangerous careers working undercover in some of the Australian Federal Police Force's most dangerous operations. Not the kind of stability needed to raise a child. At least, that's how he'd felt. He'd assumed Alex felt the same.

Until it became obvious she didn't.

And then there had been the fatal covert operation in Jakarta.

Even now, more than four years later, the devastating memories almost overwhelmed him. The screams of his men as they were attacked in their beds. The blood. Harry, with a hole in his chest Brandon could have put his fist in.

His jaw clenched. Indirectly, his marriage had been the cause of the carnage. So, he'd come home and ended it. At the time, there had seemed to be no other choice.

He'd refused to risk the safety of his men again.

It had taken him years to recover. Even now, there were moments when he was back there and it was happening all over again. He'd seen therapists until he couldn't stand to talk about it again. He'd read the notes of the various health professionals—*Post Traumatic Stress Disorder.*

It didn't matter. No label, no diagnosis would save him. He'd forfeited his marriage. No matter how much he told himself he should have fought harder for it, it didn't change anything.

He'd taken the easy way out. He'd given up on them with barely a fight.

The guilt of it still burned into him. He'd walked out on her the night of their twenty-eighth birthdays. They hadn't even cut the cake.

Chapter 5

Alex stared out the window into the inky darkness from her usual spot behind her desk. She cast a look toward the regulation government-issued clock on the pale gray squad room wall and sighed. It was just after nine. Only three hours into her twelve-hour night shift.

Despite her best efforts, her gaze drifted to Brandon. He sat side-on to her at his desk, less than ten feet away, staring at the illuminated computer screen in front of him. She was acutely aware of him—had been for the last three hours—and it was annoying her no end.

It had been more than a week since they'd spoken. Until now, with some clever manipulation of the roster, she'd managed to avoid sharing a shift with him, but not wanting to disclose too much to her boss, she'd known that sooner or later, her luck would run out. Tonight, she'd drawn the short straw.

Brandon looked good, but then, he always did. His crisp white business shirt was tucked into a pair of charcoal-gray suit pants. An expensive-looking maroon and gold tie complemented both.

He looked like he'd spent hours choosing his wardrobe but she knew for a fact he never spent much time getting ready. He had an innate sense of style that came naturally and it hadn't diminished over the years. But he was also different... A "good different" in lots of ways. Less restless, edgy, anxious. *Had he found peace with someone else?*

The bold thought intruded, entirely unwelcome. As was the stab of jealousy that came from nowhere. What did she care who he was seeing? It was none of her business. Just like her life was none of his. She'd told him as much. She'd be all kinds of hypocritical if she stuck her nose into his business. And a hypocrite, she wasn't.

Still, Alex couldn't squelch the tiny seed of curiosity that lodged itself in her brain and refused to die. *Was he seeing someone? Did that account for his new level of awareness and maturity?*

With a snort of disgust, she forced her gaze back to her computer. A comment flashed on the screen in front of her and her stomach clenched. It was from Justin. The name was obviously a pseudonym. That's just the way it was. But "Justin" had tweaked her curiosity. He was one of the persons of interest she'd been tracking over the last few weeks and he'd just responded to her mention of a netball game being played next Saturday.

Tonight, she'd logged in as Angel—a thirteen-year-old girl who liked to swim, play netball and whine about her homework. Alex tried to keep the facts as much like her as she could. It helped keep the lies straight, especially when she used so many different profiles.

She generally based the physical description on herself, but bent toward a younger version. The hair she usually wore loose became a ponytail. The odd freckle on her face became more than just a smattering. And of course, a zit was a major catastrophe.

Although she didn't have any experience with other teenagers, she had been one herself and after doing some online research on YouTube and discovering what was selling in the iTunes Store, she quickly came up to speed. Besides, there was nothing like spending time in an online chat room to rapidly become acquainted with the current-day teenagers' vernacular and the things that held their attention.

Which changed daily, of course. At least, that's how it felt.

Right now, she was chatting to Justin. A few nights ago, it had been Zac.

"Justin" had told her he was fifteen. He played cricket in the summer and football in the winter. She'd asked him to send her a picture, but he hadn't yet complied and even if he did, it wouldn't mean it would be the real him. Anyone could source a photo online. Most parents would be aghast if they knew what a predator could do to their child's picture once it was uploaded onto the web. Or how someone else could use it to misrepresent themselves.

Alex pushed the thought aside and concentrated on the words appearing on her screen. She'd been chatting to him for several weeks and her radar had begun to hum. There was just something about him that had the smell of a predator.

For one, his manner was way too obliging for a teenage boy. He was also way too interested in her and her friends. The average teenager was self-absorbed. They didn't want to know any more about you than you offered. And most especially teenage boys. They couldn't care less about your snotty Maths teacher or the fact that you'd had a fight with your best friend.

But Justin did. At least, he said he did. He responded to Angel's moaning and groaning with an uncharacteristic sensitivity and even encouraged her to elaborate. He asked lots and lots of questions. He agreed with everything she said.

Yes, the person posing as Justin had ignited her curiosity and as she began to read his most recent reply, her heart rate accelerated.

My sister plays netball, Angel. Which team do you play for?

Alex wasn't on speaking terms with any teenage boys, but she couldn't imagine one that cared a fig about netball and even less about his sister. She quickly typed back a response.

I play for the Bondi Babes.

A few seconds later, another reply came.

Great name. Which position do you play?

Alex kept it easy by using the position she usually played on the few Saturdays she had off and found time to enjoy a game.

I play Wing Attack. What about your sister?

That would test him. Not many fifteen-year-old boys would know the positions of a netball team.

Goalkeeper.

Alex contemplated his reply. Most sports had a goalkeeper of some sort. Even if he knew nothing about netball, it was a fairly safe response. It didn't mean he was a predator. But then again, it didn't mean he wasn't.

Another comment crawled across on the screen.

Who takes you to your games?

Alex tensed, then took a deep breath and tried to relax. Another seemingly innocuous question. It was probably only her and the other members of the CPU that would read insidiousness into that query. Then again, it paid to be sure. Her radar was humming louder and it hadn't failed her yet.

She typed a reply.

I usually catch the bus and meet my friends there.

The response came quickly.

Are you playing at Bondi this weekend?

No, we're playing away this weekend. Over at Clovelly.

She waited, holding her breath. A few minutes later, he responded.

Too bad. I was hoping we could meet and say hi. Maybe you could come over to my place after the game. I live just around the corner from the Clovelly netball courts.

Alex's heart thumped hard and her chest went tight. Was that it? Had Angel just received an invitation from a pedophile?

She stood and leaned over the top of her cubicle. "Hey, Boland. Come and take a look at this."

Ryan looked up from his screen. "What is it?"

Alex bit her lip. From the corner of her eye, she saw Brandon glance in her direction.

"I've been chatting with a kid who calls himself Justin.

Says he's fifteen. But he's asking a hell of a lot of questions. He has my radar up."

Ryan's eyebrow rose. "Justin? Can't say I've had the pleasure, yet."

"Come and take a look. Sometimes I think I just overreact. This job has a way of making you paranoid. Even Santa Claus would trigger my suspicion some days."

Ryan rolled his eyes. He stood and made his way around to her desk. "I can't believe you just said that, Cavanaugh."

"What? Santa Claus? Don't tell me you never thought he was just a bit *too* jolly?"

Nudging her out of the way, Ryan sat at her desk and threw her a droll look. "Santa's not real, Alex, remember? Boy, you really need a holiday." He grinned. "The offer for a cruise up the Hawkesbury still stands, you know. We could even stay somewhere overnight."

Catching movement from out of the corner of her eye, Alex saw Brandon push away from his desk and walk toward them. She stiffened, knowing he'd heard every word. Leaning over Ryan's shoulder, she stared with fierce concentration at the text on the screen in front of them.

"See, start reading from here. We've been chatting for the last few weeks. He's asking all the right questions, don't you think?"

Ryan's eyes narrowed at the screen. He read in silence.

"What's going on?"

The words thrummed along Alex's spine. She drew in a quick breath and released it slowly, refusing to acknowledge the affect her husband still had on her.

"Alex thinks she might be onto something," Ryan replied, throwing Brandon a quick look over his shoulder. "And from what I've read, I might agree."

Ryan turned in the chair, forcing Alex to stand upright, in closer proximity to Brandon. She tensed when he moved nearer and she tried not to notice how delicious his cologne smelled. Fresh. Woodsy. Familiar.

He leaned in closer to read the text over Ryan's shoulder and her traitorous heart accelerated.

"To a casual observer," Ryan explained, "it might be easily dismissed as a young boy's curiosity—exactly what he says he is. But to anyone trained in the way these sickos work, it has all the hallmarks of a predator." He swung back around to Alex. "You've done good, partner. This one needs to be watched." He pushed back her chair and stood. "I'll go and tell the boss."

Ryan started off in the direction of Patrick's office. Alex watched him disappear, panic starting to rise. Brandon's gaze burned into her, but she refused to look at him.

"How long have you known Boland?"

The words took her by surprise. She looked up in confusion. "Ryan? Um, I'm not sure. He's been here as long as I have. Three years or so, I guess."

He tensed. His face closed.

Comprehension dawned on her. "Oh my God, you think he's Sam's father?"

"Sam? Is that his name?"

Alex bit her lip in silent castigation, but gave a brief nod.

Brandon pounced. "Boland has the same dark coloring, the same curly hair. Good looking." He held her gaze. "I can imagine you falling for a guy like that. You always did have a thing for a pretty face."

Anger burned through her. "How dare you!"

He lifted a shoulder in a casual shrug. "Just saying it how it is, sweetheart. Or at least, how it was."

"You bastard. You know that was only one of the many things I loved about you. At the end of the day, I couldn't have cared less if you were as ugly as a beast or as fat as a toad—it wouldn't have made any difference to the way I felt about you. You and you alone destroyed what we had when you left without a word of explanation and you damned well know it. It had nothing to do with your looks."

The color on Brandon's cheeks heightened, but he scoffed. "What's the big secret? What difference does it make who your son's father is?"

Before she could respond, his expression changed. A

sudden look of understanding filled his handsome features and his lips curled up in a sneer.

"I've got it. It's someone I know, isn't it? You were so desperate for a baby, you crawled into bed with one of my mates. Or maybe you didn't do it that way at all? Maybe you did it the modern way and just went off and got artificially inseminated? Ordered a donor off the Internet. Maybe that's the big secret—that even *you* don't know who his father is."

Fury, hot and thick, gushed into her veins and throbbed at her temples. She could barely speak around the surge of emotion that threatened to choke her.

"Do you really hate me that much?" she managed, her voice harsh.

A deep, red stain spread over Brandon's neck and across his cheeks. He looked away. A few seconds later, the tension left his body. When he looked back at her, his eyes were full of remorse.

"I'm sorry, Alex. That was uncalled for. I'm a prick. I'm a bastard. I'm every lowlife name you've ever thought of and more. I should never have said anything. It's none of my business—like you said. Please, forgive me?"

She stared at his outstretched hand and wished she could take it. But for too many years, the anger and hurt had gone unabated, stored in a secret place in her heart where it had been left to fester and grow into a cancerous mass that sat heavily in her belly, mostly ignored but never forgotten.

"You vowed love; you vowed honor; you vowed to stand beside me 'til death do us part," she rasped, fighting tears. Shaking her head, she swiped at her eyes and snatched another breath. "It was a lie. It was all a lie. You—"

"No, Alex, no. You've got it all wrong," he implored her. The pain in his eyes and the desperation on his face gave her pause, but she stifled the flash of guilt that shot through her and hardened her heart.

"I don't think so, Brandon." Renewed anger heated her veins. "You forfeited any chance at forgiveness the night you gave up on us."

CHAPTER 6

He'd always been a loser. Even in primary school, no one had wanted to know him. Pale and weedy, life had gotten worse when he'd entered puberty and acne had visited with a vengeance.

He'd learned early on the need to escape the humiliation of the playground and had gravitated toward the quiet, secret confines of the school library. The tall rows of shelves had secluded him from the torment of the rest of the world and the safe smell of books had soothed him in their silent, stale embrace.

It was in the library that he'd first discovered the Internet and his life had changed forever. Finally, he'd found a place to call home. It was a world where he could be anyone he wanted to be. The cocky captain of the football team, the fastest kid on the track team, or Mr Popularity 101. There were no rules; there were no boundaries; there were no truths. Just thousands of other kids wanting to be friends—begging, pleading, *happy* to be friends.

With him.

He'd thought he'd died and gone to heaven.

Now, years later, with the nightmare of puberty and high school behind him, he was free to live his life the way he'd always wanted. His boring day job as a traveling IT salesman gave him the freedom to play on the Internet whenever the urge took him. It also provided the necessary funds to finance his life's passion and if everything fell into place, soon he wouldn't even need that.

With a thrill of anticipation winging its way through his arteries, he unlocked the door to his grungy ground-floor apartment that boasted a spectacular view of the asphalt car park at the rear of his four-storey building.

In stark contrast to the attention he paid to his appearance, the unit was filthy. Ignoring the stack of dirty plates and cups piled high in the sink and the stench of garbage left too long in the trash bin, he headed straight for his sanctuary.

Leaving the light switch off, he made his way across the familiar dimness of his bedroom. The blinds were in their customary position, drawn tightly against prying eyes from the street outside. He cracked open his window. A gentle breeze seeped through, spreading the stench of unwashed clothes and bed linen throughout the room.

With a sigh of contentment, he turned on his computer and waited for it to boot. Clicking onto the Internet connection, he typed in the address of his favorite chat room and let the anticipation build.

His breath caught. She was already online. With his excitement growing, he reached for the zipper on his jeans. Life couldn't get any better.

Cassie's heart skipped a beat when Justin entered the chat room. She'd run all the way home from the bus stop and had gone straight up to her room. She hadn't even stopped to investigate the smell of freshly baked muffins wafting from the kitchen. Her Mom must have left work early.

She'd been daydreaming about Justin all day—during her dreary math class with Mr Purvis and in English with Mrs Pennant. She'd even missed the ball twice at netball practice.

She giggled. Her friends were beginning to wonder what was wrong with her. She couldn't bring herself to share him with them. Not yet. He was her secret. The feelings he evoked in her were too new, too exciting to share. He made her feel warm and wonderful all over. Like a woman.

She ran her hands over the soft buds of her breasts loosely encased inside the satiny A-cup bra and sighed. So far, the bra was just for show, but in a few months, she'd turn thirteen.

She thought of her upcoming birthday and sent a silent prayer that her body would take flight into puberty and she'd wake in the body of a real woman. A woman like her mother. With generous breasts that spilled out of the neckline of her dresses. And rounded hips and a butt. A real butt. One that was taut and curvy and moved with a sexy sway whenever she walked. Not the skinny, flat-assed one Cassie had carried around, to date.

Focusing on the screen in front of her, she read Justin's opening words. Her breath hitched.

Hey there, gorgeous. Just thinking of you. What a coincidence. You and I are like the same person.

Cassie blushed. Taking a deep breath, she tried to get her pulse rate back under control. Her fingers stumbled over the keys.

I can't stop thinking about you, either.

His response was swift. *I want to see you.*

Excitement surged through her. A grin stretched her mouth wide. She wanted to sing.

You don't even know what I look like!

I already know you're beautiful on the inside. That's all that matters to me.

Cassie's heart melted. Could he be any more perfect? She shot off another reply.

I want to send you a photo. Just so you know.

Only if you want to.

I want to.

Then I'll send one to you, too.

Her heart filled with love. Nothing could change the way she felt about him, but she'd been dying to know what he looked like. It would make her feel closer to him. Whenever she thought of him she'd be able to picture him as he was, not just the way she'd imagined him to be.

Clicking on a file, she quickly searched through her folder of pictures, choosing and discarding several before she settled on one that had been taken a few months ago at her Uncle Brandon's birthday. Her hair was loose around her shoulders and her braces were barely visible. She wore her favorite little black party dress that made her feel so grown-up and emphasized the coloring of her golden-blond hair. But best of all, her new push-up bra had given her a cleavage that until then, she'd only dreamed about.

A few short clicks later and the photo uploaded. She didn't have to wait long for his response.

I always knew you would be beautiful.

Happiness spread through her, leaving her feeling giddy. He couldn't have said anything better. She typed a reply.

You're so incredibly sweet.

Just wait until you meet me.

Her heart skipped a beat.

I can't wait.

Me, either, but first, I'll send you a picture. Fair's fair, after all.

Cassie held her breath in anticipation. Less than a minute later, a picture appeared on her screen. The air left her body in a rush. She stared in surprise. Oh God, he was gorgeous. Even cuter than Uncle Brandon.

Warm brown eyes sparkled out of a Hollywood-handsome face that showed the first signs of the man he would become. Shadow darkened his cheeks and she realized it was stubble. *Stubble?* Wow, he *shaved.* The only boys she knew who shaved were in the senior years, at least four or five years older than she was.

She tugged the keyboard toward her.

You look so much older than fifteen. You're so sexy.

Her fingers stumbled over the last word and she blushed. Oh, God, what if he thought her too forward? She didn't have to wait long for his reply.

I'm so glad you think so. I hope I don't look too old for

you. I've been shaving for nearly a year. A gift from my Italian heritage. Most people think I'm at least seventeen.

Cassie smiled and nodded at her screen.

I was thinking exactly the same thing, she typed.

Hey, I'd never lie to you. You know that, don't you?

Cassie stared at the words and her heart swelled.

Of course, I do.

Do you trust me?

She didn't hesitate.

With my life.

His next words filled her with emotion.

You make my heart smile.

Cassie thought she'd burst with happiness. How had she gotten so lucky? How had she, plain old Cassandra Lillian Munro, stumbled across the most gorgeous, wonderful, funny guy in the whole wide world and even better, a guy who liked her. *Really* liked her. He was her first boyfriend. Well, second, but holding hands with Warren White in the fifth grade didn't really count and it didn't even compare to the delicious feelings that filled her heart at the thought of Justin.

She hugged herself and smiled, embracing the happiness that bubbled up inside her.

Life didn't get any better. She couldn't wait to tell the girls.

————————

He stared at the picture on his screen and fondled his crotch. She was everything he'd imagined. Big blue eyes, a wide smile, flawless skin all surrounded by a halo of white-blond hair. She was the quintessential girl next door. Perhaps that was why she looked vaguely familiar?

Need tightened his groin. His cock twitched. With her picture enlarged before him, he tugged down his zipper.

CHAPTER 7

Alex squared her shoulders and stared up at the small mountain of stairs that led into the team's squad room. Another night shift, her last one before she had time off. Twelve hours and it would be over, at least for a couple of days. She'd be free to sleep in, take Sam to the park, touch up the highlights in her hair, talk to her mother. It felt like they'd barely spoken the last couple of weeks, doing not much more than passing in the night—or morning, as it had been lately. She'd had a string of night shifts and was at last coming to the end of them. For now.

Her reluctance to leave the parking garage had nothing to do with the job. She'd checked the roster in Patrick's office on her way out the door yesterday morning and had cringed when she realized she was working with Brandon again.

His harsh words the night before had sent her reeling and she'd left the squad room at the end of her shift still angry and shocked.

She'd had no idea he thought she was so low... To accuse her of not knowing the father of her child? It was unbelievable. It hurt her that he'd even thought that.

Okay, so their marriage breakdown hadn't been amicable. A spouse's decision to walk out on their marriage with no explanation tended to do that. But she hadn't dreamed he'd turn so nasty. After all, *she* was the one who'd been wronged. It wasn't like he knew she'd lied to him about Sam.

A swift stab of guilt pierced her and she let it run its course. Brandon may have broken his marriage vows by leaving, but she wasn't exactly without sin. Having a child without the father's knowledge was up there on the scale of dishonesty, even if the said father had long vowed he didn't want anything to do with children.

Her shoulders slumped on a sigh. It was clear he was going to be in the unit for the foreseeable future. She needed to find a way to work with him or she wouldn't survive.

"Hey, Alex, you going up?"

Ryan had walked up behind her and she blinked and hurried to reassemble her thoughts. Work. *Right.* Upstairs. *Right.* With Brandon. *Not so right.*

Gritting her teeth, she drew in a deep breath, determined to get past it. Ryan shot her a curious look, but followed her up the stairs in silence.

Brandon spotted Alex the minute she stepped into the room. His heart stuttered. Nerves gripped his belly.

He hadn't spoken to her since their confrontation the night before. From the moment the ugly words had left his mouth, he'd wished them back. He burned with the shame of it then and now, and wondered how he could make amends.

She looked great. With her hair loose and flowing around her shoulders, she looked a lot younger than her thirty-two years. Her tailored navy skirt and matching jacket hugged her curves.

His hands clenched at the memory. The thought of another man caressing that satiny skin knotted him with jealousy. He knew on some sane level that she'd have found comfort in someone else's arms, but to discover the harsh reality was taking some adjusting to.

She had a son. The child she'd always wanted. The child

he hadn't been willing to give her. Thoughts of her sleeping with another man long enough to create a baby were driving him crazy.

Of course, he hadn't expected her to remain celibate. After all, it had been four years. But he hadn't expected to find out she'd jumped into bed with someone else quite so soon after he'd left.

It just wasn't right. No, scrap that. To be truly honest, he'd admit he was hurt. He hadn't thought she'd replace him quite so easily and quite so soon.

She'd been his one true love. He'd have given his life for her. But he hadn't been able to bring himself to give her the one thing she'd pined for.

Then Jakarta had happened and it was all over.

An exotic mix of expensive perfume and freshly brewed coffee tantalized his nostrils. He looked up from where he sat at his desk and braced himself. Alex had stopped beside him, brandishing two coffee cups.

"I just came from the tearoom. I thought you might like a cup."

Brandon stared up at her, trying to gauge her sincerity. "Thanks," he said and took the offered mug.

Their fingers touched and his breath stilled. Silently he cursed his reaction. Setting his mug down, he met her gaze again. She stared at him, her expression somber.

"Brandon, I'm going to come right to the point. You said some pretty awful things last night and you really took me aback. I had no idea you thought so poorly of me."

He opened his mouth to speak, but she cut him off with an impatient wave of her hand. "When I left here, I was mad as hell and I called you every name under the sun and then some. But bygones are bygones. It's been more than four years and I don't think I've done too badly getting my life back on track, despite what you might think."

Heat spread up his neck. "Alex, I'm—"

Once again, she cut him off. "Apparently, we're going to be working together for the foreseeable future, unless you're thinking of putting in for a transfer?" She lifted a querying brow. He lowered his gaze and shook his head.

Her lips thinned. "That's what I thought. And since I'm not going anywhere, we need to find some neutral ground and call a truce. You may have been a real shithead who mucked up our marriage, but I refuse to drag all that up again, no matter what I might have said. Agreed?"

She extended a slim, manicured hand in his direction and Brandon gaped. Her upfront, no-nonsense approach had taken him completely by surprise, although it shouldn't have. She'd never tolerated pretence and had always called a spade a shovel. Guilt tightened his throat.

He took her hand, reveling in its softness as it pressed briefly against his before withdrawing. It took all his concentration to focus his thoughts before speaking.

"First of all, I don't think badly of you and, despite what you might think, I don't hate you. Last night, I was spoiling for a fight. I don't know why; I guess I was taken by surprise by the discovery you have a child. I thought..." He stopped short, unwilling to admit she still had the power to wound him. She looked at him expectantly.

"It's not about me," he continued, "and I'm ashamed of my behavior. I deserved every name you called me. Alex, I hope you believe me when I tell you I can't say how sorry I am that it happened."

Alex stared at him, distrust evident in the dark depths of her eyes.

He held her gaze and his voice shook with emotion. "Have I ever lied to you, Alex?"

She closed her eyes and looked away. "No," she replied, her voice low.

"Please." He held out his hand again. "Forgive me."

He held his breath, his chest tight. *She wasn't going to accept his apology. Oh, Christ, she wasn't going to accept it.*

She stepped back, her eyes fierce. "You ask too much of me. I may have agreed not to revisit the tattered remains of our marriage and how it got that way, but you simply can't expect me to forget about it. You broke us apart without even a word of explanation. That kind of pain doesn't go away. I admit, four years ago we were having a few problems, but it never occurred to me you were ready to leave. Now, I don't think any explanation you gave me would make a difference."

He accepted her outburst in silence, his head bowed. It was nothing less than he deserved. It was too late. He'd been wrong to imagine things could be any different.

"So where do we go from here?" he murmured, keeping his eyes averted.

She heaved a sigh, the sound so desolate it tore through him. He looked up, his gaze clashing with hers.

"I'm sorry, Alex. Coming here was a mistake. I'm sure there'll be somewhere else I can transfer to. I-I'll speak to Patrick tomorrow."

The words, tasting sour on his tongue, were the last words he wanted to utter, but he forced them out. He'd come to make amends and set things right. He'd come to win her back. It was time to admit it. He was still in love with her. He'd always been in love with her.

But it was never going to happen. He could see that now. She'd moved on without him. She had a flourishing career and the child she'd always wanted. She had no need for him in her life.

"That might be for the best."

The quiet words shredded his heart. He almost gasped from the pain of it. Instead, he turned away and stared at the computer screen that blinked in front of him. He knew the very second that Alex turned on her heel and left.

Alex glanced at her watch and sighed. Her break was nearly over. Despite the late hour, she'd escaped the confines of the office and had spent the time wandering past the brightly lit store fronts that lined the city's central business district. The late fall air was crisp enough to cool her cheeks, but she welcomed the discomfort.

She'd managed to avoid any further conversation with Brandon by burying herself in her work, but the chat rooms were slower than usual and there had been nothing to spark her interest. The usual suspects were busy elsewhere tonight, it seemed.

She'd always had a passion for children. It was only when it had become a problem for them that she'd realized Brandon hadn't shared her passion. She'd taken it as a given that during the course of their marriage, they'd welcome children. It's what people did. It wasn't something people negotiated and had to put into writing.

But when it had become obvious they were on completely different pages when it came to having a family, she realized her mistake. By then, it was too late to avoid the inevitable arguments and the anguish. Even then, she'd never dreamed it would be a deal breaker.

Her thoughts turned to Sam and she sighed. It wasn't the first time she'd felt guilty about him not having a father. Even worse, it was her fault his father didn't even know he existed. In the early days, she'd often defended her decision against her mother not to let Brandon know. She'd been so angry and hurt and bewildered; the last thing she'd wanted to do was gift him with her much longed-for child.

But now, four years down the track, the pain of his abrupt departure had lessened, despite what she'd told Brandon. She knew him well enough to know when he'd pledged his life to hers, he'd taken his marriage vows seriously and although he hadn't shared with her the reasons why he'd irrevocably changed his mind, she'd come to hope they were at least valid. Perhaps it was time to come clean? Perhaps she owed it to both Brandon and her son to make them aware of each other's existence? The thought filled her with equal parts optimism and terror.

Finding herself back at the entry to the AFP offices and no closer to an answer, she squared her shoulders and headed back inside.

Alex frowned at the hub of excitement in the squad room. A crowd of agents surrounded Brandon's desk. She stowed her handbag beneath her desk and sauntered closer, doing her best to look disinterested.

"What's going on?" she asked the agent nearest to her.

"Brandon's got a bite."

Alex moved a little closer and peered at the entries on Brandon's screen. Her eyebrows rose and her instincts kicked into gear. It certainly appeared like he was onto something.

Brandon was posing as a thirteen-year-old boy. A chat room user, logged in as "Adam," had posted some increasingly suspicious questions in response to Brandon's innocuous comments. As if aware of her presence, Brandon twisted in his chair and stared at her. She flushed and averted her gaze.

"What do you think, Alex? You've been here longer than I have."

His question was issued in a moderate tone, but Alex caught the gleam of challenge in his eyes.

"Yes, well, he certainly warrants closer attention. These are exactly the kind of questions these scum tend to pose. You've done a good job drawing him out."

Brandon's eyes widened at the praise. He smiled warmly, appearing to genuinely appreciate her comment.

"Thank you, Agent Cavanaugh. Coming from you, that means a lot. From the way everyone around here speaks about you, it's obvious you're highly thought of."

Alex blushed and looked away. *He'd been discussing her with the other agents?* She didn't know whether to feel upset or flattered.

"I wish I'd worked with you years ago. Instead of going in different directions, maybe we could have...you know." Brandon's comment was little more than a murmur, but Alex heard every word. Her heart clenched and her eyes stung with sudden emotion.

"Maybe," she whispered huskily.

As if in silent agreement, the agents surrounding Brandon dispersed one by one and returned to their workstations. Alex turned to leave.

"I'm really sorry, Alex. It was wrong of me to transfer here. This is your turf. I get that. You love it here and you're good at it. Better than good—you're great. The kids out there need you. They need you to protect them from the pond scum that seek them out, luring them with a level of deceit that takes my breath away."

He took a deep breath and let it out on a sigh. "I promise you I'll go and see Patrick in the morning and request a transfer."

Alex closed her eyes. Her shoulders slumped. There were a thousand good reasons why it was best for both of them if he left as quietly as he'd arrived. She opened her mouth to wish him luck.

"There's no need to do that. You're making progress... You've picked it up in no time at all and God knows, we can use the extra manpower. It wouldn't be fair to the rest of the team or to the kids to ask you to leave."

He stared at her in surprise. "But, what about...?"

Her lips tightened. "I meant what I said, but we're adults. I think we can put aside whatever personal issues we may have for everyone's sake, don't you think?"

He smiled again and her heart did a somersault. "Yes, of course we can. From now on, cool and professional will be my middle name. You won't even know I'm here unless we need to speak about work."

A reluctant grin tugged at the corner of her lips. "I'm not sure you need to go to that extreme. People might talk."

He hesitated and then held out his hand. "Truce?"

A lifetime of seconds dragged by, each one haunted by memories. The pain of his leaving would never be forgotten, but it was time to forgive. She took his proffered hand. "Truce," she murmured.

His gaze held hers for long seconds. Her heart thumped hard. Panic gripped her. Was she really ready for this? She pulled her hand away. Brandon lowered his gaze.

"I guess it's asking too much to suggest we could be friends?" he asked.

She bit her lip. "Friends? Is that even possible after all we've been through?"

He looked up at her, his eyes burning with intensity. "We used to be best friends."

A pang of regret went through her. "We used to be a lot of things."

Guilt flooded Brandon's face and he looked away. She sighed. He wasn't the only one who felt guilty.

"I guess it's not too late to try." The words fell out of her mouth. His gaze found hers, hope igniting in their depths.

"I guess not," he murmured.

A fleeting smile lifted her lips. "So, how was your coffee?"

He grinned back at her. "Hot."

She chuckled. He smiled back at her. "You remembered," he said. "You remembered how I take it."

"Black with one? Of course."

His gaze locked with hers again and her heart squeezed tight. The seconds multiplied. She was relieved when he cleared his throat and broke the tension.

"So, tell me about the investigation. I mean, I understand we're trying to crack a pedophile ring that's using the Internet to solicit children, but why are the AFP involved? Don't the State police usually investigate this kind of thing?"

Alex nodded, thankful for the change of subject. "Yes, each state has its own Special Ops Team, but this investigation shows plenty of signs of being international— hence our involvement. The intelligence we've received indicates the main source of the illegal pornography is coming out of Belgium. The images are being emailed to a handful of accounts around the world. The owners of these accounts are the facilitators. They purchase the images from the head office in Belgium and then on-sell them to their customers."

Brandon nodded, his lips pursed. "Sounds complicated."

"It is," Alex agreed, "and time consuming. Hence the barrage of twelve-hour shifts. But little by little, and with the help of INTERPOL and the FBI, we're collating information about the users of these accounts. The aim is to identify them, find them and lock them up for a very long time."

"And the names on the whiteboard?" He nodded in the direction of the board hanging on the far wall of the squad room. Already, more than half a dozen names had been listed with various descriptions in abbreviated shorthand underneath.

"They're the potential targets we've identified through the chat rooms. Each of us compiles our own list of information based upon the targets we come in contact with."

"How do you weed them out from everyone else in there? I've only been here a short while and it does my head in when I consider how many people visit these places. It was only when Adam, a guy in the chat room, triggered something inside me that I called some of the others over to take a look. Is that how you know when it's someone you need to look at a little closer? Is it based merely upon gut reaction?"

Alex nodded with understanding. "Gut reaction has a lot to do with it. The rest of it comes with experience. You have to remember, I've been doing this for a few years and while most of these guys lie about who and what they are, the good news is that a lot of them stick to the same basic story."

She moved to prop her hip against his desk. "There are a few basic things to look for. They generally pose as schoolboys, tend to reside in the same suburbs, have the same sporting interests and these basic facts stay the same as they move from chat room to chat room." She shrugged. "I guess it helps them keep things straight in their heads. Only one set of lies to remember, so to speak. I use much the same technique myself."

She pursed her lips. "I thought Patrick briefed you on all of this?"

Brandon nodded and smiled. "He did, but it's useful to get the operational lowdown from the foot soldiers. When does a user make it to the whiteboard?"

"Each investigator will compile a list of similarities between individual chat room users. Once you take time to analyze it, you see a pattern of common information begin to emerge. In this way, we can narrow down a list of potentially hundreds of suspects. Once we're confident about a suspect and his online aliases, he goes up on the whiteboard."

"It must be tough to stay sane while you're joining so many dots, but you thrive on it, don't you?" He said it softly, his voice full of admiration.

Alex blushed. "Yes," she said simply. "I do."

"So, how are your parents? Do they still live in Canberra?"

Adjusting to the change of subject, Alex shook her head, regretting that Brandon had missed so many important events in her life. "No, Dad passed away about three years ago."

"I'm sorry, I didn't know."

"Why would you?"

She said it without malice, but he didn't reply.

"Mom hated being in the house on her own," she continued. "She said it held too many memories. She moved into a duplex just around the corner from me not long after we buried Dad." Alex smiled, chasing the shadows away. "She's a great help with Sam and it's lovely to have her so close. I guess it worked out well for everyone."

"I guess so."

Brandon looked at her like he wanted to ask more questions. His mouth opened and then he closed it again. A sudden yearning to return to the way they had been almost overwhelmed her. What had the past four years been like for him? Had he missed her even a little bit? Had he returned to Jakarta? Was there anyone special in his life?

She clamped her jaw shut. It was none of her business.

They'd agreed on friendship, nothing else. If she wanted him to respect her privacy, she had to respect his. It was only fair. "So, what about you? Do you have any kids?" The words fell out of her mouth and into the silence.

Alex snapped her teeth together the minute she said the words. She couldn't believe she'd uttered them. What the hell was she doing? Hadn't she just told herself to mind her own business?

Brandon looked surprised and slightly confused. Who could blame him? She was up and down, hot and cold. All over the place. She gritted her teeth and silently wished for her life to be returned to normal. Back to a time before her way-too-good-looking husband intruded into every corner of it.

She had no business asking him about his kids. He was none of her business, just as she was none of his. Besides, what the hell did she care whether he had children with someone else? She couldn't care less.

Liar.

The word branded itself inside her head. Heat crept up her neck and across her face. She turned away and pretended interest in the view of the city lights outside the darkened window.

She should have known better. Brandon had always been way too observant. It was what made him such a good cop.

"No, I don't have any kids."

Her gaze flew back to his and she was startled at the regret that lingered in the deep blue of his eyes.

"That's good. You always said you didn't want any," she replied dismissively, hoping he bought her act.

He stared at her. "I said a lot of things. Four years is a long time, Alex. A lifetime, for some. People change."

"Have you?" She tried to keep the challenge out of her voice, but only partially succeeded.

He took a long time to answer. "In some ways, I guess I have."

In what ways, dammit?

The words formed in her mind and she bit down on her lip and swallowed her thoughts before they could escape. Whatever they'd had together had ended more than four years ago. They were no longer husband and wife, no matter what the law said. She had no room in her life for regrets.

"Here comes Patrick. He probably wants to take a look at my notes on Adam."

Alex blinked. She was at work. Now wasn't the time to get sidetracked.

She watched their boss advance in their direction.

"I guess I'd better leave you to it, then," she muttered, more than pleased for a reason to escape.

He leveled her with an unfathomable look. "I guess so."

CHAPTER 8

Alex's thoughts were jumbled as she pulled her Toyota into the garage of her modest three-bedroom Bondi apartment in Sydney's eastern suburbs. If she stood on tiptoe and looked out the kitchen window, she could catch the tiniest glimpse of the sparkling blue of the Pacific Ocean, but even without the view, the cool, salty smell wafting in on the early morning breeze always managed to lift her spirits.

She sighed and rested her head back against the seat for a moment. Why had she offered Brandon an olive branch? What had she been thinking? It had taken four years, but she'd moved on—hadn't she?

She didn't need this complication. Not now. And what was she going to do about Sam?

Exiting the car, she slung her handbag over her shoulder and pulled the garage door closed behind her. Taking a deep breath, she headed up the short flight of stairs to her first-floor unit. She opened the door and stepped into the quiet sanctuary of the entryway. *Home.*

She dropped her bag in its usual spot on the low table near the door. A few short steps took her into the kitchen where her mother sat at the dining table frowning over the morning newspaper, a steaming cup of coffee near her elbow.

"Hi, Mom. I'm home."

Warm, brown eyes captured hers. Martha Cavanaugh smiled. "Hi, darling. How was your night?"

Memories of the last twelve hours with Brandon rushed to the surface. Alex pushed them aside and forced a smile. "Not too bad."

"You look tired."

"I am. It was a long night. How did it go? Did Sam sleep through?"

"Almost. He woke about three and needed to go to the bathroom. He came in and asked me to turn on the light."

Alex grimaced. "I keep forgetting to pick up a night light from the shops. It only seems like yesterday he was in diapers. Now he's getting up and going to the bathroom by himself."

"I know what you mean. It seems like only yesterday I was taking *you* to the bathroom. And here you have a child of your own." Martha picked up her cup and brought it to her lips, a gentle smile on her face.

Alex smiled back at her and gave her mother's shoulder a squeeze. "Thanks, Mom."

"For what?"

"For everything. You know this would be impossible without you."

"You've always been resourceful, Alexandra. I'm sure you would have worked out a way."

Alex walked over to the cupboard and took out a mug. Flicking on the electric jug, she turned back to her mother.

"Maybe so, Mom. But I'd never have been able to take on night shifts and that would've really restricted the types of positions I could apply for."

A surge of emotion tightened her throat. She swallowed. "I'm—I'm so grateful for everything you've done for me. Life would have been very different for us without you."

Martha stood and came over to her. Pulling her in close, she pressed a kiss against Alex's hair. Tears stung the back of Alex's eyes.

"I love you, Alex, and I love Sam. He's my only grandchild. Where else would I spend my time?"

Alex shook her head. Her voice was muffled against the thick softness of her mother's house coat. "You don't have to say that, Mom. I know you had plenty of friends down in Canberra, plenty of clubs you were part of. I've hardly seen you go anywhere since Sam was born."

Pulling slightly away, Alex dashed the moisture from her cheeks and met her mother's gaze. "When I'm not feeling so damned grateful about having you in our lives, I feel guilty about taking you away from all that, away from your life."

"Don't be silly, Alex. You and Sam are my life. When your dad died..." Tears welled in Martha's eyes. She brushed them away and cleared her throat.

"The truth is, when your dad died, I was lost. I didn't know where to turn or what to do. We'd been together for nearly forty years. A lifetime. We'd always done everything together. And suddenly he was gone. And it was just me."

Martha moved slightly away and directed her gaze out the kitchen window. Alex remained silent, giving her mother the space she needed.

The older woman's voice choked with emotion when she spoke again. "When you asked me if I'd move closer to you and Sam and help you look after him, it was like a gift from above. Suddenly, I had a purpose in my life again, something to look forward to, a reason to get out of bed."

She turned and looked at Alex. "You gave me that, sweetheart. And I'll always love you for it."

The boiling kettle gave Alex an excuse to turn away. She took the opportunity to swipe at the moisture in her eyes and poured water into her mug.

Martha cleared her throat. "Enough about me. Why don't you sit down and tell me what's bothering you. For the last couple of weeks, I've been able to tell something's not right."

The urge to confide in her mother was suddenly overwhelming. Alex drew in a deep breath, picked up her mug and made her way back to the table. Martha followed her.

"You're right, Mom. Something's not right."

Her mother sat beside her, her gaze filled with love and encouragement. "Talk to me, Alex."

"I-I don't know where to start."

"Start where it matters."

Alex sighed and fixed her gaze on the checked tablecloth. "It's about Brandon."

"Brandon? As in, your husband?"

"Ex, Mom. Ex-husband," she said dryly.

Her mother shrugged. "If you say so. I don't recall seeing any divorce papers."

Alex bit her lip. "You know we're not divorced, Mom. The fact that we're still legally bound to each other doesn't make him my husband."

"If you say so, darling."

Irritation surged through Alex and she began to have second thoughts about confiding in her mother. Martha seemed to sense her daughter's change of heart.

"I'm sorry. I shouldn't have said that. But you know I always liked Brandon. It broke my heart to see the two of you go your separate ways. I've never given up hope you might one day reconcile."

"There's no hope of that, Mom. But, you might yet get to see him again."

Martha frowned. "What do you mean?"

Alex pressed her lips together. "I mean, he's back."

"Back?"

"Yes, Mom. Brandon's back."

Her mother's eyes went wide. "He's back? In Sydney? For how long?"

"Yes. As for how long—who knows? He's just transferred to the CPU. He started a fortnight ago."

"Oh, Alex. Honey. What are you going to do?"

"Do? I'll do what I always do. I'll get out of bed, put a smile on my face and go into work. I've been there for more than three years, Mom. I love that job. He's not going to march in and take over my turf. If anyone's going to leave, it will be him."

Her mother looked doubtful. "If he's only just arrived, I can't see him wanting to move on any time soon. Did he know you worked there?"

Alex shrugged and took a sip of coffee. "I don't know. Something tells me he must have known. It just seems too big a coincidence, otherwise. But then, why would he choose to come and work alongside me? I'm sure he hasn't forgotten how things ended between us. Why would he want to fraternize with the enemy?"

"Maybe he doesn't see you that way anymore?" It was offered quietly, without inflection.

Alex hung her head in her hands. "I don't know, Mom. I don't *know*. I don't know what he's doing here. I don't know what he wants. He says he's changed, but I don't know that either."

"Changed? In what way?"

"That's the thing. I don't *know*." Restless energy surged through her and she pushed away from the table and paced the length of the small kitchen.

"It's driving me crazy. I'm so tied up in knots at the thought of working with him, it's interfering with my concentration. We're in the middle of something huge at work and all I can think about is him. I remember the way we were before we broke up and then I remember why we broke up and the anger just about consumes me. I know it wasn't all his fault. There were problems with our marriage before he left for Jakarta, but he was the one who returned home one day and announced we were over."

She dragged in a ragged breath. "He never told me why. He refused to discuss it. He simply told me it wasn't working and packed his things and left. I've never had the chance to rant and rave at him with my fury and my hurt and my shock and my disappointment. I feel like I've been robbed of that. That it was my right to scream at him and demand to know why. He owed that to me."

Alex met her mother's steady gaze and tears welled again at the love and sympathy she saw there. All of a sudden, the fight went out of Alex. Resuming her seat at the table, she picked up her coffee mug and took another sip.

"I don't know why I keep resurrecting these old hurts. It

was years ago. We've both moved on. What good can it do to keep reliving it?"

"*Have* you moved on?"

Alex's fingers tightened around her mug. She forced air into her lungs and concentrated fiercely on the tablecloth.

"Of course I have. Why are you asking?"

"Please don't get defensive, darling. I'm talking about what I see. It's been more than four years since your marriage ended. I haven't even heard you speak about someone who might have caught your interest, let alone seen you go out on a date. You're a beautiful young woman with her whole life ahead of her and yet, for some reason, you're not willing to take the next step." Martha shot her a pointed look. "*That's* what I'm talking about."

Alex squirmed in her seat. "Just because I haven't dated anyone doesn't mean I'm not over Brandon." She shrugged and tried to hold her mother's gaze. "I've been busy, Mom. Sam's only young. It's not like I can just leave him to go out drinking or dancing or whatever."

"Why not?" Martha challenged gently.

Heat rose up Alex's neck. "Well, because... I don't know. He's only a baby. He's my responsibility. I don't expect you to babysit him so that I can have a social life. I knew what being a single Mom would entail and I embraced it with open arms. I love Sam with everything that I am. I'm certainly not lamenting my lack of social life or a—a *boyfriend*."

"I know you're not, sweetheart," Martha agreed softly. "But I wish you'd stop using Sam as an excuse. He's no longer a baby. He's a little boy who's growing bigger by the day and one day, he'll go off and find his own life. What's going to happen to you, then?"

Alex brushed off her mother's concern. "That's so far away, Mom, I can't imagine even giving it a moment's thought."

"It's not as far away as you think, Alex. Look how fast the last four years have gone."

Alex worried at a thread that had come loose from the

tablecloth. Her mother picked up her coffee mug and took another sip. They sat together in silence, each lost in their own thoughts.

"Have you told Brandon about Sam?"

Icy tension gripped Alex's belly and her fingers stilled. She refused to look at her mother. "No."

"You are going to tell him though, aren't you? Now he's back in your life—"

"He's *not* back in my life." Her gaze clashed with her mother's. "We're work colleagues. That's all. You're not listening to me."

"I'm not the only one not listening, Alex. I told you more than four years ago you were making a mistake keeping Sam a secret from his father. My feelings haven't changed. Brandon has a right to know."

Anger blazed through her. "Brandon has no rights. He didn't then, and he doesn't now. He chose to walk out on me and our marriage. He gave up on us. He promised to love me until 'death do us part.' Four years in and he does a runner."

"That's not fair, Alex. He didn't know you were pregnant."

Alex heard the steel in her mother's tone, but chose to ignore it.

"Would you have stayed if you'd been in my position? If Dad had come home from an overseas jaunt and confessed he wanted to end your marriage? Would you have told him you were pregnant? Would you have chosen to live with the feeling every single day thereafter of not knowing whether he'd even *be* there if it wasn't for the baby?"

Alex choked on the last word and struggled to catch her breath. "I couldn't live like that. I couldn't risk telling Brandon about the baby. I didn't want him to stay with me out of a sense of duty. I didn't want to be someone's *duty*. I wanted to be cherished and loved and adored. I wanted us to be the way we were before babies and broken vows had become a part of our everyday existence."

Her voice broke. Alex turned away and tried to stem the

traitorous tears that threatened to spill over. "But it was never going to happen. I couldn't turn back time. Neither of us could, even if we wanted to."

"Good morning, Sam. How did you sleep?"

Alex stiffened at her mother's words and hurriedly swiped at her tears. Taking a few seconds to regain control, she plastered a smile on her face and turned to greet her son.

"Hey, baby. Did you have a good sleep? Come and give Mommy a kiss."

He hurtled toward her, his chubby little arms extended. She kneeled and pulled him in close, breathing in his sleepy, little-boy smell. Her heart filled with overwhelming love. He was her life. She'd do anything for him. No one would ever come between them.

She thought of Brandon and desperation nipped at the edges of her consciousness. Despite her earlier fanciful thoughts, she couldn't run the risk of Brandon discovering he had a son. No matter what her mother said. Sam was hers and hers alone.

Guilt twisted inside her. She ignored it with brutal determination. Brandon was nothing more than a sperm donor. He hadn't wanted kids. Not with her, not with anyone. He'd made it clear over and over again during the tumultuous last year of their marriage. She was the one who had wanted a child.

He had no claim on Sam. Not now, not ever.

———————

Brandon spat a mouthful of toothpaste into the bathroom sink and rinsed his mouth. Staring at his reflection in the mirror, he grimaced at the age lines and shadows of regret that life had etched on his face. The strain of working alongside Alex was beginning to show. What the hell was he doing? Why was he torturing himself like this?

With an impatient swipe of the towel across his mouth, he tossed the linen aside and left the room. The sun was slowly climbing up over the horizon, its gold and orange fire glittering across the deep blue of the Pacific Ocean. His comfortable unit afforded unobstructed views over Bondi Beach and its mix of trendy apartments and old family homes.

It was the home he'd shared with Alex. Even though their marriage had ended, he hadn't been able to bring himself to part with the property they'd purchased together. It had been their dream home, the place they'd planned to grow old in.

It hadn't worked out that way, but when Alex's lawyer had raised the question of selling the apartment, he hadn't hesitated to buy her out.

Walking into the open plan kitchen and dining room, he slid one of the double sliding glass doors open and stepped onto the balcony. His eyes were gritty from lack of sleep after another long night shift, but he could still appreciate the beauty of the morning and the sharp, tangy scent of the salt spray from the rocks on the beach below. Early morning joggers dotted the sand and he yearned for their seemingly carefree existence.

Leaning over the balcony, he filled his lungs with the fresh, salty air and tried not to remember the countless mornings he'd spent here with Alex. His wife.

Despite the years they'd been separated, he'd never stopped thinking of her that way. It was probably one of the reasons his half-hearted relationships with the handful of women who'd come in and out of his life in the time since, hadn't been able to hold his interest.

That, and the fact he was still in love with her.

For so long, he'd strived to create a life without her, to move forward—and on the surface, he'd succeeded. His career had flourished.

Without the responsibility of a wife, he'd taken on some of the most dangerous assignments, no longer placing any value on his life. With the increase in danger came an increase in his salary and his financial status was enviably secure.

The same couldn't be said for his personal life, but that was something he kept firmly to himself and no one, not even his family, could guess at the depth of his deception.

Until the night he'd opened up to Tom, he'd never given anyone the tiniest hint that he was anything but happy over his single, happy-go-lucky existence. He'd done a good job of always having an attractive date at family get-togethers and work functions and, apart from the occasional look of concern thrown his way by his mother or one of his sisters, no one had been any the wiser.

But, the truth was, he was lonely. His heart had never recovered from the death blow he'd dealt his marriage and even though he'd spent the first couple of years afterwards in a quagmire of pain and anger and confusion, time and countless therapy sessions had eventually had their effect and the end result was that now he simply missed his wife. Missed her laughter, missed her touch, missed her love.

His thoughts returned to his conversation with Alex the night before and he frowned. He was still confused about her about-face. She'd been furious with him over his dig at her son's paternity the day before and yet less than twenty-four hours later, she'd agreed to a truce.

Her mixed signals were doing his head in and he hated the way his traitorous heart had leaped in joy at the scrap of kindness she'd offered. It was pathetic. *He* was pathetic.

He didn't know what he was trying to prove by inviting himself into her domain. It wasn't fair to either of them. It did his pining heart no good at all to have her within reach but completely unattainable.

Maybe he was being conceited? Maybe she couldn't care less that he was there. She'd managed to move on with someone else and have a child. The Alex he knew, or used to know, didn't give her heart out freely. The bloke must have been pretty darn special or she wouldn't have given him the time of day, let alone created a child with him.

Irritation washed over him and he cursed long and loudly.

It was over between them. She'd moved on. She had a life of her own. She had a career, a home and a son. She had everything she wanted.

And that didn't include him.

He should never have requested the transfer. There were plenty of people who needed him. Plenty of units that wanted and would appreciate his help. Alex wasn't one of them, despite her peace offering.

It was time to let her go and to accept once and for all that what they had together was over. He'd suggested friendship and she'd even baulked at that.

How many ways did she have to tell him, show him? It was over. *They* were over.

All he had to do was convince his heart.

CHAPTER 9

He stretched in his chair and languidly stroked his semi-hard erection, his gaze fixed on the screen in front of him. It was late Friday night, his favorite time to play. The weekend spread out before him, with all its glorious possibilities and he didn't have to show up to his dead-end job for two whole days.

He'd rushed home to his apartment, pushing and shoving his way through the crowds of commuters, all anxious to start their weekend. Impatiently, he'd unlocked his front door and stumbled into his hallway.

Dropping his bag to the floor, he'd made a beeline for his bedroom and with a few quick movements had brought his computer to life. With fingers flying over the keyboard, he'd logged into his favorite chat rooms. It was only then that his body relaxed and the familiar promise of pleasure coursed through him.

He was home—in his favorite place in the world. Surrounded by dewy, sweet little girls who thought he was funny. Who thought he was cute. Who were so, so eager to please.

And better still, who wanted to meet him.

He thought of Lady G. He'd been chatting to her for weeks before she'd posted her photo. Finally, he'd had a face to put to the girl he'd been grooming.

She'd looked at once warm and familiar and just the type he enjoyed. More than that, she was opening up to him. Up until now, they'd mainly talked about school and movies, but tonight, she'd told him about her girlfriends and their netball team. Anticipation surged through him. Slowly, but inexorably, he was drawing her in. The game was on.

His cock hardened and his breath came faster. His hand pumped the engorged flesh. His balls tightened in anticipation. With his gaze still fixed to the screen, he gave a yelp of relief as Lady G came online.

Sticky, white fluid pumped out of his cock, covering his hand in wetness. He collapsed against the chair and savored the last of his orgasm. His body filled with joy.

He reached over to the nightstand and tugged out a handful of tissues from the box that sat there and wiped his hand and now-flaccid cock. Tossing the tissues to the floor, he drew his keyboard closer and began to type.

Hey there, gorgeous. I was just thinking about you.

The reply was halting and he smiled. Lady G was not a good typist.

I'm glad. I'm always thinking about you.

So, are you playing netball this weekend?

Yeah. Tomorrow morning.

Anticipation coiled in his gut. *I'd love to come and watch you.*

He waited for her response, his heart pumping hard. It seemed to take forever.

Okay.

Relief and excitement gushed through his veins. His cock twitched. His fingers shook on the keyboard.

Where?

We're playing at Manly. We start at nine.

I'll be there.

Really? Oh, my God! I can't wait!

Cassie scanned the pockets of people that dotted the netball courts, looking for Justin. She'd printed out the picture he'd posted and it was tucked inside her bra strap. The Saturday morning crowd wasn't thick, and most of the spectators were mothers, but she still couldn't spot him.

She was kicking herself for not telling him which court she was playing on. He knew her team, but she didn't know if he'd be bothered to find out which court they'd been assigned. There were at least twenty teams congregated around various courts. If he didn't ask someone where the Manly Musketeers were playing, he'd never find her.

With a sigh, she turned away and focused on her team mates gathered around their coach.

"Cassie, I need you to play Center today. Marcie Richards is home in bed with the flu."

Cassie snapped to attention, a protest forming on her lips. She hated playing Center. Besides, she'd told Justin she played Goal Attack. She wanted him to see her at her best.

"But, Mrs Johnson, it's been ages since I played that position. Perhaps Jane could—"

A stern look was thrown her way and Cassie swallowed the rest of her argument.

"Right. Now that's settled, everyone listen in. This is an important game. I need you to..."

Cassie tuned out the rest of the coach's instructions and scanned the crowds once again. She still couldn't see anyone who looked even remotely like the picture he'd sent her. Disappointment surged through her. He wasn't going to come.

James Gibbons took refuge from the sunshine under a tall gum tree and lowered the brim of his baseball cap. After making a few innocuous enquires about the whereabouts of the Manly Musketeers, he'd made his way to the court where Lady G's team was playing. From his vantage point in the shade, he could see members of the under thirteens stretching and warming up in anticipation of the game ahead.

His gaze fell upon the girl wearing the GA bib and his jaw dropped. She looked nothing like her photo. *The cunning little bitch.* No wonder she'd sent the picture of the cute teen.

Although her hair was light, it wasn't the golden wave of shiny blond that had illuminated his computer screen over a week ago, keeping his fantasies at fever pitch. And she'd put on at least twenty pounds since the shot had been taken, if it was a photo of her at all. After seeing her in the flesh, he had his doubts.

The girl he'd wanked over was tall and lithe and had the body of a dancer. This girl was only average height and her thighs were so thick they were probably rubbing together beneath her short little sports skirt.

Disappointment surged through him and it was tinged with anger. He'd had such high hopes for little Lady G. She seemed perfect. Beyond perfect. Photos of her beautiful young body would have fostered a premium price—maybe one of his highest yet. Flawless beauty like hers—well, like the girl in the photo she'd sent him—was highly sought after in the circles he frequented. His customers would have been begging him for more, willing to pay whatever price he demanded, to have a piece of her on their screens. He may have even had a chance of attracting the attention of some of the bigger international buyers.

The players took their positions and the whistle blew. Girls ran and bounced across the court, but he'd seen enough. He'd forget about her and the promise she'd held and instead, he'd turn his attention to a couple of other promising young playthings he'd been courting online. Hopefully, they'd prove more successful than his experience with this little bitch.

Turning away, he jammed his fists into the pockets of his jacket and strode toward the car park.

———————

Cassie looked up as a man with a red baseball cap pulled low over his eyes walked away in the direction of the car park. She couldn't tell how old he was, but even from this distance, it was obvious he wasn't a teenager. Dark sunglasses hid his eyes and only a few tufts of brown hair escaped the confines of his cap and tickled the back of his neck.

His clothes spoke of money, but had been put together in a rather haphazard way. His denim jeans were wrinkled and the light fabric of his black jacket was no match for the fall crispness that permeated the early morning air.

She wondered who he was. Definitely not Justin, but she hadn't seen him here before. He was probably an uncle of one of the girls, perhaps visiting from the country. Sometimes her father's brothers came down to Sydney from the north coast and occasionally, they'd come and watch her play.

"Cassie!"

She was jolted out of her musings when the ball came hurtling her way. Snatching it out of the air, she threw it to a team mate and watched as it made its way to the Goal Shooter. She waited, tense and expectant, as the girl prepared for the shot.

The ball bounced once, twice upon the steel rim and then dropped out over the line. The whistle blew. Cassie's shoulders slumped. It was a shitty start to a shitty day.

A couple of hours later, weighed down by hurt and disappointment, Cassie dragged her netball kit up the stairs. On the one hand, she was glad Justin hadn't showed. The stand-in Goal Attack had been hopeless and they'd been soundly defeated. But Justin had told her he would come. He'd told her he'd wanted to meet her and say hi. He'd told her he'd wanted to watch her play.

He'd done none of those things and she was beginning to wish she hadn't said anything to her girlfriends. They'd quiz her mercilessly when she got to school on Monday. In fact, her best friend Madeleine would probably text her any minute wanting to know how things had gone.

She felt like an idiot. She should have known better than to think a boy as hot as Justin would be interested in her. Even some of the girls in Grade Nine and Ten couldn't get their boyfriends to watch a netball game. And he was a boy she'd only just met. Not even met, if you didn't count the Internet.

Closing the door to her bedroom behind her, Cassie dropped her bag on the floor and flopped onto her bed. She could almost hear her mother scolding her for lying on her bedspread with her Nikes on, but right at that moment, she didn't care.

She'd never been so humiliated. She was mad at herself, more than him. She was the fool who'd thought he actually meant it when he'd called her beautiful.

She picked up the pretty pink-and-white cushion that decorated her bed and squeezed it hard to her chest. It wasn't fair. It just wasn't fair. Why couldn't he have been different? Why couldn't he have been there, smiling and cheering for her and making her heart sing?

She tensed at the gentle knock on her door.

"Cassie, I heard you come in. Are you all right?"

Her mother's soft voice, full of concern almost brought tears to her eyes, but she bit her lip against the surge of emotion. She wasn't a baby any longer and it was high time she stopped acting like one. How was she ever going to capture the interest of a boy like Justin if she blubbered over every little disappointment like a baby?

The knock came again and she knew if she didn't say something, her mother would come in.

"I'm fine, Mom," she managed. "Just tired from netball. It was a hard game."

"Can I come in?" The request was voiced softly, without demand and Cassie ignored the guilt that assailed her. She'd always tried to be honest with her parents, just like they'd taught her to be and it made her uncomfortable to lie to her mother now. She knew her parents wouldn't approve of Justin. They hadn't even let her have a Facebook page.

Despite weeks of begging and pleading, they'd refused to give in. It was one of the disadvantages of having a father who was a long-serving detective. He'd seen too much of the wrong side of society to be anything but overprotective of his own kids and her mother was in full support of his decision.

Not that she couldn't understand their attitude. In fact, most of the time she was glad to know they cared. Plenty of kids weren't as lucky to have parents like hers. But there were times, like now, when her parents wouldn't approve of her behavior. They hadn't exactly banned her from online chat rooms, but they'd cautioned her long and hard about the risks associated with them and they'd no doubt be horrified to know she'd struck up a friendship with a boy she'd met there.

But life was so different now compared to when they were young. The Internet hadn't even been invented when they were teens. They just didn't understand how vital it was to be part of it. To talk to your classmates, to meet new friends. She appreciated their concern, she really did, but they just didn't—and perhaps, couldn't—understand.

Knowing if she didn't respond as her mother expected, she'd become suspicious, Cassie sat up on her bed and hung her sneakered feet over the side.

"Sure, Mom. Come in." She plastered a smile on her face and waited for the door to open.

The house stood in darkness and had been quiet for more than an hour when Cassie finally found the courage to open her laptop and login to her favorite chat room. Her heart skipped a beat when she saw he was there.

She chewed on her thumbnail. Should she acknowledge

him? What should she say? What if he ignored her? God, she couldn't bear it if he ignored her.

Hey, there, gorgeous. I was wondering if I'd get to talk to you today.

Her heart skipped a beat. He'd noticed her and wanted to talk. Her tension eased slightly, but she bit her lip. He'd made no mention of failing to show up at her game. Should she play it cool, like it hadn't really mattered? Was that the best way to handle it?

Before she could decide, he commented again.

Sorry I couldn't make it to your game today. Dad had a list of chores for me that took me most of the day. I couldn't believe it. I had to wash the car and mow the lawn. He even made me sweep out the garage. All I wanted to do was to be at your game. How did it go, anyway?

Relief surged through her and she felt giddy with happiness. She giggled and swiped at the tears in her eyes and hurried to type a response.

Sorry to hear about your day from hell. Mine wasn't so hot, either. We lost 10-4. Our Center was away and I had to switch positions. The girl who played in my position didn't get a single goal. It was so frustrating. I'm glad you weren't there to see it.

His reply came quickly.

I wish I had been. Even watching you lose would have been the highlight of my day. I would have given you all the sympathy you wanted. When do you play again?

Cassie went warm all over. Her heart filled to bursting and she wrapped her arms around her chest and held on tightly. She wanted to hold onto the feeling of joy and excitement for every second that it lasted—and even longer.

She knew he was the real deal. He hadn't been stringing her along. He *did* think she was beautiful. She smiled in contentment. She couldn't wait until the next game.

James read the words as they crawled across his screen. His excitement stirred. It hadn't been her. The fat little Goal Attack hadn't been her. He hadn't even noticed the Center. He'd been too furious at what he'd thought was Lady G's duplicity.

Hope and anticipation surged through him. Maybe all was not lost, after all.

CHAPTER 10

The squad room door opened, drawing Alex's gaze. Brandon strode in and she quickly averted her eyes. She tamped down on the fluttering of her heart and the nerves that tightened her belly. No matter how many times she told herself she was over him, her body continued to betray her.

They'd been working together for nearly a month, yet he still had the power to distract her. Thank God they'd both been too busy concentrating on the job at hand to spend much time in idle chitchat.

Patrick strode out of his office and headed toward the whiteboard. Detective Sergeant Larry Perkins, his second-in-command, was by his side. Both men looked tense. Alex's stomach clenched in anticipation.

"All right folks, gather around. We need to talk."

Alex pushed her chair back and joined the handful of other officers who had pulled the morning shift. She chose a spot next to Ronald Gregson, a veteran agent with more than twenty years behind him and who looked more like a cuddly grandfather than the hardened agent she knew him to be. Brandon pulled up next to her.

Her nerves escalated and it had nothing to do with the upcoming briefing. She studiously ignored him and trained her gaze on her boss.

"Okay people, here's what you need to know. I've just gotten off the phone from INTERPOL. Over the last few weeks, every agency involved has ramped up their efforts and we're very close to identifying the suspected ringleader. There is one Internet Service Provider, or ISP address that consistently appears in the sites offering pictures of young children for sale."

Patrick glanced around the group of officers. "The information just in from INTERPOL is that they've narrowed the search to an address in a small farming village on the outskirts of Antwerp. The Belgian police have been notified and are putting together a taskforce as I speak."

"What role do we play in it?" asked Jack Nelson, one of their newer members.

Patrick acknowledged the question with a brief nod in Jack's direction. "At this stage, nothing. We've been asked to sit tight until INTERPOL and the Belgians formulate a plan." He met the gaze of each one of them, his expression grim.

"You can all appreciate the need for utmost secrecy. If even a whisper of this gets out, these guys will disappear into the cyber ether and we'll have lost any chance of identifying them. Any hint their ringleader is under suspicion and it will be all over for us and our investigation."

"What do you expect will happen, sir?" Brandon asked, his voice low.

Patrick turned and faced him. "I expect the local Belgian police will put the house under surveillance and, when the time's right, storm the place with a search warrant. That's what normally happens in these situations." Patrick turned to his second-in-command. "Larry has some images of the house in question courtesy of Google Earth. You might all like to take a look."

Larry moved toward the SMART board next to the whiteboard on the wall and logged in to Google Earth. Less than a minute later, a non-descript farmhouse perched amongst green fields on the edge of a town filled the screen.

Alex stared at it, unable to believe how perfectly innocent it looked. If the intelligence was accurate, this unobtrusive structure housed a monster. She shook her head. Brandon leaned closer.

"Scary, isn't it? How normal it looks?"

She nodded and kept her gaze focused on the screen, unwilling to engage him in conversation.

Patrick walked to the SMART board and picked up a pointer. "You can see that although it's on acreage, there are a couple of neighboring properties here and here that are uncomfortably close. The taskforce will need to take the proximity of these houses into account when formulating any plan to storm the building in question. We only hope, when the time comes, the occupant or occupants surrender peacefully."

Ryan stepped forward. "How many people do they think are involved?"

"At this stage, I understand there's only one suspect. The house is owned and occupied by Nicolas Janssens. He's a public servant who works in some administrative capacity with the Antwerp Water Works, also known as the AWW. As far as they can tell, he lives alone."

Alex cleared her throat. "I assume once the search warrant has been executed, the taskforce will seize the suspect's computer and analyze the data?"

Patrick turned to her. "You assume right. The computer will be sent to the FBI at Quantico. Their experts will go over every inch of it and analyze whatever information they find. Obviously, we're hoping the computer will help identify the suspect's suppliers and customers, including those residing in Australia."

His gaze moved around the room. "That's where you all come in and where your lives are going to get busy. You might have thought you'd been busy before, but let me tell you, it will have nothing on the hours you're going to have to put in once we've identified the ISPs based in Australia."

Larry paced in front of them. "Time will be of the essence. Once they've carried out the raid on the suspected ringleader, every minute will count. It will only be a matter of time before this guy's clients figure out something's not right.

Overnight, people will shut down accounts, delete browser histories and destroy hard drives. This will be a complex operation and one that requires the expertise and finesse of the very best in law enforcement." His gaze encompassed the team of officers standing in a loose semi-circle. "That's why you're here."

Alex shared nods and glances of acknowledgement amongst the officers. She could feel Brandon's gaze on her, but refused to look at him.

"According to INTERPOL, Janssens has been operating for a substantial period of time. They're anticipating the discovery of thousands of ISP addresses and even more customer email addresses stored on his computer," said Patrick.

Jack groaned. The super's gaze narrowed on him. "You're right to groan. It's a mammoth task. Just be thankful it's not your responsibility to plow through them all. Every credit card transaction found on that hard drive and linked to a suspicious online purchase will be checked out and either discounted or added to the list of suspects."

His gaze returned to encompass the group. "Fortunately for us, given that we have a proportionately smaller population than Europe or North America and going on past experience, we anticipate only a very small number of those will originate from Australia. Even so, as Larry said, when this breaks you're going to be busier than you ever thought possible."

Brandon straightened and Alex tensed and then cursed under her breath. She hated that she was so sensitive to his every move.

"From what you say," Brandon said, "tracking down suspects' ISP addresses is going to take them considerable time. What do we do in the meantime?"

Patrick cocked an eyebrow in Brandon's direction, his mouth twitching. "Angling for some time off already, Munro? If you can't handle the pace..."

Most of the officers chuckled. Brandon flushed. Alex felt a wave of sympathy, even as a smile formed on her lips.

Patrick waved them silent. "Sorry, Munro. I couldn't help myself." He cleared his throat. "While the FBI is doing their bit, I expect each of you to keep the users you suspect might be predators engaged and interested online. I want you to increase your presence in the chat rooms and provide a distraction. We don't know how many of them are going to turn up on Janssens' hard drive. We don't want them suspecting anything's amiss and we want to keep them too involved to worry about contacting their supplier. Keep collating data and adding it to the whiteboard. You never know what might be helpful."

Larry clapped his hands. "All right people, that's about it. If anyone has any other questions, please feel free to ask. Otherwise, you can all get back to work. Thanks for your time... And good luck."

The group of officers dispersed. Brandon followed a couple of others in the direction of the tearoom. Alex swallowed a sigh of relief and headed back to her desk.

It was only mid-morning, but already she was tired. The long hours were wearing her down. She'd almost forgotten what her son looked like.

She couldn't wait for the end of the week and the promise of a couple of days off. They'd be all the more precious now that she knew there'd be no time off once the investigation hit full swing.

She was planning to take Sam to the aquarium at Darling Harbour and she couldn't wait to see the look on his face when she told him.

"I thought I'd return the favor. White with one, right?"

The deep, familiar voice drawled close to her ear and Alex's traitorous heart took off at a gallop. Lost in her plans for the weekend, she hadn't even noticed his approach.

Brandon leaned over and placed a steaming mug of coffee in front of her. His arm brushed her shoulder. Her breathing stilled. Heat stole up her neck and spread across her cheeks and she cursed silently, knowing she was now going to have to attempt some form of conversation.

"Thank you. I... I can't believe you remembered."

He stared at her, his face only inches from hers. "I remember lots of things."

The seconds lengthened. Try as she might, Alex couldn't drag her gaze away. Her heart thumped against her rib cage. The look on his face intensified.

"So do I," she murmured.

An indefinable emotion flared hotly in his eyes. Her breath caught. She couldn't believe she'd said that. *What the hell was she thinking?*

She turned away and shuffled papers around on her desk, needing to keep her hands busy while her mind tried to regain its equilibrium. The heat of his gaze seared the back of her neck. She had to say something. The problem was, she couldn't think of a single, sensible sentence.

Brandon propped a hip against her desk and crossed his arms, obviously in no hurry to leave. Panic nipped at her heels.

"I miss us."

His quiet admission rocked her to the core. Her gaze flew to his and she almost gasped at the raw need she saw reflected in the dark blue shadows of his eyes.

Her heart constricted. Somewhere deep inside of her, she recognized his pain and responded to it. The feeling was familiar. Way too familiar. No matter what she'd told herself over the years, she loved him. Had always loved him.

A heavy weight settled in the pit of her stomach and she couldn't even bring herself to look at him. What sort of a future could they have? Even if she accepted the reasons why he'd left the way he had, when he discovered the level of her deceit, he'd never forgive her.

No, it was best to leave things the way they were. Acknowledge the past and move forward into the future. Alone. Just her and Sam. And her mother.

She snuck a peek at him and quickly looked away. No, she didn't need anyone else. Most especially, her way-too-good-looking husband who now stared at her with undisguised yearning.

It was way past time to let him go. Let *them* go. And move on.

Her thoughts turned to the half-completed online dating application she'd filled out a week ago, when she'd vowed to put Brandon Munro out of her life once and for all. What better way to get over him than to return to the dating game? She'd put that off for way too long.

Like her mother said, she was young and passably attractive with her whole life ahead of her. There was no reason she couldn't go out with other men and have fun. The fact that she didn't have the slightest inclination to start another relationship didn't matter. A casual date here and there with an attractive man could be exactly what she needed.

"Tom and Lily are having a barbeque on Saturday. I was wondering if you'd like to come? I checked the roster. I know you have the day off."

Alarm sealed Alex's vocal cords and she fished around in increasing desperation for an excuse.

"Um, I…um… Thanks, but I promised Sam I'd take him to the Aquarium. With all the stuff that's been going on here at work, I've barely had time to say hello to him."

"It's a night time thing. Dinner. I think the Aquarium closes at five. Why don't you come afterwards?"

Alex's heart accelerated. *Oh, God, how did she get here?*

"Er… Thanks, that's really kind of you, but my mother's away for the weekend, so I won't have anyone to look after Sam. She leaves as soon as I get home this afternoon."

"Bring him with you."

Her panic escalated to sheer terror. She flailed around for another excuse.

"Oh, wow. That's…that's really kind of you, but Sam won't be in any state to socialize after a day out. He'll be exhausted. He'll need to be bathed and put to bed. Believe me, you don't want to be around a tired thr—two-year-old." Her cheeks flamed and she prayed he hadn't caught her slip.

His expression hardened. He pushed away from her desk, his body tense.

"It's okay, Alex. I get it. You don't want to see any more of me than you have to. I just thought…" His jaws clamped together and he gave a sharp shake of his head. "Don't worry; I won't bother you again."

The hurt and rejection that shadowed his eyes almost did her in. "Brandon. I didn't mean… I… It's not what you think. It's just that…I can't…" Guilt settled heavily in her belly. Sharp tears pricked the backs of her eyes. But there was no help for it. Until he knew the truth, she couldn't have him around Sam. She couldn't have him, or his family, looking and comparing and wondering, no matter how she might wish things were different.

She had to tell him. But not here at work. Perhaps she could meet him somewhere afterwards? Somewhere neutral, somewhere free from interruption. Hope sprang to life inside her and then quickly fizzled. The timing was off. Both of them were buried knee-deep in a high-stress investigation. Very soon, they'd be working around the clock. Neither of them needed the extra pressure of dealing with unforeseeable, traumatic personal circumstances.

Brandon's shoulders slumped and he turned away. Alex swallowed a sigh. Could she have Brandon's family meet Sam and keep the secret of his paternity concealed?

Was it possible?

Brandon had seen Sam's photo and it hadn't seemed to trigger any suspicions. Her lie about his age had seen to that. Knowing she was going to regret it, but somehow unable to stop the words from forming, Alex stood and called to his retreating form.

"Okay, we'll come."

Brandon stilled and then slowly turned around. His gaze was icy, his voice scathing.

"Don't do it out of pity, Alex. I don't need you to feel sorry for me."

She shook her head, suddenly anxious for him to

understand. "Of course I'm not doing it out of pity. Surely you know me better than that?"

He gave her another hard look, his eyes narrowed. "I don't know what I know anymore."

"It...it would be nice to see Tom and Lily again," she added, the words coming out in a rush. "Give me the details and we'll meet you there."

His body relaxed and he gave a tentative smile. "Really? Great. I'll let them know there will be a couple of extras." He shot her a quick grin and turned away, heading in the direction of the staff amenities.

With a sigh, Alex plopped back down in her chair and tried to focus on the computer screen in front of her. Why, oh why couldn't she have simply declined?

———

It was hours later, with the house adjusting to the oncoming night and Sam tucked into bed that Alex switched on her laptop and opened up the page to the dating website she'd been toying with. She may have agreed to go to a family barbeque with Brandon, but that didn't mean they were going to have a future together. It was time she accepted that and got on with her life.

She clicked open a link on the dating site and was inundated with photos of good-looking, carefree couples strolling along the beach, enjoying summer picnics and sharing laughs. They seemed to mock her with their picture-perfect happiness.

This could be you, they seemed to say. *See how happy we are? You, too, could find your perfect match. You, too, could enjoy a romantic weekend away, watch a perfect sunset with the perfect date. All you need do is sign up and wait for the fun to begin. There's someone out there waiting for you, wanting you. We guarantee it. It's all just a click away.*

Alex opened the profile she'd compiled a week ago and

reread it. Unlike a lot of people who frequented these sites, she'd tried to be honest with her answers. *Who knew?* Maybe there was a like-minded man out there with a similar moral compass?

Her hand closed over the mouse. Nerves tickled her belly. Taking a deep breath and a mouthful of the merlot in the half-empty glass by her elbow, she clicked on "Submit." Her application for the search for everlasting love disappeared into cyberspace.

It was done.

CHAPTER 11

The house in the much-sought-after northern Sydney suburb of Chatswood was larger than the single-storey structure Tom and Lily had lived in four years ago. A big front yard bordered by huge Moreton Bay fig trees embraced a wide stretch of manicured lawn. Several cars, some costing more than a couple of years of Alex's salary, lined the long pebbled driveway and her already-frayed nerves ratcheted up another notch.

She found a place to park and switched off the engine. She hadn't seen Tom and Lily since the separation but she could still recall the hurt and bewilderment in Lily's voice when Alex failed to respond to the countless messages Lily had left on her voice mail in the days and weeks after the breakdown of her marriage.

They'd been more than sisters-in-law. They'd been friends. Good friends. And despite the fact she'd had no choice, Alex still felt guilty about turning her back on her.

A renewed flutter of nerves tightened her belly. What the hell was she doing? Why, oh why, had she said yes? She and Brandon were over. How had she let herself be persuaded by a gorgeous pair of baby blues, shining with hope and vulnerability?

She should have just told him no and that would have been the end of it. He wouldn't have asked again. She knew him too well. Stubborn and proud, he wouldn't have risked rejection twice.

Therein lay the problem. To be honest, she didn't want to let him go. She might be a fool for even entertaining the idea that they could be something to each other again, but there it was. The thought of shutting that possibility down forever terrified her. And she saw her uncertainty and a glimmer of hope in his eyes too.

But what about Sam? If there was even a chance they were going to have a future together, she had to tell Brandon about his son and whichever way she looked at that little dilemma, she couldn't imagine a happy ending.

"Whose house is this?" Sam's sleepy voice came from the back seat.

Alex suppressed a sigh and kept her tone light. "I told you, remember? It's the brother of a friend of mine from work. I knew them a long time ago, before you were born. They asked us over to a barbeque."

"Do they have any kids?"

She nodded. "Yes, they do. A boy and a girl. They're both a bit older than you, but I know they'll make sure you have a good time."

"Will there be lollies?"

She smiled and shook her head. "I don't know, honey, but I'm certain you'll find something yummy to eat. Come on, we'd better go inside."

Wishing she felt as confident as she sounded, Alex opened the car door and did her best to ignore the surge of butterflies that vied for space in her belly. Collecting Sam from his car seat, she headed toward the graveled path that led to the front door.

"Alex, hi! How wonderful to see you!"

Before she had time to catch her breath, Alex was enveloped in a warm hug. She breathed in the scent of expensive perfume—a mix of spicy oriental and vanilla.

Lily Munro hadn't changed a bit. Her glossy blond hair

was still shoulder length and hung in soft, shiny waves around her face. She hadn't gained a pound on her slight frame and from the welcoming smile on her lips, it was as if the years of separation had never been.

"Hi, Lily," Alex murmured, grateful the woman seemed to hold no animosity toward her. "Thank you for inviting us."

"Why wouldn't we invite you? When Brandon told us he'd caught up with you again, we practically threatened him with annihilation if he didn't bring you around to see us. And where's your little boy? Brandon said you have a son."

She searched Lily's eyes for any sign of suspicion, but the bright blue orbs held nothing but pleasure and a mild curiosity.

Sam had planted himself behind Alex and now clung tightly to the leg of her jeans. She gently disengaged his fingers and knelt down beside him. Giving his arms a reassuring squeeze, she stood and made the introductions.

"Sam, this is Mrs Munro. She's married to the brother of my friend from work."

Lily stepped forward and held out her hand, her eyes twinkling in delight.

"Hello, Sam. I'm Lily. It's so lovely to meet you."

Sam ducked his head shyly and tightened his hold on Alex's leg.

Lily smiled. "He looks just like you, Alex. A total mini-you."

Alex nodded and averted her eyes, ruffling the top of Sam's curly, dark hair. "Yes, that's what everyone says," she murmured, relieved when Lily didn't pursue the matter any further.

"Come outside and meet the others. We've invited a handful of friends over and I think there might just be a couple of children around your age, Sam. What do you think?"

Sam nodded cautiously and they followed Lily across the foyer and into a large open kitchen. The walls were decorated in neutral colors that contrasted nicely with a red and silver glass splashback. The late afternoon sun poured through tall French windows and glinted off an array of stainless-steel appliances.

"Your house is lovely, Lily. This space is so wonderful. It seems to go on forever," Alex said, tilting her head back to take in the twelve-foot ceilings. A wide expanse of caramel-colored bamboo flooring ended in a carpeted area that housed a modular-shaped red leather couch and an enormous flat screen TV.

Lily smiled with pride. "Yes, it's a little larger than the last place. With the kids growing bigger and bigger every day, we needed a bit more space. There's another room through that door where the kids have their things." She pointed in the direction of a wooden doorway at the far end of the open-plan living room. "They have a TV and computer set up in there, along with a couch that's no stranger to spills. They practically live in there."

Alex smiled back at her. "I know what you mean about spills. Sam and I live in an apartment. Three bedrooms, one of which I've converted into an office. Then there's a single living area. Sometimes it drives me mad that I don't have more space. Who'd have thought a child could need so much stuff?"

Lily eyed her with frank curiosity. "Where are you living now?"

Alex looked away. "Still in Bondi," she murmured. "I love being close to the beach. Somehow, I couldn't bring myself to leave."

"I know what you mean. I'd love a place by the water. Unfortunately, I'd have to sacrifice some of this space and with a teenager and a half in the house driving me and each other insane on any given day, I'd rather have the space!"

She laughed and Alex laughed with her, their nervousness easing. She didn't know what she'd been so worked up about. Lily was as lovely and gracious as she'd always been. Alex should have known she'd be far too well mannered to pry into matters that were none of her business.

Sam tugged at her arm and Alex leaned down. "What is it, Sam?"

"Where are all the kids, Mom?"

Lily smiled down at him. "They're outside, sweetheart. How about we go out the back and see if we can find them?"

She turned to Alex. "I'm afraid Cassie's in bed with the flu. She's really upset to be missing the party. She was beyond excited to hear that you were coming."

"She must be so grown up now. I wondered if she'd even remember me," Alex murmured.

"Of course she remembered you. She was nearly nine when you and Brandon separated and it hasn't been *that* long."

Alex's smile was strained. "No, I guess not."

"She'd love it if you went upstairs and said hello. I'm sure she's past the infectious stage; she just wasn't feeling up to getting out of bed and with the night air getting chillier, I thought it was probably best if she stayed there."

"Of course," Alex said. "It would be great to see her again."

"Brandon's her favorite uncle. She'd be thrilled to see the two of you back together again."

Panic gripped Alex's belly and she had to swallow against a throat that was suddenly dry. "We—we're not getting back together, Lily. I'm not sure what Brandon told you, but we're work colleagues, that's all. When he asked me to come over, I thought it would be nice to see you all again, but please, don't read any more into it than that."

Lily eyed her solemnly. "I was so sad when it didn't work out for the two of you, but that's life, isn't it? Some things just don't go to plan, no matter how we wish it could be different." She moved closer and clasped Alex's arms, forcing Alex to look at her.

"It's none of my business what happened between the two of you or what is going on with you now. I'm just so glad to see you and I really hope we can be friends again. I've missed you."

That simple admission almost did Alex in. Tears pricked her eyes and her lip wobbled when she tried to smile.

"Thanks, Lily. I-I'd like that. I missed you, too."

Lily put her arms around Alex and gave her a hug. "Let's go outside and I'll introduce you around. I'm sure Tom and Brandon are wondering what's happened to you."

With arms linked together, they stepped through the double French doors and onto a large, paved outdoor area. Sam trailed behind them.

Stylish outdoor furniture had been arranged to encourage conversation and Alex glimpsed an in-ground swimming pool behind some low green shrubbery.

The size of the backyard was just as generous as the house and Alex could see why Lily preferred it to a cramped unit in Bondi.

"Aunty Alex! Aunty Alex!"

A young boy of about ten came hurtling toward her, almost knocking her over in his enthusiasm.

"Hey, Joe. Wow, look at you. I can't believe how tall you are!"

"It's so cool to see you again, Aunty Alex." Joe turned to Sam. "Who are you?"

"I'm Sam. Who are you?"

Joe stuck out his hand. "I'm Joe." Sam looked at the outstretched hand for a few seconds and then shook it solemnly.

"Nice to meet you, Sam. Do you want to come and take a look at my bike? I got a new BMX for my birthday last month. It's got pegs and everything. It's really cool. You coming?"

Sam looked up at Alex, his eyes shining. "Can I, Mom? Can I?"

She laughed and bent down to give him a hug. "Of course you can, sweetheart."

His answering smile lit up her heart. "Just be careful," she called out to his retreating back.

"Don't worry, Aunty Alex," Joe called back to her. "I'll look after him."

"It looks like they're friends already." Lily smiled.

"*Mm*," Alex replied over the lump that had lodged itself in her throat.

"Oh, I just remembered I've left the garlic bread in the oven," Lily exclaimed. "I'll be back in a minute. Make yourself at home."

She dashed back toward the house. Alex wandered into the garden and admired the pots of colorful daisies and geraniums that sprang from an artful display. A man with his back to her was talking on a cell phone. She began to move away, but he turned and offered her a smile, shaking his head in silent apology.

She acknowledged him with a nod and wandered off a short distance to admire a beautiful glazed urn that stood almost as tall as she, and was filled with sweet-smelling jasmine that cascaded down the side.

"I'm sorry; that was very rude of me. I'm at a party and I shouldn't be on the phone."

Alex turned and laughed, taking in the man's short, graying hair and lithe athletic build. He was only about her height, but the cut and cost of his clothing and the glint of humor in his dark eyes gave him an air of confidence and authority that belied his medium stature.

He held out his hand and smiled again, showing a set of even, white teeth.

"I'm Jim, by the way."

Alex returned his warm handshake. His brown eyes, glinting with curiosity, crinkled behind his wire-rimmed glasses.

"Alex. I'm a...friend of the family."

A nicely shaped eyebrow arched. "You say that like you're not quite sure."

Alex blushed and looked at her feet. "No, no, I'm sure. I'm an old friend of Tom and Lily."

"Funny, I haven't seen you around here before."

"Well, um...it's been awhile."

Although the curiosity in his eyes flared brighter, he didn't push. She breathed a silent sigh of relief when he changed the subject.

"It's been awhile for me, too. My work often takes me out of town. Every now and then, Lily sends me an invitation that happens to coincide with when I'm around."

"How do you know Lily?"

"We're related by marriage," Jim answered with a smile. "My father married her mother when we were kids. I was nearly sixteen and I think she was about nine. I left home not long after, so we didn't have much to do with each other, but Lily makes an effort at keeping in touch." He shrugged and grinned ruefully. "She's better at it than I am."

Alex smiled back. "What do you do? You said you're often out of town? Are you in sa—"

"There you are. I was beginning to think you weren't going to show."

The low drawl behind her sent a rush of butterflies through her stomach. Alex turned and found Brandon much too close for her equilibrium. She snatched a quick breath and did her best to still her racing heart.

"Brandon. Hi. Have you met Jim? He's Lily's—"

"Stepbrother. Yes, we've met."

Alex frowned at Brandon's brusqueness, but Jim seemed to take it in stride.

"I'd better go and mingle or Lily will have my head. She's always saying I spend far too much time working. Nice to meet you, Alex."

He wended his way through the garden in the direction of the crowd that had gathered around the barbeque. Alex followed his progress with her eyes, trying to delay the moment when she'd have to talk to Brandon.

"How did you get caught with that jerk?"

She looked at him, surprised by his rancor. "I'm not sure what you mean. He seemed perfectly civilized to me."

"*Humph.* Don't fall for the smooth tongue. There's something I don't trust about him. Ask Tom."

Alex shook her head. "Yes, well…thank you for warning me. I'll keep that in mind next time I happen across a handsome stranger."

Brandon frowned again, his expression dark. "Stay away

from him, Alex. There's something about that man I've never liked."

"How long have you known him?"

"Long enough." He made an impatient sound. "Forget about him. I'd rather talk about you." He ran an appreciative gaze over her simple white blouse and denim jeans. She'd topped it with a black leather jacket. "You look great, by the way. Thank you for coming."

Thank you for inviting me. Us. It's lovely to see everyone again."

"Where's Sam? I hope he's not too overwhelmed by all the attention. Joe's been nagging me every five minutes, wondering when he was going to arrive."

She smiled and turned to look in the direction her son had disappeared. "Sam's probably loving every minute of it. He's never had a cousin to play with."

Brandon eyed her askance. "Not exactly cousins, but who's quibbling?"

Heat stole up Alex's neck. She bit her lip. "Y-you know what I mean," she stammered.

"Do I?"

The question hung between them. Panicked by her slip, she fished around for a suitable reply, but could think of nothing.

"Here you are, Alex. It's good to see you again."

Her legs nearly collapsed with relief when she caught sight of Tom. She turned to greet him with a smile firmly in place. "Hello, Tom. It's lovely to see you, too. You have a beautiful home. Thank you for inviting me."

"Oh, that was all Lily's idea. Once she heard you and Brandon were working together, she insisted on having you over."

Alex ducked her head in embarrassment. Brandon frowned at Tom.

"We've all missed you, Alex," Brandon said. "Cassie and Joe were beyond excited when I told them you were coming and Lily's been cooking up a storm since yesterday. It's great that you could come." He shot another look toward his brother. "Right, Tom?"

Tom sent her a tight smile. "Of course. Can I get you something to drink?"

"A glass of red would be lovely, thank you," she replied, relieved when Tom moved off in the direction of the house.

"Don't mind him," Brandon said. "He's just doing the protective big brother thing. I was a bit of a mess after we separated."

Anger pumped through her. "What do you mean, *you* were a bit of a mess? *You* were the one who made the decision to end it."

Brandon glanced around them and then drew her closer toward the shrubbery. "Okay, okay. I know." He bit his lip and then met her gaze again. "I only told Tom the truth about what happened about a month ago."

Surprise shot through her. "Do you mean to tell me all these years they didn't know it was *you* who left our marriage?"

Brandon shifted his weight and averted his eyes, a flush staining his cheeks.

Alex frowned in disbelief. "Don't tell me they think *I* was the one who walked out? That it was *me* who gave up on our marriage?"

The look on his face and his continued silence confirmed it. Her anger burned hotter. "You let *me* take the blame for it? How could you?" She shook her head in disgust. "No wonder Tom's less than friendly. For the last four years he's probably hated me."

"Alex, no. It wasn't like that. I didn't tell Tom about Jakarta. I didn't tell him about any of it. We were having problems in our marriage long before that happened and the fact was, we were over. What good would it have done to drag up all our dirty laundry with the family?"

She scoffed. "It certainly worked out well for you. You didn't have to admit to the people who cared most about you that you'd given up on your marriage without a word of explanation. That you weren't as perfect as they thought. Your family have always looked at you as some sort of super hero. Good looking, great body, slayer of dragons, righter of wrongs. They have no idea it's an illusion—that you're fallible, like the rest of us."

Pain darkened the blue of his eyes. He stared at her beseechingly. "No, Alex. Please. That's not the way it was. It wasn't any of their business. They were upset because I was hurting, but they're smarter than you give them credit for. They knew there were two sides to the story, but they respected and loved me enough not to pry."

"*You* were hurting!" she shouted. "You were the one who'd ended it!"

"You're right. I came home on leave and quit our marriage. I did it because I didn't think I had a choice. It was either my career or my marriage—I could no longer do both." He heaved a heavy sigh. "I still had three months to run on my term. I couldn't abandon my men or throw away the months of hard, dangerous work collecting intelligence, infiltrating terrorist cells, gaining the trust of people who thought nothing of committing suicide for their cause."

He dragged a hand through his hair. "When I left our apartment that night, I ended up at Tom and Lily's. Despite what you might think, I was a mess. They could see I was in no condition to be interrogated and I made it quite clear that I wouldn't tolerate their interference, no matter how well meaning. This was between me and you and I wasn't going to sully the memory of us—the memory of our marriage—with sordid stories of who was to blame."

He looked so genuinely distraught, Alex softened. Yes, he'd walked out on her, but this was the closest he'd come to providing an explanation and what he'd said was true: The cracks in their marriage had already started to appear long before he arrived home from Jakarta and she was just as responsible for those as he was. She was the one who'd assumed they'd have children somewhere down the track.

It was true that when they'd first married, babies were the farthest thing from her mind. She'd been happy to pursue her career in the AFP and carve out a name for herself. She'd put her hand up for every dangerous assignment that came her way and had thrived on the thrill of it. She'd been young and strong and bulletproof. Brandon had supported her every step of the way.

But then things had changed. She'd crept toward thirty and suddenly her exciting career hadn't seemed quite so satisfying. She began to find fault in the people and places around her and Brandon had borne the brunt of her discontent. His emotions had ranged from surprise and bewilderment to plain old anger when she'd raised the subject of having children and couldn't let it go. For over a year and a half, they'd argued about it. Then Brandon had been posted to Jakarta.

It was a twelve-month posting and they'd both breathed a little sigh of relief when he'd come home with the news. It was normal for spouses to accompany the agent to the posting, but Alex had been involved in her own investigation and they'd both agreed it was better if she stayed home.

It would give them time to step back and breathe and repair the damage the last eighteen months of constant bickering had done to their relationship.

His visits home were sporadic. Three months had passed before she'd seen him the first time. The second gap had been even longer and he'd slept in the spare room.

She'd stopped taking the pill. It hadn't been a conscious decision. Not really. More like, there was no longer a need. Brandon was away for months at a time. The time he'd come home and slept in the spare room, they'd barely spoken.

But then he'd surprised her. He'd arrived on the doorstep of their Bondi unit completely out of the blue, exhausted and depressed. His undercover operation, infiltrating a terrorist cell in Jakarta, was going nowhere and the daily fear of discovery was eroding his mind and his body. He could barely find the words.

He'd come to her for sustenance. He'd come to her for strength.

Without hesitation, she'd taken him in her arms and had

loved him the way they had loved in the beginning. All night, they'd kissed and made love and she'd held him until finally, he'd fallen asleep. Once again, he was the Brandon she'd fallen in love with. He'd needed her and she wanted him home. She'd never loved him more.

But his stint in Jakarta wasn't finished and he wasn't a man to let others down. The team of AFP officers he'd left in Jakarta were depending upon him to return and he'd had no choice but to go back to them.

After a tearful farewell, Alex had promised to be waiting for him when he got back. He still had a few months to run on his posting. If arrests weren't made during that time, his placement would be extended. He was working undercover. He couldn't simply disappear and be replaced by someone else.

Six weeks after his visit, Alex discovered she was pregnant. She was elated and a little scared of Brandon's reaction, but had been confident they would work things out. He was due home just before their twenty-eighth birthdays.

She'd planned everything down to the last detail. The meal, the wine—she was sticking to soda water—the music. She'd even made a cake.

She'd taken the ultrasound image of their baby, scanned at twelve weeks, and had placed it in a small gift box lined with tissue paper. She'd hoped and prayed he would accept her gift with joy.

But things hadn't turned out that way. Before she'd had a chance to give him her present, he'd quietly told her they were over.

Shock and disbelief had paralyzed her. She'd begged him for an explanation. Over and over again, he'd refused until at last anger had overtaken her and she'd told him to leave and to never come back. At the time, she'd meant every single word.

But time had a way of softening even the harshest of memories. Brandon's worried face came back into focus and Alex's shoulders slumped.

"I'm sorry, Brandon. I shouldn't have flown at you like that.

I'm surprised you didn't tell your family about our troubles, but in a way, I think I'm glad you didn't. It was nobody's business but ours."

His face filled with hope. "You don't know how much that means to me, Alex. I've tortured myself for years about that night. I wished I could have done it differently. You don't know how many times I wished I'd chosen us and our marriage."

"We've all done things in our lives we're not proud of," she whispered.

"Can you ever forgive me, Alex?"

Tears sparkled in his eyes. Her throat tightened with emotion. She took a step closer to him and rested her palm on his smooth cheek. "I think I already have."

His lips found hers and she melted into him. Memories bombarded her from every corner of her mind. Her arms came up around him and he pulled her in tightly against him. His lips continued their sweet torture, igniting a fire deep inside her belly.

"Hmm."

The noise slowly penetrated the fog in Alex's head. She pulled slightly away and caught sight of Lily standing only a few feet away, carrying a glass of red wine. Heat flared in Alex's cheeks.

"Lily, oh, God—I know what you must be thinking. It's not what it looks like. I—"

Lily didn't miss a beat. She waved her hand nonchalantly.

"Hey, no problem. You've already told me you weren't getting back together. I believe you, I really do. By the way, Tom asked me to bring this to you." She handed Alex the glass. "I also wanted to ask if Sam was allergic to anything? We're about to sit down and eat and I wanted to make sure before I filled his plate."

Alex's embarrassment burned hotter. She'd completely forgotten about Sam. Her son. Her baby.

Unable to look at Brandon, she straightened her blouse and patted her hair and turned to follow Lily.

"Thanks, Lily. Sam can eat anything you have." She stumbled, but didn't dare stop as she made her way to the table.

Brandon called after her. "Save me a seat."

CHAPTER 12

Alex was acutely aware of Brandon seated beside her at the table crowded with Tom and Lily's family and friends. Although it seated a dozen people comfortably, more than half that again were perched on stools and other chairs as food was passed from one to the other.

Sam had squeezed himself in between Joe and the five-year-old daughter of one of Lily's friends and seemed to be having the time of his life. His little face was animated as he chewed his way through a sausage. Joe turned and said something to him and he laughed in delight.

A pang went through her. It was such a shame he'd missed out on this sort of connection. She snuck a look at Brandon and found him staring down at her. Flustered, she quickly shifted her gaze to her plate. Oh, God, he'd kissed her. She'd kissed him back. What the hell had she been thinking?

The only good thing to come of it was that he'd barely noticed Sam. Apart from a perfunctory nod when she'd made the briefest of introductions, throughout the meal his attention had remained firmly on her. Uncomfortably so.

She squirmed in her seat and did her best to ignore Brandon by concentrating on slicing into her steak and forking a piece of it into her mouth. She took her time, chewing it slowly, knowing she wouldn't have to answer any of his burning questions while her mouth was full.

Working the meat until it was little more than mush in her mouth, she finally swallowed. He pounced the second her throat stopped moving.

"Are we going to talk about this like adults?"

Alex coughed and reached for the glass of merlot Lily had given her. Taking a sip, she prayed for the right words. She so didn't want to get into a conversation about this in front of everyone. She hadn't had any time to think about the kiss—what it meant and how she felt about it.

There was no denying it had been wonderful, like coming home after a long, long absence, but things were way too complicated now. The biggest complication sat right across from her, dunking pieces of sausage into the ketchup and sucking it off the ends. The sauce was smeared across his lips and over his cheek. As she watched, his little pink tongue came out to swipe at it.

A reluctant smile tugged at her lips. "Sam, use a napkin, honey. You're getting it everywhere."

Brandon's gaze landed on Sam and he frowned. Alex held her breath and cursed silently for drawing his attention to her son. Brandon turned back to her, his eyes shuttered.

"You're overthinking things, Alex," he murmured close to her ear. "Let's discuss what just happened in the garden— like adults."

She tensed as his warm breath tickled her skin. "Really? And how would you know what I'm thinking?"

"I know you. It wasn't that long ago I knew you better than you knew yourself."

The observation stung. It was a claim she couldn't refute. She set her jaw, determined not to be pressured into discussing the issue. "It's not a matter of being adult about it, Brandon. There are so many other things to consider."

"At least you don't deny there's something to discuss."

She bit her lip and wished she'd done just that. It would have been the wisest thing to do. Laugh off the kiss as if it was nothing.

But that wouldn't be honest and she vowed not to deceive him again. Her conscience weighed heavily enough on that score. She wasn't about to compound it. It would be tough enough to deal with the fallout when he discovered he was a father. And until she was ready to tell him about that, she'd be wise to stay as far away from him as possible.

Decision made, she turned to him, determined to put an end to any fledgling hope he might have about a reunion.

"Can we do this somewhere else?" She glanced meaningfully around the crowded table.

He pushed back his chair and waited for her to stand. Taking hold of her elbow, he steered her toward a part of the garden that lay in shadows, away from the revelry of the barbeque and any curious onlookers.

Alex drew in a deep breath and prayed for the right words. She cleared her throat.

"I've always been attracted to you, Brandon. You know that. And, regardless of all that's gone on with us, you still have the power to turn me on."

Even in the dimness, she saw his eyes darken with emotion. Ignoring it, she plowed on.

"That's just the way it is, Brandon. It doesn't mean anything. It doesn't change anything. Let's call it how we see it."

He started to protest and she quickly continued. "It is what it is, Brandon. Let it go. I have a new life, now. A life I'm very happy with. I have my son whom I adore, a job I love and...it's great. Everything's great."

"What about you? Who looks after you?"

He'd leaned in close, too close. His deep voice rumbled over her and she shivered from the impact. He'd always been so good at taking care of her, of making sure she always had everything she'd needed. It was one of the things she'd loved about him. She turned away and clenched her hands to stop from reaching out for him.

She was wrong to think they could ever have a future together. Too much had gone on and nothing could change the biggest deception of their relationship. A deception she'd initiated.

Plastering a bright smile on her face, she turned back to him. "I-I've actually started seeing someone. A man who is very sweet and charming and who treats me really well."

The lie tasted like poison. He recoiled as if she'd bitten him. The shock on his face horrified her. *Where the hell had that come from?* And what about her decision two minutes ago to be honest?

She thrust around wildly for some way to justify her comment. It wasn't a total untruth. She'd seen some very attractive men come through on her dating page. Just last night, she'd decided at least two of them looked like genuine possibilities. She hadn't decided whether she really wanted to take the next step, but the more she thought about it, the more it made sense. She had to move on. Too much had happened. Too much had been said. Too much had been left unsaid.

Brandon stared at her, hurt and disbelief clouding his features. His lips twisted into an ugly sneer.

"You really take the cake, you know that? I would never have believed it of you, Alex. The girl I knew may not have been perfect, but she had more integrity than anyone I'd ever met."

He shook his head in disgust. "You had the nerve to kiss me? To tell me how I still turn you on. Does he know? The poor bastard you have dangling on a leash? Does he know you still fantasize about your husband?"

Heat scorched her cheeks, but she took the tongue-lashing without comment. It was nothing less than she deserved. She'd have reacted the same way if their roles had been reversed. She didn't know why she'd said it. She'd panicked and said the first thing that had come into her mind.

That was no excuse. It was unforgivable. She shouldn't have said it. But now that she had, it gave him a reason to pull away, to leave her and her son alone, to get on with his life without her—without them.

Pain arced through her heart, but she refused to give it heed. This was for the best. She should never have dreamed otherwise. She was a fool to think, even for an instant, that they could return to the way it used to be—to the time when they'd lived for each other, when they were so attuned they'd completed each other's sentences.

It could never be that way again and it was time, once and for all, to accept that.

Turning her back on him, she hurried back to the table, averting her eyes from the gazes of everyone seated there. Sam was where she'd left him. She tugged him by the arm.

"Come on, honey. It's time to go."

"But, Mom, I haven't finished my other sausage. And I want to play with Lucy. And Joe said we're having ice cream after."

"I know, Sam, but it's getting late. You've had a big day. We need to get home."

From the corner of her eye, she saw Tom push away from the table. Panic seized her. She didn't want to explain herself to anyone, least of all, Tom.

Taking hold of Sam again, she lifted him out of his chair and hugged him close. Burying her face in his shoulder, she headed toward the house.

Lily was in the kitchen.

Alex came to a halt. "Lily, um…there you are. Thank you so much for having us over, but we have to leave."

Surprise widened the other woman's eyes. "Leave? We haven't even had a chance to talk properly. Do you really have to rush off?"

Alex grimaced. "I'm afraid so. Sam's had a big day out at the Aquarium and it's all beginning to catch up with him. It's time I got him home to bed."

Lily eyed her intently and Alex did her best not to squirm. The seconds dragged on, but finally, Lily shrugged and looked away. Alex bit her lip and wished things could be different.

"Would you do me a favor and say hello to Cassie? I just came down from her room. She's asking about you."

Alex bit down on a sigh and nodded. "Of course. I'd like

that. Do you mind watching Sam for a minute? I'd rather he not breathe in any residual flu bugs."

Lily smiled. "Sure." She bent down until she was at eye level with Sam. "Would you like to have some ice cream? I have chocolate, vanilla and strawberry."

Sam's eyes went wide and he looked at Alex. "Can I, Mom? Can I?"

She nodded again. "Yes, sweetheart, but don't forget your manners." She looked back at Lily and mouthed *thank you*. "I won't be long."

"Take all the time you want. I'll look after Sam until you get back. She's second on the right from the top of the stairs."

———

Alex knocked softly on the closed door that announced it was Cassie's room in bold, bright letters carved from wooden blocks. The knock was answered by a husky voice. Alex pushed open the door and stepped inside.

The room was painted a soft pink and was gently illuminated by a bedside lamp. A matching pink-and-white floral bedspread covered most of the bed. The walls were decorated with posters of Katy Perry and One Direction, but there were also a few older ones of the young Harry Potter crew, and, what really impressed her, an old Dire Straits picture.

She smiled and cocked an eyebrow at the girl that lay in the bed. "Dire Straits? Wow, I'm impressed."

Cassie's face lit up with a smile. "Aunty Alex! You came! Mom said you were downstairs. She didn't tell me you were coming up to see me."

Alex perched on the side of the bed and leaned over to kiss her niece on the cheek. "Cassie Munro, of course I was coming up to see you. It's been like *forever*. You didn't think I'd come by and not drop in and say hello, did you?"

Cassie lifted a shoulder in a shrug and stared down at her

hands that were resting on top of the quilt. "I don't know. After you and Uncle Brandon split up, we didn't see you again. I didn't know if you'd even remember me."

Alex's heart clenched. "Oh, honey. I'm sorry I haven't stopped by. It's not that I didn't want to. I just... Things just got a little...complicated. You know what I mean?"

Cassie looked up at her shyly and nodded. "Yeah, I think so. That's what Mom said. Things were *complicated*."

Alex forced a smile. "Hey, look at you? You're so grown up! I love what you've done to your hair. It looks so glamorous, so Hollywood, styled like that."

Smiling, Cassie blushed and twirled a long, blond strand around her finger. "I've been growing it since I turned ten. It's way longer than all the other girls in my class."

"It's gorgeous, sweetheart. I bet you've caught the attention of every boy in your year."

Cassie's blush deepened and Alex smiled. To be almost thirteen again. So full of hope and promise. So full of expectancy that life was going to be wonderful. Before broken hearts and broken promises dashed the hope to pieces.

She forced the dark thoughts aside and picked up Cassie's hands. "Your mom says you've been sick? That's no good."

Cassie nodded. "Yeah, some bug I picked up from school. Penny Jones had it last week. Hopefully, I'll be right by tomorrow. It would be a shame to spend the *whole* weekend in bed."

Alex nodded toward the laptop that sat on the desk nearby. "At least you have your computer. I suppose you're on Facebook and Twitter and all those other things?"

She shook her head. "No, Mom and Dad won't let me open up those accounts. They say it's too dangerous. I think they're being way too over protective, but what can I do? They'd take my laptop away if I broke the rules."

"Your mom and dad are right, sweetheart. I know you think those sites are just a way to stay in contact with your friends, and they're great for that, but there are people out there who use them for much more scary reasons. You're best to stay off them if you can."

Cassie groaned. "You sound like Mom and Dad."

Alex laughed softly. "I'm sorry, honey. I don't mean to come across all doom and gloom, but there are some people out there who are up to no good. Your Uncle Brandon and I are working to stop some of them right now."

Cassie's eyes widened. "You mean some of those people live in Australia?"

"Yes, sweetheart. Some of them might even be in Sydney. They could be anywhere. You never know. That's why it pays to be careful and not talk to strangers. The same rule applies whether it's someone online or down the street. You wouldn't give your personal details to someone you'd just met at the bus stop, would you?"

"No."

"The same thing applies in the cyber world. I know it seems safer, in the security of your bedroom, but believe me, these people have a way of finding you."

Cassie shivered and Alex pulled back, suddenly aware she was probably scaring the girl. Which was probably a good thing, except it wasn't her place to lecture her. She was only her aunt and a largely absent one at that. Besides, from what Cassie had said, her parents had things firmly under control.

"So," Alex teased in an effort to lighten the mood, "do you have a boyfriend?"

The telltale blush spoke volumes. Cassie looked down at her hands and fiddled with the tassels on the end of the bedspread. She gave Alex a shy grin.

"Maybe," she murmured.

Alex smiled. "That's lovely, sweetheart. What's his name?"

Cassie blushed again and bit her lip. Alex's eyes widened in sudden comprehension.

"You haven't told your mom, yet. Is that it?"

A nod was followed by a peek from underneath golden-tipped lashes.

"It's okay, honey. You don't have to tell me. Is he cute?"

She giggled. "Oh, yes, even cuter than Nick Jonas."

"Wow, that is seriously cute. How old is he?"

"He's fifteen. I know it's a bit older than me, but we have so much in common. We talk for hours and hours."

Alex's eyebrow lifted in surprise. "Fifteen? Wow. But then, boys quite often go out with girls who are a bit younger than them. Girls tend to mature quicker than boys."

Cassie's eyes shone with happiness. "Exactly. Oh, Aunty Alex, I'm so glad you understand." She leaned forward and threw her arms around Alex's shoulders, hugging her tightly.

Alex returned the embrace, her eyes prickling with unshed tears. She'd missed so many moments like this with her self-imposed separation from the rest of Brandon's family. Despite what happened in the future, she vowed to remain a part of their lives.

Cassie's voice was muffled against Alex's blouse. "It's so good to see you again, Aunty Alex. Does this mean you and Uncle Brandon are getting back together?"

Alex tensed, unsure how to respond. She slowly pulled away.

"I don't think so, sweetheart. Like your mom said, it's complicated. But it doesn't mean you and I can't still visit each other."

The girl's face brightened. "Really? That would be so cool. I'd really like that."

Alex leaned forward and pressed a kiss to the top of Cassie's forehead. "I'd really like that too, sweetheart. Now, I'd better get going. Sam's probably torn half of your mom's kitchen apart by now."

"Mom said you had a little boy. Sam. Is that his name?"

"It's Samuel, actually but I usually call him Sam."

Cassie grinned. "I'd love to meet him."

"And you will. Just as soon as you're better. Right now, you'd better get some rest. I'll see you soon."

"Bye, Aunty Alex."

"Bye, sweetheart."

Alex walked over to the door and pulled it open. With a

final wave to Cassie, she stepped through the doorway, pulled the door gently closed behind her and headed down the stairs.

"Is she gone?"

Lily looked up from the dessert she had prepared and nodded as Brandon stepped into the kitchen, sliding the French doors closed behind him.

"She left a few moments ago. She said Sam was tired and needed to go home."

Brandon shook his head in disgust. "She didn't even say good-bye."

Lily shot him a questioning look, but he ignored it. He should have known better than to expect that she'd stay quiet.

"What's going on with you two? Alex walks in here after disappearing without a trace for more than four years and the first thing she tells me is that you aren't getting back together. Less than an hour later, I find the two of you locked in what could be loosely described as a rather amorous embrace in the middle of my garden. Fast forward another hour and she's beating a hasty retreat out my front door, mouthing some lame excuse about her son needing his bed."

She flung her arms up in the air. "Call me stupid, Brandon, but something seems way too weird right about now. Would you care to explain?"

Brandon grimaced, regretting his impulse to enquire about Alex's whereabouts. It was obvious Tom hadn't said anything to his wife. He was grateful his brother had kept his confidence, but it would have gone a little way to making it easier to explain to Lily if Tom had already clued her in. Now he was caught, and knowing his sister-in-law, there was no way she was going to accept a brush-off. Not this time.

Pulling out one of the leather-topped, stainless-steel

barstools, he lowered himself onto it and rested his elbows on the black granite counter top.

He sighed heavily. "The truth is, Lil, *I* don't even know what's going on. She's hot and cold and everything in between. One minute we're having a relatively decent conversation and the next, she's blowing me off." He shook his head. "It's confusing the hell out of me."

"So, why not walk away?" Lily asked simply. "She's been out of your life for four years. Why go and complicate things with this...this attempt at a reunion—if that's what it is?"

"I wish I knew, on both counts."

"Knew what?" Tom came up beside him and pulled out another barstool.

Brandon groaned.

"We were talking about Alex," Lily supplied.

Tom glanced at his wife and then looked at Brandon. "I haven't told her."

Brandon grimaced and then sighed. "Yeah, I figured as much."

Lily rounded on them, her face clouded with suspicion. "Told me what?"

Brandon drew in a deep breath, bracing himself for what was to come. "I've never told you about why Alex and I split up."

Lily stared at him, her eyes wary. "I thought she called it quits? You were completely devastated. I just assumed it had been her decision."

Brandon shook his head. "When you asked, I told you I didn't want to talk about it, that it was none of your business and that it didn't matter, it wasn't going to change things. Alex had gone. Our marriage was over. All of those things were true." He ran his fingers through his hair. The silence was strained.

"Why did your marriage end, Brandon?" Lily's voice was tempered steel.

Brandon lifted his head and met her gaze without flinching. "It ended because I came home one night and told her it was over. Alex ranted and raved and demanded an explanation, but I refused to give her one. I packed my bags and left. And that was it."

"What? I don't understand. Why would you do something like that?"

Brandon threw a look toward his brother, hoping he'd intervene. Tom cleared his throat.

"It's complicated, Lil. The gist of it is, Brandon was suffering from undiagnosed Post Traumatic Stress Disorder. He'd been subject to some horrible things in Jakarta and he couldn't take it anymore. Alex bore the brunt of it and by the time he was treated and recovered, it was too late for Brandon to do anything about it."

"Why didn't you seek professional help earlier, Brandon?" Lily asked, shaking her head in confusion. "Alex meant the world to you. I can't believe you threw away everything you had together without a fight."

Brandon closed his eyes against the memories. When he opened them again, he looked straight at Lily. "You're right. I was in love with her from the moment I saw her. I still am. Now that I've had time to heal, I can't believe how badly I handled it. I should have given Alex the chance to help me, to help us."

At Lily's questioning look, he explained. "We were having problems well before I left for Jakarta. Alex wanted a baby." He shook his head. "And I didn't."

Surprise filled Lily's face. "Wow," she murmured, "I had no idea."

Tom turned toward him. "I take it you guys didn't have this conversation before the wedding? Whether you wanted kids or not?"

"No, mate. That would have been way too sensible. We were young. We were in love. We were invincible. Nothing was ever going to come between us." He included Lily in his look. "You two remember how it was."

Lily looked chagrined. "Well, it was a bit different for us. I was already pregnant before we'd even decided whether we had what it took to make a couple. Remember? The conversation was kind of taken out of our hands."

A faint blush stained Tom's cheeks. "Yeah, well. It worked out okay."

Lily punched him lightly on the arm. "Only okay?"

Tom grinned. "All right, all right. More than okay. Much more." He leaned across the counter top and placed a kiss on his wife's lips. "Better?"

"*Mm*, much better." She smiled.

Brandon's belly clenched and he looked away from the love that radiated from both of them. He missed having that special someone. Someone who knew him as well as he knew himself. Someone who loved him for who he was, imperfections and all.

He'd had that with Alex. And he'd lost it.

Lily shook her head. "Poor Alex. All these years I've thought she ditched us like she ditched you."

"No," Brandon implored. "It wasn't Alex's fault. I should have told you the truth when it happened, but I wasn't in a fit state of mind to talk to anyone. After what happened in Jakarta, I didn't think I had a choice." His voice cracked with emotion. "Being single seemed like the only option." He shook his head, and covered his face with his hands, a familiar despair settling heavily on his shoulders.

A strong hand gripped his arm. He turned and took comfort in his brother's embrace. Pain he'd thought long gone seized him, tightening his chest. His breath caught on a sob.

"It's all right, mate. Let it out."

It was all the invitation he needed. Powerful emotions gripped him, shredding his control. He shuddered. Memories battered him from all sides. There was no escape.

He sucked in oxygen, his chest heaving with the effort. He'd done all his crying years ago. He was supposed to have moved on from the night more than four years ago when he'd destroyed the only good thing in his life.

Regaining a semblance of control, he lifted his head and offered a shaky smile to the people who cared about him most.

"I'm okay. Really. It happened so long ago. I don't know

why it still gets to me like that. I guess seeing Alex again has stirred up all the old memories, especially the painful ones."

Lily leaned over the counter and gave his hand a squeeze. "Tell me, Brandon. What happened?"

"Jakarta," he whispered. "That's what happened."

Lily regarded him with a mixture of surprise and acceptance when he finally finished his story. "Did you explain any of this to Alex?"

Brandon shook his head. "I was in no state to provide explanations. The whole way home on the plane from Jakarta, there was only one thought going around and around in my head. I never wanted to be put in a position like that again—where I had to choose between the commitment to my wife and the commitment I had to my men and their safety. I knew what I had to do. Extricating myself from my marriage and the responsibility that came with it seemed like the only way." He sighed raggedly. "I wish I'd known how much I'd come to regret it." Silence settled around them. It was finally broken by Lily.

"Sam's a nice-looking little boy."

Her comment snapped Brandon out of his dark reverie. "Yeah. He looks just like his mother."

She pursed her lips. "He certainly looks like Alex, but I was talking to him for awhile and I kept catching glimpses of someone else." She looked at him intently. "Is there any chance he could be yours?"

Brandon ignored the stab of regret. "No. Alex said he's two. There's no way he could be mine."

Lily shook her head. "Two? I don't think so. He's way more articulate than that. If I'd had to guess, I would have said at least three. Besides, look at the size of him. He looks more like a four-year-old than a two-year-old."

Brandon frowned. Why would Alex lie about Sam's age? It didn't make sense. There was no way she wouldn't have told him if the boy had been his. He'd meant it when he'd told her she had more integrity than anyone he'd ever known.

No, Lily must be wrong. After all, not all kids fit the average model.

"Maybe his father is extra tall. It does happen," he said.

Lily looked unconvinced, her expression thoughtful. "Who knows?" she murmured as she began stacking dessert things, including bowls and spoons and fresh napkins, onto a tray.

"I'd better get back to the rest of our guests before they begin to think we've abandoned them." She picked up the tray and headed toward the French doors that led outside.

"Tom, can you bring the tub of ice cream and the apple meringue pie?"

"Yep."

Brandon pushed back his stool and stretched. "I might call it a night, mate. As tempting as that pie sounds, I have to be at work first thing in the morning."

"No worries. Thanks for coming."

The brothers embraced. Tom pulled away, concern lingering in the depths of his eyes. "Take care, all right?"

Brandon smiled wryly. "What, no well-meaning advice to stay away from Alex?" He shook his head. "Don't worry, bro. After tonight, I got her message loud and clear. Besides, she told me she was seeing someone else."

Tom's brow furrowed. "Really? So, why did she come?"

Brandon shrugged. "Maybe it was to see you and Lily. Then again, I did find her deep in conversation with your favorite brother-in-law. What's that loser doing here, anyway?"

Tom exhaled. "It was Lily's doing. She still feels guilty for the way her family has kind of written him off. She tries to make up for it by inviting him over whenever he bothers to return her call. I haven't seen him for more than twelve months. Who knows what brought him out tonight?"

"Yeah, well, Alex seemed to find him palatable. They looked very cozy when I happened across them."

"I guess there's no accounting for taste," Tom said, a sly grin curling his lips. "She chose you, didn't she?"

Brandon thumped him in the arm. "Low blow, bro."

"Hey, I thought it was funny."

"Yeah, about as funny as a condom in a convent."

"Now look who's being obscene."

Brandon smiled, feeling better than he had for awhile. "See you later, mate. And thanks...for everything. Give Lily and the kids a kiss for me."

CHAPTER 13

Cassie Munro's fingers flew with two-fingered speed over the keyboard of her laptop. She'd waited all day to speak to him. School had gone on forever. She'd even skipped netball practice so she could get home quicker and go online. It had been more than a week since he'd been in the chat room. It was driving her crazy.

Had he gone away? Somewhere weird where there was no Internet access? Was he sick? Lying on death's doorstep in one of the city's hospitals? Or maybe—and this was the one her mind kept shying away from—maybe he'd moved on, forgotten about her. Found someone prettier to chat to.

Her stomach clenched and she felt sick. God, please not that. She'd rather find out he was dying from some rare, incurable disease than to discover he'd passed her over for someone else.

Especially after she'd shared him with her aunt.

Not that she exactly *shared* him, but she'd told Alex more about him than she'd told anyone, except her two best friends. Madeleine and Lucy were wild with envy. They'd squealed with jealousy when she'd showed them his picture. They couldn't believe how lucky she was to have such a hot guy talking to her online.

Cassie began to key in the strokes that would allow her to enter the chat room. Her fingers faltered. Holding her breath, she forced herself to complete the actions.

Oh, God. *He was there.*

She let her breath out on a gasp of excitement. Her heart thumped erratically against her ribs. She couldn't believe her eyes. After nine days of nothing, there he was. In bold, black type. *Justin.*

Would he say hello to her? He'd know by now that she was there. Should she make the first move? Oh, God, she didn't know what to do. Indecision gnawed at her belly.

Hi, there, Lady G. Great to see you here.

Cassie read the words on her screen and almost collapsed with relief. He'd said hello! He'd acknowledged her! She hurried off a reply.

Where have you been?

She hit enter without thinking and then worried that she sounded too accusatory. She didn't want him to think she was keeping tabs on him. After all, they weren't exactly going out.

A reply came right back.

Yeah, sorry about that. I've been at my mom's in the boondocks. She lives like, miles from the nearest town. I don't think they've even heard of the Internet out there. It was the longest week and a half of my life.

Relieved, she smiled and shot off another reply.

I was worried you'd been taken off to hospital with some rare disease. Glad to hear it was nothing more serious.

Nothing more serious? I couldn't check emails, surf the net, talk to you—for a whole nine days! What could be more serious?

Cassie went warm all over. He'd counted the days, just like she had.

I missed you.

There, she'd said it. Put it out there. She waited with bated breath for his response. And then it came.

I missed you, too.

Giddiness swept through her. She collapsed back against her bed and clutched her laptop close to her chest. All that worry for nothing. He'd been away, that was all. And, he'd missed her.

Are you playing netball again this week?

She sat up and typed back.

Yes, we're at home this week. Down at Manly Oval.

I'd love to come and watch you play. Hopefully, Dad won't have a list of chores for me this time.

Cassie's smile couldn't get much wider.

I'd really like that.

I can't wait to meet you.

She nearly burst with happiness.

Me, either. See you on Saturday.

Counting the days. Again.

CHAPTER 14

Alex stared at the list of names on the piece of paper near her keyboard and frowned in concentration. The FBI techies had managed to hack into the email account of Nicolas Janssens and had provided the dozen or so international agencies involved in the investigation with thousands of email addresses. The addresses originated from all over the world. One hundred and sixty-five of them had come from computers using an Australian Internet service provider.

Patrick had divided the list up between the members of the CPU. Alex had scored ten of them. She'd been laboriously tracking through each one since she'd arrived at work that morning. So far, she'd only managed to cross one entry off her list.

It was tedious and time-consuming work. Each email address had to be tracked back to an owner. That owner's credit card and banking details were then retrieved and examined, cross-referencing any possible link with their Belgian suspect. Mind-numbing and monotonous, yes, but it was the only way to build evidence against their list of suspects and ultimately make arrests.

A soft sigh escaped. Her gaze flicked to Brandon. He sat a few feet away, totally immersed in the information on his screen. At least, that's how he appeared.

From the corner of her eye, she saw him lean back and stretch his arms over his head. She stilled and kept her gaze firmly on her screen, trying to ignore the rush of emotions that pumped through her veins, bursting into bloom across her face.

She'd been ignoring him since the barbeque. She was determined to put him back in the past, where he belonged and focus on her future. With Phillip. Maybe. Or Jason. Maybe. Or Andrew. No, not Andrew. There was something about his profile that just didn't feel right.

She glanced at the clock on the wall in front of her. It was nearly lunchtime. Six more hours to go and she'd be out of there and getting on with her new life. She'd agreed to meet Phillip for brunch the next day. She'd read somewhere that brunch was the safest option for a first date. It wasn't meant to last as long as lunch and if the date wasn't going well, you had a valid excuse to leave after an hour or so.

On the other hand, if sparks were flying and you wanted to spend more time together, brunch could move into lunch with very little effort and you still had the safety of daytime to conduct the entire operation.

Her mother had been happy to look after Sam and had even congratulated her on finding the courage to take the next step toward her future.

Alex didn't feel quite as confident about it. Phillip looked pleasant enough in his picture and based on the information he'd provided in his profile, they certainly seemed to have a lot in common, but still, she couldn't help but feel just a little bit cynical.

The picture could have been taken years ago, or worse still, be a complete fake. The profile could have been made to say whatever he thought would take someone's fancy. Or maybe he was an axe murderer? There had to be some reason why a good-looking guy who seemed to be what every girl was hoping for was still single.

But, then again, what about her? She prided herself on staying fit and attractive and had a healthy self-esteem. She wasn't some mad woman with baggage that would overload Mascot Airport.

Okay, she had a couple of tiny trust issues, but who

didn't? Nobody got to be her age without someone letting them down. That was life. Sometimes, it sucked.

More movement on the periphery of her vision snagged her attention. Brandon had pushed away from his desk and was now headed straight toward her.

Alex's heart rate accelerated and she fought to get it under control. She was being ridiculous. He was just a man. A man she worked with. Nothing more. She sucked in a deep breath and held it.

Brandon was frowning when he casually propped a hip against her desk. "Alex, I was wondering if I could ask you some questions about what we're doing. I'm a bit confused. You've been at this a lot longer than I have."

Alex let her breath out. See, it was a work thing. That's all. Just like she'd been telling herself.

"Er...um... Yes, of course. Fire away." Her gaze flitted between his handsome face and the designer tie that was knotted with perfect precision around his neck.

"It's like this. I understand these addresses have come from a suspected pedophile in Belgium, so obviously the owners of the accounts have had contact with the slime, but how is going through their credit card histories going to help us work out if they're part of a pedophile ring or if they're just ordinary people? Surely, he must have friends and acquaintances that he emails that aren't caught up in this?"

Alex nodded, her breath coming easier. "Of course, that's what makes it so difficult. Someone has to comb through every single email address and decide which ones look suspicious and which ones don't and it all has to be done anonymously. We don't want any of the people involved getting a whiff of what we're investigating or there will be no hope of tracking them down. Accounts will be closed, ISP addresses removed—they'll disappear into cyberspace without a trace."

"So what are we actually looking for? I was assuming if there were a number of transactions between the suspect and the email account holder, that would be enough to put them on a suspect list, but that might not be true. This Janssens guy in Belgium owns a legitimate online sex toy shop. How do we know if these shoppers aren't buying dildos or strap-ons or adult movies...or whatever, as opposed to child pornography?"

"Yeah, it's tough. And the truth is, there are times when we don't know. Sometimes it comes down to gut instinct. Knowing when something doesn't look right. The other difficulty is that a lot of these slime balls share their images for free. They join an online club for a minimal fee and share kiddie pics around the table, so to speak."

Brandon's jaw tensed. "I had no idea how many of these sick fucks are out there."

Alex understood how he felt. It turned her stomach every time she thought about it. That was one of the things that kept her going after finishing a string of all-nighters. Someone had to put the scum away.

She cleared her throat and reached for a piece of paper and the pen that lay on her desk. "Okay, here's a rough guide on how these things work. As I said, once upon a time, no one made any money out of kiddie porn. They just got together online and shared their sick fantasies with each other—pictures and all.

"But recently, we've had some budding entrepreneurs stick their heads up. People who are so depraved, they've decided to turn child pornography into a business. It's bad enough that pedophiles exist; it's stomach-turning to know that someone's getting rich from it."

"How does it work?"

"Something like this. One of these lowlifes—let's call him Rick—prowls around these online clubs and lets it be known he has images for sale. Sometimes it's DVDs, too. That's where the real money is."

A look of distaste crossed Brandon's face. Alex acknowledged it with a terse nod.

"Yep, this is why we come to work every day."

"I'm beginning to see why you're so passionate about it."

"Passionate? Yeah, I guess I am. Although I'd be much

happier if the world was rid of this kind of filth once and for all. I'd happily go into retirement if I could be assured another pedophile would never step foot in our world again."

Brandon's eyes narrowed dangerously. "Death would be too good for them. I'd like to see them go a round or two with one of those Russian KGB interrogators from the '80s. They really knew how to inflict pain. These scumbags would wind up wishing they were dead."

Alex shuddered. "I can't even bear thinking about it." She drew the piece of paper closer. "Anyway, as I was saying, the Ricks of this world usually set up a legitimate online shop front—an adult shop or something similar, and they let it be known in the chat rooms and clubs that they have other stuff under the counter."

"So to speak?"

Alex offered a slight smile. "Yeah, so to speak. The legitimate sales are usually one-offs and for smaller amounts. For example, a regular adult DVD sells for around twenty US dollars. Millions of them are sold around the world every day. It's a thriving business. The illegal ones, on the other hand, sell for much, much more."

"As you'd expect," Brandon murmured.

"That's right. A child porn DVD might sell for as much as five hundred US dollars. Then of course, there are the still images."

"What are they worth?"

"Anywhere from fifty to one hundred and fifty bucks and we're talking thousands of transactions."

Brandon whistled. "That's some serious coinage."

"Yes," Alex agreed. "And that's why these shop fronts are popping up all over the place. It's big money. And the demand seems endless. Then there are the website subscriptions."

"What do they entail?"

"In addition to purchasing single images, you can pay a monthly membership fee, sign up to an Internet site and have unlimited access to their online images."

"What's the going rate?"

"Somewhere in the vicinity of thirty to forty US dollars a month. It's a lucrative business."

"But what about the clubs? I thought you said members shared their images for free?"

"I did and they do. But not everyone knows about these clubs and not everyone can become a member. In fact, they're becoming very secretive and selective about who's admitted. They've realized how far law enforcement can and will go to track them down now and they've become more reticent about advertising their activities."

Brandon shook his head. "God, it's just unbelievable. Until I started working here, I had no idea about the extent of the problem. And given the difficulties in tracing them, it's a wonder you have any success in bringing them down."

Alex wanted to bask in his admiration, but was unwilling to let him see how much she appreciated his sentiment. Instead, she offered a shrug.

"Yeah, well, we work hard and we're good at what we do and each one of us is utterly determined to nail every single one of these scumbags." She grimaced. "The problem is, for each one of them we put away, another five take their place. Some days it feels impossible."

Empathy etched lines into Brandon's face. "You just have to keep on keeping on and hope like hell that sooner or later, you'll get on top of them. It's all you can do."

"Yeah, that and try to educate as many parents and kids as we can about the dangers of sharing information, and particularly photos, online."

She looked up at him. "I'm glad to hear Tom and Lily have had the talk with Cassie."

"What do you mean?"

"I spoke to her the other night, at the barbeque."

Brandon frowned. "I thought she was in bed sick?"

"Yes, she was. Had the flu, I think. But I went upstairs and said hello to her before I left. She told me she's not allowed on Facebook or Twitter."

"Good to hear, although I'd expect nothing less from

those two. They've both seen firsthand how dangerous those social networking sites can be."

"I agree, but I can't help thinking that it's only a matter of time before she breaks the rules. She's a teenager, after all. It's what they do."

"Well, hopefully her parents have instilled enough caution and common sense into her by that time, she'll be sensible about it."

"Yeah, I hope so. They've done a really good job so far. She's a nice kid."

Brandon's gaze increased in its intensity. "So is Sam."

Nerves tightened around Alex's throat. "Thanks," she managed.

"He's pretty tall for his age."

The words struck her like a physical blow. Her mind spun. Had he guessed she'd lied to him? Did he realize Sam was his son? Oh, God. She was so not ready for this conversation.

"Right and I guess you've been around lots of three-year-olds?"

"You said he was two."

Alex shrugged and attempted to keep her breathing even. "Two, three—what does it matter?"

"Lily thought he looked older than two." His gaze drilled into hers.

Alex tried to get a handle on her frantic thoughts. Shit, they'd obviously been talking about her—and Sam. She should never have gone to the barbeque. She'd known it before she'd accepted the invitation. And yet, she'd gone. Now look at the mess she was in.

Plastering a smile on her face, she gave him another shrug. "Everyone says that. What can I say? His dad's tall."

Brandon's shoulders slumped. "That's what I told Lily."

Guilt rushed through her and she almost called out at the dejection that clouded his eyes. God, she couldn't keep doing this.

"I'm sorry." His apology startled her out of her reverie. Before she could respond, he spoke again, his voice rough with emotion.

"Please, Alex. Forgive me. It's none of my business. I know I've said that before, but I'm saying it again. I'm sorry. I won't ask you about your past again. We were over. You had every right to be with someone else. I've been acting like an idiot. We're still over. I'm sorry."

He turned and stumbled away in the direction of the locker room. Alex burned with shame. Every pore in her body radiated heat. She lay her head down on her desk and groaned. Why, oh why did he have to choose *her* unit? Why couldn't he have stayed safely in the back of her mind, like he had for the last four years—existing, but not *co-existing*? So what if she'd spent more hours than she'd like to admit thinking about him, wondering how he was, hoping he thought of her—if only occasionally. So what if in the dark, lonely hours before dawn she'd longed for him. She'd never imagined it would happen—that he'd come striding back into her life and send everything into a turmoil, awakening feelings she'd forcefully put behind her.

The strain of keeping the truth about Sam from him was wearing her down and she had only herself to blame. She was the one who continued to vacillate over telling him. In the beginning, her mother had urged her over and over to rethink her decision and tell Brandon about the baby, but she'd refused. He hadn't wanted a child when they'd been together; she'd seen no reason to tell him once they were separated.

She'd known him too well not to know he'd feel duty-bound to stay with her. She'd never met a man with a greater sense of honor. And that's what had hurt and confused her more than anything. What had happened to that honor the night he'd chosen to walk away from his wedding vows? Only he knew, but their marriage had been irrevocably broken because of his refusal to talk about it, to explain himself, and it had stayed that way.

"You okay?"

Alex lifted her head as Ryan moved up beside her, concern in the dark depths of his eyes.

She managed a weak smile. "Yeah, I'm okay." She

motioned with her head in the direction of the locker room. "Just a few teething problems with the ex. We haven't seen each other for more than four years. It's taking a little adjusting having to work with him every day."

"What's he doing here?" Ryan's voice held a note of distrust.

"Your guess is as good as mine."

Emotion darkened Ryan's eyes to black. "Just as long as he doesn't go breaking your heart again. I haven't forgotten how you were when you first turned up here still licking your wounds. You could barely string two words together that weren't related to work. I don't want that happening to you again."

Alex smiled and reached out to squeeze his hand, surprised at the depth of his caring.

"Thanks, Ryan. I really appreciate you looking out for me. You're the big brother I never had."

Ryan blushed and his voice turned gruff. "Yeah, well, you do remind me of my little sister. She lives in the country. We don't get to see each other very often. She's as headstrong and stubborn as you. That makes it even harder to look out for her."

Alex felt a surge of longing for the siblings she'd never had and for the camaraderie that came with them. And she thought about her son Sam, being raised without his father and cousins... "She's lucky to have such a caring brother."

Ryan offered a lop-sided grin, still embarrassed. "Yeah, well, I'm sure she'd agree with you—or not. Anyway, I just wanted to make sure you were all right. I passed Brandon on his way to the locker room and he looked like he was about to murder someone."

"Yeah, well, that would be me, I guess."

"If you want me to have a word with him..."

Alex was touched by his offer, but shook her head. "Thanks, Ryan. I really appreciate it, but I'm fine. We're fine. We just have to give it time, let things work themselves out. It's probably best if we keep everyone else out of it."

"I understand. I do. I had to work with an ex once before, too."

Curiosity tilted Alex's lips up. "Really? Who was she?"

"No one you knew. She left a couple of months before you started working here. Clarissa Neil. We'd been together a few years, but it didn't work out. We were both in the CPU when we broke up. It took her about six months to get a transfer. It was pretty tense for the first little while, but as you say, time has a way of working these things out."

He shrugged. "After the first month or so, people kind of accepted we were no longer a couple and moved on. Once she started seeing someone else, it was almost as if the world had forgotten we'd ever been close, which made it easier to work together."

Alex smiled. "So, what about you? Are you seeing anyone new? How's that boat of yours going?

Ryan grinned. "As a matter of fact, I asked out the instructor who took me for my license test. You wouldn't believe how well she can steer a boat."

Alex smiled back at him genuinely pleased. "Well good on you, Ryan. I'm happy for you."

"Yeah, it beats pining over an ex."

His words struck her hard. Whether he meant them to or not, Alex couldn't tell, but they reverberated through her head long after he'd moved away.

Was she still pining over Brandon? Was that what she'd call the all-to-frequent late-night wistful dreamings that things had worked out differently?

Surely not. No, what they'd had together had been great, for awhile. And then it had been awful. Time to put that to bed, once and for all and get on with her life. A life that didn't include Brandon.

CHAPTER 15

Brandon listened to the rhythmic thud of his running shoes on the pavement and tried to concentrate on the gorgeous Sydney morning unfolding before him.

The sky was clear and crisp with only the whisper of an occasional feathery cloud to break up the blue. The morning sun had enough warmth in it to chase away the overnight chill. The ocean sparkled like diamonds.

It was his favorite jogging route, high above the sand of Bondi beach, and it never failed to lift his mood. On a day like today, with most people kick-starting their weekend, the footpath was crowded with other joggers, mothers with prams, tourists and even older people, all enjoying the unseasonably warm winter weather.

He hadn't had a decent run for nearly a week. With the investigation heating up, he'd been drawing long hours at his desk and even longer back in his unit. As the new kid on the block, he'd felt an obligation to come up to speed and help his colleagues in any way he could. He'd spent more than a hundred hours of his own time collating the information he'd gathered from chat rooms and other sites and was now comparing it to the people whose addresses had been found on Janssens' computer.

One name on his list kept coming up: James Gibbons. The name itself meant nothing, but the man had an active presence on the net and was a regular visitor to sites that were known to be frequented by pedophiles. His email address had also been among those found on the hard drive of the computer in Belgium.

Brandon wanted to talk to someone about what he'd found. No, not just to someone. He wanted to talk this over with Alex. But he'd promised to leave her alone and he'd meant it. She wanted to move on with her life. He had to do the same. He had to put aside the yearning that things could go back the way they had been and face the fact he would live the rest of his life without her.

Alex was never going to love him again. She may have forgiven him, but things between them would never be the same. He knew that. In his head, he knew that. It was his heart that still held out hope. Especially after that kiss.

She'd melted against him. He'd felt her hunger. If Lily hadn't interrupted them…

But then she'd shut him down. She'd even claimed to be seeing someone. It had knifed him when she'd said that, but the more he'd thought about it, the more it seemed likely to be a few throw-away words said in the heat of the moment from a woman desperate to regain control.

His head had been spinning, too. Their kiss had triggered a torrent of emotions—shock and amazement and hope and love—he'd barely been able to put two words together afterwards. He'd known exactly how disorientated she'd have been feeling. He'd felt the same way.

A spurt of hope rushed through him. What if her declaration she was involved with someone else had been merely a smokescreen? A blockade to buy herself time to adjust to the sudden change in their relationship? Was it possible she felt more for him than she'd admitted? Could he be that lucky?

Slowing his steps, Brandon jogged around a young couple and their dog. He was on the downhill run. Along the pavement, past the cafes and shops fronting the beach and up the final hill to his apartment and he'd be done. His legs were tired and his T-shirt was soaked, but he felt good. He felt strong and alive and ready for whatever might be thrown at him. He savored the moment.

And then he saw her.

He stopped short and doubled over, feeling as though he'd just taken a fist to his gut. People behind him stepped around him, muttering their annoyance. He stumbled and tried to get out of the way, dragging in desperate breaths.

She sat with her back to him, but he'd have known her anywhere. The man sitting opposite her laughed at something she said, displaying a set of even white teeth that could have come straight out of a Colgate advertisement. There were plates half-filled with breakfast food on the table between them and coffee mugs off to one side. An air of calm intimacy surrounded them.

Alex nodded and responded to something the man said and the million-dollar grin flashed again.

Brandon's gut clenched. Christ, he was such an idiot. She hadn't been lying. She *was* seeing someone—a good-looking, successful someone, from the look of him. Designer sunglasses hid the man's eyes and impressive shoulders filled out a five-hundred-dollar jacket.

A shaft of jealousy speared through him and he had to look away. It was one thing to know she'd been with another man since he'd left. It was quite another to be confronted with the proof smack bang in the middle of Bondi.

Did she still live around here? Was that why she was breakfasting on his turf? Or maybe her boyfriend did?

His mind rebelled against the word. *Boyfriend*. It jeered him, reminding him of all he'd lost. A surge of helpless anger nearly bent him over. She was still his wife, dammit. She had no right parading around with a boyfriend.

The anger dissolved as quickly as it had ignited and the tension left his frame. He was deceiving himself. She wasn't his wife really. In name, maybe, but that was all. And everyone knew that amounted to zilch. What was in a piece of paper, anyway?

Veering off the pavement, Brandon jogged across the

crowded car park and made his way back to his apartment via a circuitous route. He climbed the final hill toward home. His heart still beat a furious tattoo against his chest, despite the fact he'd slowed his pace.

How could he have been such a fool? He'd almost convinced himself Alex had been lying about her boyfriend, but it was obvious she'd been telling the truth.

She *did* have a boyfriend. And one she was very chummy with if sharing breakfast was any indication. It was closer to lunchtime than breakfast, but maybe they'd had a late night, slept in and finally went in search of food.

Images of her lying naked and sprawled across the toned limbs of her mystery man sent a shudder of pain through his heart. God, what he'd give to turn back the hands of time, to choose differently, to be the man she deserved, the man she'd loved.

He came to a halt outside the entrance to his apartment block and dragged in some huge breaths. His eyes burned with pent-up emotion and his body had begun to shake.

Fitting the key inside the lock on the gate, he jogged up the final few steps and opened the door to his unit. Closing it behind him, he strode across the carpeted living room and collapsed onto the couch.

The leather was cold on his damp skin and he shivered at the impact. Leaning forward with his head in his hands, he gritted his teeth against the emotions that threatened to overwhelm him. For so long, he'd held it back, pushed it to the far recesses of his mind. Apart from the few times he'd released the tension by getting good and drunk with Tom or his other brother, Declan, he'd resisted the urge to wallow in his self-pity or waste time reliving his lifetime of regrets.

But he'd never given up hope that one day they would reconcile. That he'd tell her the reason he left. That she would forgive him. That she'd remember what they'd meant to each other and how much they'd loved each other. How they'd promised themselves to each other. 'Till death.

In the first few years after their separation, he hadn't kept tabs on her. It had been too painful to even think about her, let alone know anything about her life without him.

But, gradually, the pain had faded and in its place hope had taken root. He'd brought an end to his career as a covert agent taking on high-risk operations and had applied for a transfer. He'd tracked down Alex and had yearned for the day when he would see her again. His first day in the CPU had been filled with equal parts excitement and fear. He hadn't been surprised to find her in a role that had some involvement with children. In the months before their marriage ended, having a child had been all she'd talked about. And argued about.

He shook his head with regret. His reasons for not wanting a child hardly seemed to matter now. If he could have his time over, he'd agree to a hundred kids. However many she wanted. Anything to keep the smile on her face. Her much-loved face. A face he'd adored.

And one he now had to yearn for from afar. Well, from at least the distance of a few desk spaces, but it might as well be another continent away. The thought of working with her, seeing her nearly every day, suddenly became claustrophobic. Panic tightened his chest. How could he bear to see her, be near her and know that she belonged to someone else?

He was trapped in a nightmare of his own making. He should never have tracked her down, requested a transfer. What the hell had he been thinking? That she'd be glad to see him? That she'd welcome him back with open arms, sweeping away the last four years like they'd never happened?

The idea was so fanciful he couldn't believe he'd imagined it. And yet, he *had* imagined it. He might not have acknowledged the thought or given it voice, but there was no denying the secret hope he'd nurtured way down deep inside him that she'd react in just that way.

Brandon groaned and scrubbed at his face. It was too late. Even if he offered her the explanation for his actions when he'd announced they were over, it probably wouldn't make a difference. He had to let it go. He had to let *her* go.

It was way past time. He'd been in denial. But his hopes and dreams of any future with Alex had been smashed the minute he'd seen her with a man that made her smile.

———————

Alex cast a surreptitious glance at her watch and tried not to groan. She was being a bitch. Phillip sat across from her finishing his coffee and all she could think about was how much longer she'd have to continue making polite conversation with a complete stranger.

It wasn't as if he was ugly, or even unpleasant company. He looked better than his photo and she'd yet to uncover any nasty habits. Hundreds of girls would give their right arm to be sitting where she was, and given the number of admiring glances from the scores of female backpackers in tight denims and cute jackets that had sauntered past their table, there'd be someone only too happy to take her place if she happened to stand and leave.

But that would be rude and if there was anything her parents had drummed into her from the moment she could talk it was good old-fashioned manners.

Forcing a smile, she tried again to concentrate on what he was saying. They'd enjoyed a perfectly nice brunch with bacon and eggs and hot coffee and croissants and had managed to keep the conversation flowing at an even rate with only the occasional uncomfortable silence.

The problem was, there was no connection. No spark. That indefinable *something* was missing. No matter how hard she tried to find it. And she *was* trying.

He was smart and funny and knew how to dress. He was a little older than her—probably in his early forties, just as he'd stated in his profile. The fact he hadn't lied about his age— or his looks—was another plus. He was honest. She, of all people, knew that was a rare commodity.

Thoughts of Brandon immediately filled her mind and she grimaced at the intrusion. She was on a *date*, for goodness sake. How dare her husband intrude? The whole purpose of the exercise was to move on with her life—without him.

Phillip fell silent and looked across at her expectantly. She froze, clueless about what he'd just said. She nodded and smiled and prayed it was enough.

With renewed determination, she forced thoughts of Brandon to the back of her mind. She owed it to Phillip—no, she owed it to *herself*—to give this a chance. It was a first date, after all. No one expected fireworks on a first date. It took time to get to know someone. That's all she needed to do—give it time.

She reached over and touched his hand. His eyebrows flew up in surprise.

"I just wanted to say thank you for breakfast," she said. "It's been lovely."

He smiled back at her a little warily. "Why do I hear a "but" coming?"

Alex shook her head. "No, there's no "but." It's just that I have to collect my son. He has a soccer game this afternoon. But," she smiled, "if it's all right with you, I'd like to see you again."

The words fell out of her mouth before she could stop them. She held her breath and waited for his reply, her gaze fixed on the table. If he turned her down, so be it. She'd tried. She really had. If he said yes—God, she didn't know what she'd do if he said yes.

"You have a son?"

Her breath eased out. She looked up. "Yes, I do. Sam."

"How old is he?"

She paused and then decided on the truth. "Um, he's three and a half. Nearly four, I guess."

"Wow, and he's already playing soccer? That's what I call commitment. Or is it something he does with his dad?"

Phillip's voice held open curiosity and Alex couldn't blame him. Of course he'd assume there was a Dad in the picture somewhere. She could understand him wanting to know more.

"No, it's not really a soccer game. We get together with a

few of the other parents and their kids in the neighborhood and play in the park. It's kind of a long-standing Saturday afternoon ritual and one that I haven't been able to join in for awhile. I've worked a lot of Saturdays recently."

"I guess you do a lot of shift work in the police force?"

"Yes, yes I do. This is one of those rare occasions," she replied hurriedly. She didn't have the time or the inclination to get into a discussion on the intricacies of her job. It was definitely not first-date material.

"Well, then, I do feel special."

She tried not to grimace at the warmth in his tone. Things were moving out of her control. It was time to call it quits.

Gathering her handbag from the empty chair beside her, she made to leave. Phillip stood and held out his hand.

"I'm sorry you have to rush off. It was really lovely to meet you, Alex. I hope we can see each other again."

Alex shook his hand and forced another smile. "It was nice to meet you, too. I'll check the roster and see when I'm off. I'll send you an email."

His answering smile should have weakened her knees, but left her sadly unaffected. "I'll count the days," he murmured.

James Gibbons adjusted the lens of his camera until the girl on the bed was perfectly framed. She was still half-drugged on the concoction of sleeping tablets and speed he'd given her on the way to his apartment.

He'd been heading over to see Lady G play netball when he'd spied little Veronica on the swings in the park not far from where he lived. He'd seen her before, of course. He'd seen many of them before, swinging and playing and running around. There were usually at least a couple of parents around and he'd never had the opportunity to do much more than smile hello or wave as he walked through the park.

Once, he'd managed to drop his glasses not far away

from where Veronica had sat on the grass threading daisies and he'd used the excuse to ask her name. He'd told her about his new puppy.

That had been nearly a month ago and he hadn't had another opportunity to get close. It didn't do to spend too much time at the park. Mothers tended to get suspicious and fathers got downright aggressive. He'd been on the receiving end of more than one father who'd taken offence to him talking to their young daughters.

Veronica stirred on the bed and he frowned. The drugs were wearing off quicker than he expected. He'd have to work faster. He couldn't risk her waking before he was through. That was only asking for trouble.

He'd already taken numerous shots of her asleep. Her fat, childish plaits were spread over his pillow, their blondness contrasting vividly with the black satin cover. Lying naked and spread-eagled across his sheets, her pale, youthful skin shone with an iridescence that had made him instantly hard. The pictures would be exquisite.

She was a little younger than the girls he usually went for, but that didn't detract from her beauty and he knew there would be plenty of men willing to pay a good price for her image.

Working faster now, he arranged her thin limbs this way and that to capture the light and to show the artful beauty to its best advantage. Returning to his camera, he pressed the button to start the video.

His cock throbbed. Oh, God, he couldn't wait. He was disappointed he hadn't made contact with Lady G, but Veronica, dear, sweet little Veronica more than made up for it. Besides, fate had intervened. Veronica had literally fallen into his lap.

He'd spied her alone in the park and had stopped his car. He'd been walking across to talk to her when he'd seen her falling from the monkey bars. He'd dashed across and broken her fall, the two of them landing in the dirt below.

He'd told her he'd take her home. She'd asked about the puppy.

Veronica stirred again and his cock twitched. Sliding down the zipper of his jeans, he pulled out his engorged shaft and approached the bed.

Cassie peered through the scattering of people that surrounded the netball courts, hoping he was still here. She'd forgotten to tell him she didn't play until twelve. He'd probably turned up at nine. She hadn't explained how the start times changed from week to week.

He wasn't there and it was all her fault. How could she be so stupid? It's not like she could expect him to hang around for three hours.

She sighed and picked up her gym bag. It was a shame he'd missed it. Her team had won 6-5. It had been a hard-fought game and Cassie had scored the winning goal.

She shrugged off her disappointment, knowing there would be other games. But would he want to come and watch? He'd already tried twice and neither time had worked out. What if he got tired of trying?

Fear clutched at her heart. *No, please don't let that happen. Please let him want to come again. Please, please, please. I'll do anything.*

Tossing her bag over her shoulder, she headed toward the bus station.

He stood back and gazed at the girl on the bed. She was now fully dressed, but to him she remained beautiful. The photos and video would be worth a fortune. He couldn't wait to go online and share them.

She was fast asleep again. After he'd finished, he'd forced a concoction of pills down her throat and had watched while they'd taken effect. The cocktail of drugs would skewer her memory. She'd never be sure what was real and what was just a dream—or a nightmare.

He never did more than taste them. He wasn't that stupid. He took his pleasure from having them spread out before him—naked and vulnerable. He'd carefully washed away the evidence of his orgasm—the arc of creamy fluid he'd sprayed across her chest—and he would launder the sheets as soon as he returned.

She'd been missing less than an hour and soon there would be no trace of little Veronica ever having been in his apartment.

She'd be dazed and confused and uncertain about what had happened. There was a possibility she'd remember seeing him in the park, but she'd seen him there before. She wouldn't know whether it was this time or another that they'd spoken. Everything would be a jumble of confusing sensations, colors and sounds.

He smiled, secure in his knowledge everything was as it should be. His method of operation wasn't new and it had worked every single time.

CHAPTER 16

"All right, everyone, listen up."

Alex heard Patrick's order and stood and peered over the partition that divided her desk from the others. Other members of the team were doing likewise, making their way to where their superintendent stood in front of the whiteboard.

"I want to thank you all for working your asses off over the last few weeks. We've narrowed the list down to thirteen and we're close to a breakthrough. But, we're not there yet."

Alex looked around at her smiling colleagues and joined in the murmurs of agreement. Her gaze slid to Brandon where he stood a few desks away. A small smile of satisfaction nudged at his lips.

He turned and caught her gaze. Embarrassment scorched her cheeks. He acknowledged their joint achievement with a slight nod then returned his attention to Patrick.

"I want to make special mention of our newest team member. You've all been working around the clock on this, but Brandon Munro's work ethic has been beyond exceptional. The amount of data he's managed to collate in the short time he's been here has been impressive and incredibly useful. In fact, Brandon's the reason we've managed to cull our list so quickly."

Brandon ducked his head. Patrick continued.

"Brandon went over and above what I'd expect of any of you, let alone someone new to our unit. I don't know how many hours of his own time he's spent on this—I'm sure he could tell you and probably down to the last minute. I haven't received his claim for overtime yet," Patrick joked, "but when I do, I'll be happy to approve it."

A chuckle went around the room and Brandon's cheeks turned crimson.

Their boss turned and looked at Brandon, his expression sobering. "I mean it when I say you've gone above the call of duty, Brandon. Without your extra commitment, it would have taken us much, much longer to narrow down this list. I know I speak for the entire team when I tell you how much we appreciate it."

Brandon shrugged, obviously uncomfortable with the praise. "It was nothing, really. Once I got into it, I couldn't let it go. It was tedious and painstaking, but every time I managed to eliminate a suspect, the rush was unbelievable."

He gazed at the faces of the men and women around him. When he got to Alex, he stopped and her breath caught. "You're an inspiration, all of you. I can't believe you've been doing this for so long. Some of you, for years. I can only imagine the number of bottom dwellers you've managed to put away in that time. Not to mention the number of kids you've saved." His voice shook with emotion. "I'm honored to be working alongside you."

Alex's chest tightened. The sincerity in his eyes was reflected in his voice. She swallowed the lump in her throat. This was the Brandon she knew and loved. The one that worked tirelessly and selflessly to eradicate evil. The one that put one hundred and ten percent into everything he did. The one that remained humble, despite the evidence of his achievements. The natural-born leader who remained a team player.

He was the reason she hadn't felt a speck of interest in Phillip. For all of Phillip's good looks and charm, he wasn't Brandon. He wasn't her husband.

Her husband. That's what Brandon was. The man she could still call hers, if she wanted to. If *he* wanted to.

Her heart skipped a beat at the thought. He'd seemed keen to try something again. She didn't know exactly what, but he'd invited her to the family barbeque. That had to mean something. He'd been hurt and angry when she'd told him about Phillip. That had to mean something, too. You didn't get upset over an ex's new boyfriend if they no longer meant anything to you. At least, she hoped that was the case.

She wanted him back. Pure and simple. Brandon was the reason she'd been celibate for the last four years. No one else could measure up. He may have broken her heart and at the time, she hadn't been able to see a way to forgive him, but time had a way of healing even the deepest of wounds and it wasn't like she was without sin. It was time to let go of the past and try to move forward as a family.

The thought of Sam filled her with renewed guilt. She had to tell Brandon they had a son. It was wrong to keep it from him. If they were to have any chance at a future, he had to know. The longer she left it, the harder it would be to explain why she hadn't said anything.

As the team dispersed back to their desks, several of them stopped to pump Brandon's hand or pat him on the back. Alex regained her seat and waited with anticipation for the hubbub to recede. Nerves jangled in her belly and her hands went cold.

What if she'd read the signs wrong? What if he turned her down? She was the one who'd told him she'd moved on. What was she going to say? That she'd lied? And not for the first time?

Dread swirled in her stomach. Perhaps she should just deal with one lie at a time? Admit to him she still had feelings. That her time with Phillip had brought that truth home. Give them a chance to get to know each other again before she told him about Sam...

Relief surged through her at the thought of putting it off for a little longer. It wasn't going to go away, but at least she could wait and see if they could rebuild their relationship.

Hopefully, by the time she told him, they'd *have* a relationship and be in a stronger position to deal with it. Brandon would be angry, naturally. She wouldn't expect anything less. But she hoped by that time he'd love her enough, love *both* of them enough, to accept her reasons for withholding the information and everything would turn out all right.

Misgivings pricked her conscience, but she swiftly pushed them away. Her plan was far from fool proof and its success would ultimately depend on Brandon, but it would buy her some time to reconnect with him, to re-establish the loving relationship they'd had before it all went so far off the tracks. And it would give him time to get to know Sam. His son.

———————

Brandon noticed the frown lines marring the smooth skin of Alex's forehead and wondered at their cause. His cheeks were still hot from the praise he'd received from the superintendent and his colleagues.

He hadn't done it for the recognition. That had never been his way. He'd done it because he'd cared and he'd really believed what he was doing would make a difference. It was what had driven him all these years. Through the years of living undercover, the loneliness, the lies. He'd only been able to do it because he'd learned his lesson; he knew his complete dedication was integral to the success of his missions.

In the end, though it had cost him his marriage, he wouldn't have changed it—couldn't have changed it. It was as simple and as complex as that.

He glanced back at Alex and his gut tightened when he noticed she'd pushed back her chair and was walking toward him.

"Brandon, um… Can I speak with you for a minute?" Her voice was as tentative as she looked.

"Fire away."

Her gaze darted from his face to her hands and back again. He frowned at her reticence.

"Um, I was um...wondering... That is..."

Now he was confused. Since when had Alex been so tongue-tied? "What is it, Alex?"

Dark red color stained her cheeks. "I was wondering if we could talk? You and I. Somewhere..." Her gaze darted around the squad room. "Somewhere else."

"Why?"

She looked away, flustered. Taking a deep breath, her gaze returned to his. "Please, not here. It's really important. I-I don't want to get into it here."

He shook his head, confused. She mistook the motion.

"Please, Brandon. I really need to talk to you. I-I was wrong."

His heart began a slow thud. "Wrong?"

"Yes, wrong. I should never have told you I was over you."

Blood pounded in his ears. She'd spent the weekend with someone else, and now she was telling him she still had feelings for him?

"Are you for real?" he growled, resisting the urge to slam his hand on the desk. "Are you for fucking *real*?"

She bowed her head. When she lifted it, her eyes were filled with shame and desperation. He stifled the urge to offer comfort.

"I'm sorry. But, please. Please can we do this somewhere else?"

Brandon looked around the room, suddenly aware of the curious looks from some of the agents nearby. Drawing in a deep breath, he let the fog of anger and confusion recede and turned back to her with a brief nod.

"Okay, we'll do it your way. I'll meet you at the coffee shop on the corner in fifteen minutes. Don't be late."

As soon as Alex returned to her desk, Brandon pushed up from his chair and headed to the locker room. He'd said fifteen minutes and he needed every second to get himself under control. Each time he thought of what she'd said, his anger renewed itself.

What the hell had she meant, she wasn't over him? He'd seen her having a lovely time with her boyfriend not three days ago. Was she really trying to play him? Turn his emotions inside out? If she was, she was doing a hell of a job.

Leaning over the hand basin, he turned on the faucet and splashed cold water over his face. Straightening, he stared at his reflection in the mirror and cursed the tiny ray of hope that had sparked to life at her words and was now reflected in his eyes.

He couldn't keep doing this to himself. He couldn't keep riding this emotional rollercoaster. She couldn't keep blowing hot one minute and freezing the next. It wasn't fair and he was darn well going to tell her.

He grabbed his jacket from his locker and pushed open the door that led outside. His gaze automatically strayed to Alex's desk. Her chair was empty. His gut clenched with nerves and anticipation. His lips compressed. *Bring it on.*

Alex twisted the napkin in her hands and tried not to look at her watch again. He'd said fifteen minutes. He'd told her not to be late. It was now going on for nearly twenty. Where *was* he?

Perhaps he'd decided not to show? Maybe he'd changed his mind? Her belly twisted in knots and she swallowed. What if he did turn up, but didn't want anything to do with her? What if she'd completely blown it when she'd told him she was seeing someone else?

A waiter appeared before her and asked if she was ready to order.

"I'm waiting for...someone," she murmured, hoping she was right.

"Of course; I'll come back later." The waiter disappeared

and Alex picked up the laminated menu and studied it in an effort to distract herself. The coffee shop was a popular eating establishment and was filling up with a mostly professional set working in the nearby buildings.

"Sorry I'm late."

Brandon materialized before her and took a seat. Alex did her best to keep her pulse under control. She smiled a little uncertainly to cover her reaction and handed him the menu.

"I think I'll have the pumpkin soup with fresh bread. It's soup kind of weather, don't you think?" She inwardly rolled her eyes. *God, could she have said anything lamer? Is this what she'd been reduced to? Talking about the weather?*

Brandon looked back over his shoulder at the dreary, gray day outside. "Yeah, you're right. It wasn't actually raining when I came in this morning."

"You must have clocked on early. It was pouring when I arrived at six."

"Yeah, it was going on four-thirty, I think."

Alex shook her head. "Four-thirty? Don't you ever sleep? No wonder the boss was impressed with the hours you've been putting in."

Brandon nodded, but didn't reply. Alex let it drop. It was none of her business why he wasn't sleeping.

"At least the weekend was fine," he murmured, his gaze snagging hers. "I take it you had a nice time at the beach?"

Alex frowned. *At the beach?* What was he talking about? Memories slammed into her. *Oh, God. He must have seen her with Phillip. There was no avoiding it now.*

In a way, she was relieved. It gave her an excuse to tell him about her failed attempt to date someone new and the reasons it hadn't worked out.

"You saw me."

He nodded. His lips compressed as he studied the menu with a fierce intensity.

He was jealous. The thought popped into Alex's mind

unannounced and spread a warm glow through her belly. He was jealous. That had to be a good sign.

The waiter returned and took their orders. When he left, Alex lay her hand over Brandon's and gave it a squeeze. His gaze snapped back to hers.

"I was having breakfast with Phillip."

He tried to remove his hand. She tightened her grip.

"Your boyfriend."

"No, not my boyfriend. A man I'd only just met."

Brandon frowned in disbelief. "Only just met? You looked awfully cozy to me."

Alex shrugged. "I can't answer that. Maybe that's how it looked to you, but I can tell you, I "met" him a few weeks ago on an online dating site and Saturday morning was our first date. Believe it or not, but that's the truth."

Hope and uncertainty warred in the depths of Brandon's eyes.

"So, he's not your boyfriend? He's not the man you said you were seeing?"

"No, he's not my boyfriend, but yes, he is the man I told you I was seeing."

Confusion shadowed his face. "I thought you said you'd only just met?"

Alex suppressed a sigh. "I did. When I told you I was seeing someone..." She gave an embarrassed shrug. "I guess I should have told you I was seeing someone online. We hadn't actually met. I wanted you to think I was with someone because I was scared and confused about all the things that were happening and I didn't know how you felt and—I don't know. I just said it."

A smile crept across Brandon's face. "You just said it. It wasn't true. You weren't seeing anyone. You *aren't* seeing anyone."

Alex nodded, her lips stretching upwards. "That's right. I just said it. I'm sorry. I shouldn't have. It just came out."

Brandon grinned. "I should be mad as hell at you, but I'm not. You don't know how much I hated the thought of you with that guy."

"I'm sorry, Brandon. I really am. I guess I wanted it to be true. I wanted to be able to say I was over you. It wasn't until I was out with Phillip that I realized how much I'd been lying to myself."

Brandon's grin widened. He grabbed both of Alex's hands in his and squeezed them hard. "I've never been so glad to hear you've been deceitful. I've been telling myself over and over that I had to let you get on with your life, on your terms, without me. But it was hard, Alex. It's been so hard. I promise I'll do everything within my power to earn your love again. I don't expect it to happen overnight, but I won't rest until you love me with all of your heart, like you used to. I swear."

The earnestness that flooded his face nearly did her in. The guilt that filled her was a palpable ache in the depths of her belly. Sam's image swam before her, his innocent dark eyes staring at her accusingly. She shook her head and held on to Brandon's hands.

"I don't know what to say," she whispered, her voice hoarse.

"Please, say you'll give me a chance. You'll give *us* a chance. Please, Alex."

She closed her eyes against his desperation. Misreading her reticence, he pleaded with her again.

"I owe you an explanation."

"Brandon—"

"No, Alex. Let me finish. If I could turn back time, I would do everything so differently. I should have done this four years ago."

Alex's stomach clenched in dread. After begging him for an explanation when he'd arrived home and told her they were over and after spending countless sleepless nights conjuring various scenarios as to why he'd left, now the moment was upon her, she had no idea if she was ready. Wasn't it true that some things were better left unsaid? After all these years, did she really want to know?

Brandon heaved a sigh. His gaze remained fixed on hers. "Please, Alex. Please let me tell you why. You deserved to be told then, and you still deserve to know now. If there is any chance for us, you have to know."

Alex closed her eyes and drew in a deep breath, bracing herself for what was to come. Brandon lowered his gaze and began.

"My team and I had been working undercover in Jakarta for months, posing as Pakistani explosives experts looking for an opportunity to commit *jihad*. Naturally, I could never have carried off pretending I was Indonesian, but with my darker coloring and my proficiency in Arabic and the local Indonesian dialect, *Bahasa*, I was able to pull off a passable impression of an extremist with shady links to groups in Afghanistan.

"Our intelligence indicated there was a terror cell meeting regularly at a madrasa, a Muslim school, on the outskirts of Jakarta. They were suspicious at the start, but when they learned about our skills as explosives experts they gave us the benefit of the doubt."

He offered a strained smile. "Over time, we managed to infiltrate the cell and little by little, we gained the trust and confidence of the ringleader. I also gained the confidence of a female member who carried messages between the head man and other operatives outside the madrasa. Her name was Lia. She talked the talk and whether she would have actually carried out a terrorist act was thankfully never put to the test, but she was privy to the inner workings of the cell and was happy to share what she knew. The intelligence I gathered from her over the weeks we were together proved invaluable."

Brandon sighed and drew Alex's hand in his.

"Things had been going to plan. Lia seemed convinced I was legitimate. We began spending more and more time together and were often deep in discussion late into the night. A lot of the time, I would sleep in cheap accommodation not far from the madrasa. She would come to my room and we would talk and make plans."

Alex's belly clenched with nerves. The room receded around her. She held her breath, waiting in agony for what she thought was coming.

"It was late. The night had been unbelievably hot and humid. There was no air-conditioning in the room where I was staying. I'd farewelled Lia earlier, stripped down to my underwear and gone to bed."

He rubbed his chin and scrubbed at his hair. Tension came off him in waves. Alex remained still, barely breathing.

"It was completely dark inside the room. Despite the late hour, I found it hard to sleep. With the oppressive humidity and the constant danger of discovery, I'd had scant sleep since I'd been there. In spite of my fatigue, I knew the instant she entered my room."

Alex bit her lip so hard she tasted blood. She wanted to cover her ears and tell him to stop, but she stayed silent and tense beside him.

"I'd told her I was single," he admitted quietly. "She was young and attractive and she'd made it plain she was interested. Even so, I never dreamed she'd want to take things to the next level. She was Muslim, after all, and she thought I was, too."

He turned his head and stared at her, his eyes dark with remorse. "But she also thought we shared a cause. A dream of *jihad*. To rid the world of the western infidel. She caught me unawares and quite literally with my pants down."

Alex shook her head, no longer able to stay silent. "All this time, I never *once* suspected you'd been unfaithful. How *could* you?"

Brandon stared at her, his gaze intent on hers. "Please let me finish, Alex."

She gritted her teeth and looked away, not knowing how she'd bear to listen to any more. No wonder he hadn't offered any explanations on the night he'd told her they were over.

"I had to make a decision: Either play along and break my wedding vows or turn her away and risk raising her suspicions and potentially jeopardize the entire operation and the lives of the other undercover operatives in my team.

Lia was a well-respected member of the terrorist cell. One word from her to her leader that we might not be genuine and we would be in a world of hurt."

Brandon's eyes were tortured. Alex held her breath.

"In the end, there was no decision to make. You were my world, my everything. I couldn't do it. I sent her away with an excuse that it was too hot and I was too tired and I prayed she'd accept it at face value and nothing further would come of it." He closed his eyes shook his head slowly back and forth. "I was wrong."

Fear tightened Alex's chest. She barely dared to breathe. "What happened?" she whispered.

Brandon opened his eyes and took hold of both of her hands, squeezing them almost painfully. "Three days later, we were raided by members of the terrorist cell. I don't know if Lia suspected my cover wasn't legitimate or if it was something as trivial as her feeling angry over my rejection, but she must have said something and the cell became suspicious."

He sighed and scrubbed at his face. It was obvious he was finding it difficult to continue. Dread cemented in Alex's belly and she wondered if she could bear to listen to any more. She held her breath when Brandon began to speak again.

"It was the middle of the night. Most of us were asleep. Three of my men were shot dead. Two others were wounded. I was one of the lucky ones."

Horror rushed through her. She stared at Brandon, her mouth gaping, her mind spinning with the shock of it. He'd been attacked. Some of his team had been killed and all because he had turned Lia away. She couldn't imagine his guilt.

"Brandon—"

"Yes, the guilt over their deaths nearly did me in. I was a mess. The AFP got me out of there as quickly as they could, but it didn't matter. Three good men were dead. Two others would take months to heal. One of them is a paraplegic for the rest of his life. And all because of me."

Denial raged through her. "No, Brandon, that's not fair. Don't do that to yourself. It wasn't—"

He sighed deeply and brought one of her hands to his lips. She shivered from the contact. "The worst of it was," he continued quietly, "I knew if I was faced with the same situation again, I would make the same decision. It was then I knew I had no choice. I had to let you go. I couldn't afford to have to make that choice again—between my love for you and the safety of my men. At the time, it seemed like the only way. And in a way it was a punishment I felt I deserved. The families of some of the other men lost their loved ones. How could I continue with a happy life after what I'd caused?"

Alex tried hard to process his words and somehow get over the shock of his disclosure. Never in her wildest dreams had she conjured such a scenario.

"I wish you had told me years ago," she said quietly.

He looked at her, his eyes shadowed with sadness and regret. "So do I." He drew in a deep breath and eased it out. "You have to remember, we'd been struggling to make it work. You wanted a baby and I didn't. The last thing I wanted was to be responsible for another person. My head was messed up pretty bad. I wasn't thinking rationally. I thought if I let you go, you could find someone who wanted a child as badly as you did and I—I never wanted to be placed in such a predicament again."

"You could have transferred to somewhere safer, out of undercover operations." She tried not to sound accusatory.

Brandon nodded. "You're right, but I'd been buried deep in undercover operations for years. At the time, it had been all I knew. The thought of getting help and switching units and changing the direction of my career never occurred to me. It was only right that I'd been excluded from sharing my life with you—a life I no longer felt I deserved. Much later, after I'd grudgingly taken up the AFP's offer of counseling, I realized I'd suffered *Post Traumatic Stress Disorder*. After receiving treatment, I began to see things more clearly."

She smiled sadly. "Too bad it didn't happen sooner."

Brandon shook his head. "You don't know how much I regretted my decision not to tell you. I thought it would be easier to simply leave. To let you go so that you could get on with your life—the life you wanted—without me."

Tears pricked the back of her eyes. "I never wanted to do it without you," she whispered.

A tiny, sad smile appeared briefly on Brandon's lips. "You don't know how much it means to hear you say that."

Alex stared at him, her heart thumping at what she was about to say. "I still don't want to do it without you."

Surprise warred with hope in Brandon's face. He leaned closer. "I love you, Alex. I've never stopped loving you. I love *us*. I want there to *be* an us. Please tell me you want that too."

Her thoughts locked on Sam and dread cemented in her stomach. How could she continue without telling him? She couldn't. But what if her confession destroyed them before they'd even given themselves a chance? She loved him with everything that she was. She couldn't lose him now. *He loved her, had always loved her.* She pushed away the heavy guilt and allowed the tiny spark of elation to take flight and grow and warm her through.

"I've never stopped loving you, either."

His eyes darkened with emotion, and he stared at her like a man starved. Desire kindled low in her belly. His gaze dropped to her lips.

"I want so badly to kiss you, Alex, but I don't know if I should. One minute you're hot, the next you're freezing me out. I don't know whether to follow my instincts or let you set the pace. I want so badly to be with you, but I'm not sure that's what you want." He shook his head. "I'm so confused I can barely think straight. Please, Alex. Talk to me."

The request was quiet, controlled, but she could see the need in his eyes. He'd never been one for playing games. Neither had she.

"I've missed you, too, Brandon. I've missed *us*. I think from the moment you walked out, I've been in mourning. It was like a death."

"I'll regret it for the rest of my life."

"I wish we'd done things differently."

His gaze intensified. "So do I."

He leaned forward and she only had seconds to comprehend he was going to kiss her before his lips, warm and supple, were on hers.

He kissed her gently, curiously, tasting his way. Memories surfaced and fire erupted inside her. They'd always been good together. He'd always known how to turn her on. He increased the pressure of his lips. She opened her mouth and offered him access. He moaned and pressed the tip of his tongue inside.

The familiar sensations rocketed through her, turning her limbs liquid. She reached out and held his face between her hands, anchoring herself to him.

Emotions raged through her bloodstream and pounded in her ears. The noise receded around them and there was nothing and no one but Brandon.

Time ceased to have any meaning. It was only when he pulled back that she came to her senses. Blinking, she looked up and noticed the waiter standing near Brandon's chair, his arms laden with soup bowls and plates.

Nothing had existed but Brandon and his kiss. Heat flooded her face. How could she have forgotten they were in the middle of a busy café during lunch hour?

She peeked at him. A grin tugged at his lips. He looked totally unabashed. She wished she could have borrowed some of his audaciousness.

"You always did look adorably confused after a thorough snog session."

Alex blushed again and refused to look at him. "And you've always had such a way with words."

He reached out and took her hand, trying hard to look contrite. "Forgive me?"

She smiled and lightly batted his hand away. Picking up her soup spoon, she began to eat. The conversation remained general, but flowed with ease. Years before it had been that way between them and it felt good to be at ease again.

After they'd finished and the waiter had cleared away their bowls, Brandon's face turned serious.

"When can I see you again, Alex? I know we need to take it slow, but now that I've tasted you again, the waiting will be unbearable."

Desire stirred again at his words. She wanted him, too. Pure and simple. Life was too short for games. Besides, she was on borrowed time. Sooner or later, her conscience would refuse to be quieted. Sooner or later, she'd have to confess.

Her gaze captured his. "What are you doing tonight?"

Back at the squad room, Alex couldn't help but sneak a look at Brandon where he sat a few desks away. As if sensing her gaze, he looked up at her and winked. Heat rose up her neck. She was like a schoolgirl with a big secret. She smiled back at him. The hours until the end of their shift suddenly yawned ahead of her.

Knowing she'd never get anything done if she kept looking at him, she pulled her chair in close to her desk and made an effort to concentrate.

She reached over, she picked up the phone and dialed her mother's number then drew in a deep breath when it was answered.

"Hi, Mom. It's me. I was wondering if you could do me a favor? I'm meeting someone after work and I was wondering if you could look after Sam?"

"Of course I can. Are you seeing Phillip again?"

Alex sucked in another breath and then let it out on a rush. She might as well get it over with. "No, Mom. It's not Phillip. I'm seeing Brandon."

Silence greeted her. She counted the seconds. "It's just drinks, Mom."

"Brandon? Wow, that's great, honey."

"You don't have to say that, Mom."

"No, I mean it. I love Brandon. You know that. And I've told you before I don't think you've ever gotten over him. You just took me a little by surprise. Last time we spoke about this, it seemed like that was the last thing on your mind."

Alex lowered her voice. "I know. But things have changed. I really want this to work out, Mom."

"I take it you've told him about Sam?"

Alex bit her lip. "Not yet."

"Alex." Her mother's voice held a note of warning.

"I know, I know. I just want to give us a chance."

"It's not right, Alex. You need to tell him."

Alex sighed. "I know. I will. I promise. Just not right now."

CHAPTER 17

Nerves churned inside Alex's stomach. She leaned over the sink in the staff restroom and swallowed some water. Pulling her hairbrush out of her handbag, she gave her hair another few swipes and wished she'd worn something a little less businesslike. Her tailored skirt and jacket and pale blue silk blouse were appropriate for the office, but she would have preferred something a little more casual for a dinner date.

Date? She grimaced with annoyance. It wasn't a date. Not really. They were married. Husbands and wives didn't date.

It was a peace offering. An opportunity to mend fences. A chance to start again. Maybe. Hopefully.

Riffling through her handbag, she pulled out a tube of dark red lipstick and applied it with skillful precision. With a last glance in the mirror, she tossed her handbag over her shoulder and headed toward the door.

She didn't know why she was going to so much trouble with her appearance. After all, he'd been working only a few feet away from her all day. And it wasn't as if he didn't know what she looked like naked.

The thought sent a nervous thrill rushing through her veins, edged with more than a hint of excitement. It had been so long since she'd allowed herself to feel anything other than what was required to get through the daily grind.

She'd had high hopes for Phillip—that, if nothing else, her self-imposed man drought could be brought to an end. But it hadn't worked out that way and now she was going to meet Brandon.

She pushed open the door that led into the squad room. Brandon had already left. He'd suggested they keep whatever it was that was happening between them, to themselves. She was more than happy to agree.

She didn't know what was happening. She could do without the curious stares of her colleagues while they worked it out. Especially the concerned glances she'd been fielding from Ryan.

Not that she didn't appreciate where he was coming from. She was glad he cared. Glad to have him as a friend. She didn't have many of those.

When her marriage had fallen apart, she'd wanted to keep as low a profile as possible. And the fewer people who knew about her pregnancy, the better. For the most part, her old friends had been willing to leave her alone—to give her time to lick her wounds and recover from the breakdown of her marriage. She hadn't felt like returning calls or texts or welcoming visitors.

Over the years, the calls and texts had dwindled and her friends had stopped asking about her. She missed them sometimes, but usually Sam and her mother were enough. Besides, most of the time she was too tired and drained from her job to even think about socializing. Her mother took Sam to all kinds of interesting places because she had the time and knew what would engage him. Because of Alex's schedule and her lack of energy during her time off, the biggest effort she made was to take Sam to the park on the occasional Saturday.

She guessed she'd have to make more effort when he started school. He'd want to have friends over or go to their places. That involved interaction and effort with other parents. The thought didn't exactly excite her.

But, if things worked out with Brandon, it would be different. He'd help her negotiate the delicate maze of socializing with kindergarten parents on their time off. She wouldn't be on her own.

Shaking her head, Alex opened the door that led outside. She was letting her imagination run away with her. They hadn't even spent a night together and she was having him join them for the school run.

She had to take things slowly—get to know him again. Find the right time to tell him he had a son.

Tension tightened in her belly. She was walking a dangerous tightrope. Not telling him could be disastrous, but telling him at the wrong time could destroy any chance they had of rekindling their love.

She was willing to take the risk. She had no choice. She could only hope and pray she was making the right decision.

The bar, with sleek décor and dim designer lighting, was one of the newer, trendier establishments that were popping up around the city. The crowd was largely made up of glamorous advertising types, far removed from the darkly suited, conservative members of law enforcement. Alex knew that was precisely the reason Brandon had chosen it. They were as likely to run into someone they knew as it was going to start raining elephants.

Alex eased out her breath and willed the tension to leave her body. She spied Brandon at a table in a secluded corner, nursing a glass of beer.

Her gaze traveled over his profile. Dark stubble shadowed his cheeks. His hair was slightly disheveled—like he'd run his hand through it more than once—but even looking mussed, his impressive physique filled out his crisp dark blue suit and the navy pinstriped tie around his neck was still curved into a perfect knot. He'd worked a twelve-hour shift and yet could still have sold products for men in any one of the myriad glossy magazines that lined the newsstands.

"What are you drinking?" he asked as she took the seat opposite him.

"A glass of red wine would be great, thanks."

He signaled the barman, who immediately came over and took her order. When the man left, Brandon turned to look at her and smiled.

Her heart skipped a beat. Even with just a smile, he turned her on. Years ago, it used to irritate her, but now she embraced the reality. Time had shown her how quickly life could be turned upside down and how something that was good and special and beautiful could slip through her fingers like dust, blown away with the breeze, gone before she realized it.

"You look good, Alex." His low murmur sent a shiver of desire down her spine.

"I was thinking the same thing about you." Emboldened by the flash of fire in his eyes, she snared his gaze and held it. Blood thudded in her ears and her palms went damp.

The look in his eyes intensified, devouring her with its heat. Her lips parted. His gaze zeroed in on them.

"I so want to kiss you again. It's all I've been able to think about since lunch."

Desire licked low in her belly. Her hand strayed to his thigh under the table. Hard muscles bunched beneath her touch. "Me, too," she breathed, leaning in close.

Out of the corner of her eye, she spied the barman returning with her drink. Brandon cursed under his breath. Alex pulled back and waited while the man placed the glass before her. Brandon reached for his wallet and she murmured her thanks. She'd always loved his take-charge way of dealing with things.

Some women felt the need to fly the flag for feminism, but Alex had always appreciated the differences between the sexes and had loved to feel protected and cared for by the man in her life. She wasn't one of those women who felt weakened or threatened when a man did things for her. Sometimes, she thought she should have been born in the fifties.

Reaching over, she brought the glass of wine to her mouth. It was rich and full-bodied—just what she needed. She licked a droplet off her lips, savoring the taste and Brandon's heated gaze. She trembled from the force of emotion behind his dark, dark eyes.

"Come home with me, Alex."

Excitement shivered through her. "I-I thought we were taking this slow."

His breath tickled her ear. His voice was rough and low. "I've waited more than four years to feel you under me again. I'm done with slow."

Her nipples tightened. Flames burned inside her. They needed to take things slowly. They needed to get to know each other again. Didn't they?

But she needed him. Now.

Emptying her drink in three healthy swallows, she watched Brandon do the same. Setting their glasses down on the bar with a decisive clink, he took her hand and led her to the exit.

———

Brandon snuck a peek at Alex from where she sat inches away from him in the passenger seat of his low-slung, silver Mustang. He had to fold his long legs into it, but he loved the purr of its powerful engine as he cruised through the streets of Sydney.

Being early in the week, traffic was light and they made it to Bondi in less than half an hour. Alex had remained silent on the ride over and he was a little concerned she was having second thoughts.

Not that he would pressure her into this. If she wasn't ready, she wasn't ready. He wanted her one hundred per cent keen or he didn't want her at all. Well, no, that wasn't quite true. He was happy to have her any way she allowed, but if she needed more time, he'd give it to her without complaint.

He pulled over to the side of the road and parked outside his unit complex. Alex climbed out of the car and looked around.

"Wow, those shrubs have grown. They were hardly out of the ground when I was here last."

She indicated the row of potted miniature oleanders. He'd barely noticed the plants on his way in and out of the building, but they were now as high as the steel fence surrounding the complex and provided a thick screen from the street. "Yeah, I guess."

She gave a nervous little laugh. "I can see you're just as interested in all things green as you ever were."

He reached out and stopped her progress with a gentle hand and turned her to face him. "It's all right, sweetheart. We'll take things slowly. I'm nervous, too."

Her gaze skittered away and she breathed in quick inhalations.

"You're right, I am a little nervous. It's been a... It's been awhile. Maybe even more than awhile."

He pulled her in tight against him and held her close, breathing in the warm, womanly scent of her. "It's me, remember? There's nothing about you I don't love."

She buried her face against his shoulder, her voice muffled against the fabric of his jacket.

"I'm sorry, sweetheart. I didn't hear you."

She lifted her head and spoke again. "You haven't seen me since I had Sam. I've...changed."

Discomfort and embarrassment clouded her features and his heart swelled with tenderness. He pulled her in hard against his chest and squeezed. "I couldn't care less what you look like. You've always been beautiful to me. Of course your body's changed. You've had a baby. A wonderful, little boy. The changes to your body are nothing but a celebration of his life. You should embrace the lumps and bumps."

She offered him a wobbly smile. "Who said anything about lumps and bumps?"

He smiled back at her. "Come on, let's go inside."

Alex followed him up the short flight of stairs and waited for him to unlock the front door. The white, three-storey building was much as she remembered. It had weathered the years well and it looked like the exterior had received a coat of paint in recent times.

Security lights shone brightly off the sides of the building, sending a warm, yellow glow into the street below. The silence of the night was only broken by the gentle crashing of the surf in the distance and the occasional vehicle passing by.

Nerves continued to bounce around inside her belly, and despite Brandon's teasing she was still uncertain about getting naked with him. She hoped he'd let her switch out the lights.

Drawing her inside, he led her across the open plan kitchen and living room and brought her up against the kitchen counter top. Taking her into his arms, he pressed his mouth against hers and eased the tension inside her with gentle pressure from his lips.

The kiss was warm and sensual. He took his time, as if re-imprinting her taste and texture on his memory. Alex tightened her arms around his neck and basked in the familiar smell and feel of him. It was like coming home.

She sighed against him and all at once, her inhibitions melted away.

This was Brandon. Her husband. The love of her life. She'd never expected to find herself in his arms again. She intended to savor every minute.

Pressing herself against him, she returned his kiss with all the passion that was overwhelming her. She felt his momentary surprise, but he quickly embraced her enthusiasm and kissed her like he could never get enough.

"Oh, God, you taste so good. You have no idea how many times I've dreamed of kissing you again." His desperate admission sent a shaft of desire zinging through her nerve endings and she thrust her tongue into his mouth, urging him on with silent ministrations.

He pulled away and slid her jacket from her shoulders. She stood still, breathing heavily, while he unbuttoned her blouse and carefully spread it open. His eyes glowed with desire as he feasted on the sight of her breasts, encased in a lacy white bra, spilling over with every one of her breaths.

"God, you are so beautiful, even more beautiful than in my dreams."

He reached out with tentative fingers and traced the outline of her breasts. She shivered from the contact and her heart thudded with desire.

His hands crept lower and spanned her waist, his thumbs stroking the side of her hips. She reached up and pushed his jacket off his shoulders and then went to work on his tie.

Suddenly impatient, he moved her hands aside and made quick work of his clothing. Within minutes, he stood before her in nothing but his boxer shorts, the evidence of his desire clearly outlined against the silk fabric.

His face filled with hope and a touching vulnerability. "I want you so much, Alex. I want to see you naked. Please?"

The last word was said with such sincerity, she melted. Stepping forward, she laid her palms against his chest, relishing the feel of his muscled warmth. She ran her fingers through the light scattering of golden hair, evoking erotic memories of other times.

Opening her mouth, she flicked her tongue across the hard pebbles of his nipples, loving the way he groaned against her touch.

Growing bolder, her hand wandered over the taut flatness of his belly and then lower. She closed her fingers over his erection. His breath hissed.

"Oh, God, sweetheart. You don't know how long I've dreamed of you doing that."

His words filled her with a sense of power and she caressed him with long, sure strokes. He was rock hard and trembling with need. The flames of desire fanned hotter inside her and her clit throbbed with need.

She squirmed and squeezed her thighs together in an effort to stem the surge of passion and need. He smiled tenderly, lovingly, and pulled her close.

His hands went around her back and found the button and zipper on her skirt. As if in slow motion, her skirt fell open and slid down her hips to the floor. She stepped out of it and carefully eased her stockings down.

Brandon watched her, his eyes heavy with desire, as little by little, she exposed herself to him. He growled low in his throat when at last, she stood before him in nothing more than her bra and matching panties.

He stepped forward and almost reverently placed his hand against the softness of her belly. Massaging the skin with his fingers, he walked around behind her and pulled her back hard against him. She twisted in his arms and reached up and pulled his head down to hers and kissed him with all the fire burning her from inside.

He met her passion head-on, his tongue thrusting into her mouth and claiming her as his own. His hand moved upwards and cupped her breast inside her bra, his fingers tugging at her nipples. She gasped at the sensation. His mouth continued to plunder hers.

Pressing back against his hardness, she moved her bottom up and down, pleased when he moaned in response.

"Let's go into the bedroom."

Nodding her assent, she squeaked in surprise when Brandon picked her up and made his way down the hall. Embarrassed, she tugged at his arm.

"Please, Brandon. Put me down. I'm too heavy."

"Quiet, woman," he growled. "I want to carry you. It's been way too long since you were in my arms. Besides, you weigh next to nothing."

Before she had a chance to respond, he'd reached the bedroom. He released her slowly, sliding her down the long, hard length of him.

Reaching behind her, he unclasped her bra and dropped it to the floor. Desire ignited in his eyes. His hands went to her breasts, cupping them in his big palms. His fingers teased her nipples and then he leaned down and took one into his mouth.

Alex gasped and arched her back, savoring the sensation of wetness and heat. He must have remembered she'd always loved being loved this way. His fingers continued to knead and tweak while his mouth worked its magic.

"Please, Brandon, please," she breathed.

"Please, what?" he murmured against the heat of her skin.

"Please, I want to touch you. I want to feel you deep inside me."

His eyes darkened with emotion, but his body stilled. "Are you sure?"

"Yes! I want you. I need you... I-I love you."

He groaned and gathered her up in his arms and lowered her gently onto the king-sized bed that took up most of the room. In some distant part of her mind, she noticed it was different than the red cedar bed they used to share.

He rolled her onto her side and pulled her in hard against him. His lips found hers, his tongue teasing and tasting her mouth. She threaded her fingers into his hair and held on, giving back as much as she took.

His erection pressed against the softness of her belly. She moved against it, the need between her legs growing. She moved up higher until the head of his cock nudged against her entrance.

"Easy, sweetheart. It's been awhile for me, too. I don't want it to be over before it's started."

She smiled softly, pleased he hadn't been in and out of bed with just anything that happened by. Her hand closed around him. "How long?"

He groaned again. "How long? You have to be kidding? What does it matter? I love you. I always have. Now, quit talking. I'm busy."

With that, he flipped her onto her back.

She gasped when he slid his body down the length of hers and settled between her thighs. His head lowered and she nearly came off the bed when his tongue lathed her with long, firm strokes.

"*Mm*, you taste so good. Just like I remember."

Alex squirmed, grasping at the bed sheets as he continued to love her with his mouth. Heat coiled, tight and hot in her clit where his mouth continued to plunder.

"Brandon, please," she moaned, almost unable to stand the exquisite torture.

"Please, what, Alex?"

"Please stop. I-I can't stand it."

"You want me to stop?" he murmured, suckling at the little hard nub of flesh until she thought she would die.

"Yes! No! I want you inside me. I need you inside me. *Now!*"

Lifting himself up, he supported his weight with his arms on either side of her body. His cock nudged at her wetness. "Do you want me?"

She opened her eyes and stared at him. "Fuck me."

With a strangled groan, he thrust into her, filling her up and stretching her wide. She gasped and he hesitated. Her nails dug into his back, urging him on. She clung to his shoulders, meeting each hard thrust of his body.

The tension between her legs continued to build until it became unbearable. She tightened her arms around his neck and used her legs to cling to his hips. He pounded into her, his body hard and taut. His face was strained as he climbed toward his own release.

"Yes, Brandon, yes. Oh, God, yes!" Her heart pounded. Her clit throbbed. Waves of pleasure cascaded through her as she reached her climax. Gasping, she tried to catch her breath.

Brandon's thrusts became more frantic. His hold on her tightened almost painfully. She watched his face take on a fierce look of concentration. With a groan of relief, he found his release.

Collapsing on top of her, he exhaled heavily and then

rolled onto his side, dragging her with him. They lay in silence, listening as their breathing slowly returned to normal.

Alex felt unaccountably shy and uncertain. She'd just had sex with her husband. Fantastic, incredible, mind-blowing sex, but what was she supposed to do now? What was she supposed to say? What did he want her to say?

"You're thinking too much, Alex. Let's just enjoy the moment for what it is and talk about it later."

Heat flared in her cheeks and even though he couldn't possibly see the evidence of her discomfort in the dimness of the room, she ducked her head.

"It's okay, sweetheart. I'm feeling a little weird, too. But in a good way." He tightened his arm around her. "In a *great* way."

"*Mm*, me too." She snuggled against him. She was so relaxed, she felt like she could float away.

He pressed a kiss to her hair. "Go to sleep," he whispered.

The sun had barely lifted its head above the horizon when Alex stirred and woke. Disorientated, she looked around the room and then her gaze fell on Brandon.

He lay sprawled across the bed, his arms flung above his head, his face a picture of innocence.

Memory returned with a jolt and with it, desire.

She glanced at the illuminated dials of the clock on the nightstand and noted the time. If they were quick, she could probably enjoy another interlude with her handsome husband before work.

The thought brought a smile to her lips. Her hand wandered across the wide expanse of his naked chest and then moved lower. He moaned quietly, but his eyes remained closed.

She reached for the part of him that had given her so much pleasure and tightened her fingers around him.

His arm snaked out and dragged her in close beside him. "Don't play with fire if you don't want to get burned," he murmured, eyeing her with a grin.

"Who said I didn't want to get burned?" she quipped and stroked him.

"Don't say I didn't warn you."

"I'm a big girl. I can look after myself."

His eyes sparkled with humor and rekindling desire. She rolled him onto his back and moved down lower, until her head was poised over his groin. His cock had come to life and lay firm against his belly. She took hold of it and covered it with her lips.

"*Mm,*" he murmured. "That feels so good."

Licking and sucking the head of his cock, she swirled her tongue up and down the thickening shaft and then opened her mouth wide and took as much of him as she could. He groaned and buried his hands in her hair, holding her head still while she continued to love him.

"Oh, Alex. Don't stop."

She increased the pace of her movements and tasted the salty evidence of his growing desire on her tongue. Hoisting herself up, she straddled his body and eased herself onto his hard cock.

"Oh, yes," she breathed. "That feels so good."

She began to move, savoring the sensations of his cock plunging into her wetness. Leaning over, she flicked her tongue over his nipples, relishing the groan of pleasure her actions evoked.

"You are a wicked, wicked woman."

She looked at him with mock innocence. "You don't like?"

"Oh, I like. I like just fine."

Before she realized what was happening, Brandon rolled and took her with him. Pulling her underneath him, he thrust into her with long slow strokes.

She moaned.

"You don't like?"

Shaking her head, she smiled back at him. "Now, who's wicked?"

His eyes widened. "I don't know what you're talking about."

Without warning, his hips pumped forward and his cock surged inside her. She gasped and clung to his arms. Tension burgeoned inside her.

With increasing urgency, she met his thrusts, crying out as she reached the pinnacle and orgasmed.

Within seconds, he'd found his own release and collapsed against her.

"This could become a habit," he murmured against her shoulder.

"*Mm,* I hope so."

Brandon drew back and looked down at her, his face serious. "Do you mean that?"

Alex frowned and tugged the sheets up around her. She hadn't really given any of it much thought. She'd just gone with her heart and her hormones. What she did know was that she wanted to be with him.

"Yes, I think I do."

A wide grin broke out across Brandon's face and he hugged her hard against him. "You don't know how much I love you for giving me another chance, Alex. I thought I'd blown it. I thought I'd never have you beside me again. It nearly killed me. I—"

"*Shh.*" She pressed a finger against his lips and then kissed him softly.

"The past is the past. All that matters is the future."

His eyes gleamed with emotion. "I love you so much."

"I love you, too."

They hugged and Alex caught sight of the clock. She pulled away. "We'd better get moving if we're not going to be late for work."

Brandon looked at his watch. "Yeah, I guess you're right. It would probably look way too suspicious if we both called in sick."

"You think?" she replied, deadpan.

Grabbing a pillow, he tossed it at her. She scrambled off the bed and looked around for something to cover herself.

Finding nothing, she reached for the sheet and swiped if off the bed, wrapping it around herself.

"Don't tell me you've gone all shy?" he teased.

She tried to act flippant while attempting to stem the blush that crept up her neck. "Just a little cool. The air's a bit chilly in here."

He smiled at her knowingly, but let it go. She looked around the sparsely decorated room. Apart from the bed and the matching nightstands, there was nothing else but a generic print of the beach on the far wall. It could have been a motel room for all its personality.

"You changed the bed," she murmured.

"Yes. It was the first thing I did when I returned. I couldn't stand sleeping alone in the bed that used to be ours."

His words found a home in her heart. She hadn't wanted to keep anything that had reminded her of him, of *them*, either.

He shrugged and stood, his expression somber. "Redecorating hasn't exactly been at the top of my list."

Trying not to gape at the naked magnificence of him, Alex simply stepped into his arms and held him tight.

Pressing a kiss to the top of her head, he gently set her aside. "I'll let you have the first shower. There are clean towels in the cupboard beneath the sink," he added as she closed the door.

CHAPTER 18

At the sound of a knock on his door, Detective Senior Sergeant Declan Munro looked up from the jumble of papers scattered across his desk and cursed at the interruption.

"Come in." He issued the curt command in a tone that was less than friendly. The door to his upstairs office in the Hornsby Police Station opened and a junior constable made his way cautiously inside.

"What is it, Kennedy?"

The young man's cheeks flushed. His gaze darted nervously around the room. Declan bit down on a surge of impatience. Christ, he so didn't have time for this.

"Spit it out, Constable. I haven't got all day."

"Um, sir, it might not be anything, but I just thought you ought to take a look at this." Constable Michael Kennedy slid a sheet of paper across Declan's desk.

"What is it?"

"It's a report I took a couple of days ago. Geoffrey Williams came in to say he thinks something happened to his nine-year-old daughter, Veronica. According to Mr Williams, on Saturday she was playing in the park not far from where they live. She goes there all the time. Apparently, he can see the park from his living room window."

Declan tapped his pen on the desk. "Is there a point to all of this, Constable?"

The young officer turned red. "Y-yes, sir. The girl—

Veronica, was playing on the swings and the monkey bars. Mr Williams said he went to make himself a cup of coffee and then the phone rang. When he looked back out the window, she was gone."

"Gone?"

"Yes, sir. He couldn't see her anywhere."

Declan gritted his teeth and wished, not for the first time, that the Academy would teach its students the art of efficient conversation.

"Then what happened?"

"He, that is, Mr Williams came downstairs and went across to the park. He looked everywhere. He went back to the house to make sure she hadn't come back in without him noticing, but the house was empty. Then, he drove down the street to the local shops. Apparently, they're only a few blocks away. Sometimes Veronica goes there for a drink or an ice cream."

Declan's eyebrow rose. "It's wintertime."

"Well, anyway, that's what her father said. I guess he wasn't thinking straight."

"Keep going."

The constable took another breath. "No one had seen her at the shops. Mr Williams went back home and checked the house again. Nothing. He was starting to panic and thought about calling us. But then, he looked back across the road, and there she was. Right near the monkey bars, where he'd last seen her."

"So, where had she been?"

Constable Kennedy shook his head in consternation. "See, sir, that's the thing. She couldn't tell him. Her father said she seemed dazed. Confused, even. She couldn't tell him where she'd been. The only thing she could remember was that she'd been talking to the man with the puppy."

Declan frowned, his curiosity piqued. "It does sound a bit peculiar, but without any evidence that a crime's been committed, what does he expect us to do?"

"That's what I told him, sir."

"So why are you here, Constable?"

The man squirmed again. "Well, it's just that I had a similar incident reported about a month ago. I only thought about it when I was at home last night. I printed the earlier report this morning." He offered Declan another piece of paper.

Scanning the contents, Declan's frown grew heavier. The report outlined a remarkably similar incident. This time, involving a girl of twelve.

While there had seemingly been no injuries, the girl had been dazed and confused and had been unable to account for the time she'd been missing from the park. Her last memory had also been of speaking to a man she'd seen there before.

Declan pursed his lips in thought. "You were right to bring this to my attention, Constable Kennedy."

The kid looked visibly relieved, which irritated Declan no end. Surely, he wasn't that much of an ogre?

"I'm not sure what's going on," he continued, "but there's something very odd about both of these cases. I'll make a couple of calls, see if this rings any bells with anyone else. Let me know if you get another one, all right?"

"Yes, sir. I will, sir." The constable turned to leave.

"You did good, Constable. Keep it up."

The kid blushed crimson and ducked his head. "Thank you, sir," he mumbled and hurried out of the room.

Declan smiled. He wasn't that old that he couldn't remember what it had been like to be fresh out of the Academy and in morbid fear of any superior officer, especially one as high up in the ranks as he was.

He should probably cut all of them a bit of slack. He'd been coming down hard on them lately. It hadn't really been their fault. The real blame lay with the recent, messy break-up of his three-year relationship with Alice. He'd kept very quiet about that but he probably had been a bit short with his colleagues...

With an impatient sigh, he pushed the analysis of his bad mood aside and reached for the phone.

———————

Brandon's phone vibrated in his pocket. He pulled it out and looked at the screen. Recognizing the caller, he smiled in surprise.

"Hey, big brother, how goes it?"

Declan chuckled. "You're sounding remarkably cheerful. Is there something I don't know about?"

"Nah, mate. Just another day, you know how it is. What have you been up to? I haven't heard from you in awhile."

"Busy at work, Bran. Same old, same old. I heard you got a transfer?"

"Yeah, I'm in the CPU."

"Tom tells me you're working with Alex."

Brandon pursed his lips and debated about answering. "Yep, that's right."

"How's that going?"

Brandon grimaced. He could understand Declan's curiosity, but he still didn't know if what he had with Alex was going to last and he wasn't in the mood to share confidences.

"How's Alice?" he asked, changing the subject. "How long's it been? Two? Three years? You must be getting ready to put a ring on it."

"You haven't heard."

"Heard what?"

"We're over. She's fallen in love with some hotshot public defender. She confessed to me last week as she was lugging suitcases out the door of our apartment.

Brandon was immediately contrite. "Oh, mate. I'm sorry. I really am. I know how much you liked her."

"Liked her? I *loved* her, Bran. And she's thrown me over for some bottom-feeding defence lawyer."

"I sympathize with you, mate. I know what it feels like to have your heart ripped to shreds."

Declan's voice quieted. "Yeah, yeah, you do."

"So," Brandon said, breaking the silence that had fallen

between them. "Is there something I can do for you, or is this just a social call?"

Declan cleared his throat. "Yeah, I wanted to run something by you. It's about a couple of strange incidents we've had at the local park."

Brandon listened in silence and made notes on the blank pad in front of him. "You're right, there is something a bit off about it. I'll run the address of the park through our database, see if it scores a hit."

"I'd appreciate that. It might turn out to be nothing, but it's got my radar up."

"It's worth looking into, that's for sure," Brandon agreed.

"Thanks, bro. We'll have to catch up for a drink one of these days. Tom invited me to the barbeque they had the other week, but I was working."

"Too bad. Lily cooked a great dinner, as usual. I'll call Tom. See when he's off. We might try and get together at the end of the week."

"Sounds good. Call me."

"Bye, mate." Brandon put his phone back into his pocket. Sliding his keyboard closer, he opened up the AFP database and conducted a search on the street address Declan had given him.

Nothing. He thought for a minute and then pulled up a map of the park and the streets surrounding it. Making a note of the names, he compiled a list, extending the search over a two-mile radius.

There were more than one hundred streets and lanes that fell within the parameters of his search. It would take him at least a couple of hours to check them all. But, he was nothing if not thorough, and sometimes a breakthrough came from the most unlikely of sources.

He didn't hold any real hope he'd help Declan with his case, but the CPU had an enormous database of pedophiles and suspected pedophiles. It wasn't accessible by the ordinary State police and he was happy to help out if he could.

He glanced across at the empty chair where Alex usually

sat. She was on a day off. He couldn't believe how much he missed her. It was dangerous to become so reliant upon her for his emotional peace of mind. The color of his day shouldn't be affected by whether or not she was there—but it was, pure and simple. And that scared the hell out of him.

But the alternative was to close his heart to the possibility that they could make it. That they could rekindle their love and build a new kind of peace with each other. It was that hope that kept him going.

He hadn't told Tom they were back together, either. Partly because he wasn't sure that they were. It had been two days since the night at his apartment and he hadn't spent more than a dozen hours with her since. And those had been working hours.

He'd wanted her to come home with him the next night, but she'd told him she had to go home. She had no fresh clothes and besides, there was Sam. She said she wanted to be there for her son.

Brandon understood—of course he did. The boy was little more than a baby. He needed his mother. But that didn't mean Brandon still didn't wish he could have her all to himself.

He sensed she held something back and he knew with time, she'd share what was on her mind. But how would he wangle more time when she had a baby to care for? It was downright selfish, but there it was. He was jealous of a two-year-old. How low could he go?

Maybe someday they'd make another child together. He couldn't believe how hard he'd fought against the idea. But how would Alex feel? She had her son, her much longed-for child. Would she even want another? With him? The uncertainty ate at his gut.

With a sigh, he forced his attention away from Alex and dragged the list of addresses closer to the keyboard. He started with the streets that were closest to the park.

The first twenty or so yielded nothing. Impatience tightened his gut. He read the next entry on the list. Randall Street. After typing it in, he hit "enter" and waited.

A couple of minutes later, it came up with a hit. He sat forward in surprise and read the text on his screen. James Gibbons lived at Unit Two, 376 Randall Street. The name was familiar. It was the same name as one of the suspects on the list that had been recovered from the computer in Belgium—one of the thirteen.

His pulse picked up its pace. *Merely coincidence, or something more sinister?* He made a note on the pad near his elbow and continued to plug the addresses into the search. Two others out of the hundred or so he searched came up with hits. Both were the last known addresses of registered sex offenders.

Switching screens, he plugged the name James Gibbons into their database of registered sex offenders, but came up with nothing.

So, the man hadn't been convicted of any assaults on children? It didn't mean that he hadn't committed them.

Tugging his phone out of his pocket, he dialed Declan's number. His brother answered on the second ring.

"Brandon, I didn't expect to hear from you so soon."

"Yeah, I know, but I had a bit of time, so I just got on with it." He explained how he'd widened the search and what he'd found. He gave Declan the names of the registered sex offenders and then added James Gibbons.

"The last character may be a person of interest in an ongoing INTERPOL investigation, but at this stage, we have nothing specific on him, so treat him with caution." His voice turned dry. "We don't want to be splashed all over *A Current Affair* for infringing on anyone's civil rights."

"No worries. And thanks, I'll let you know how we get on."

"Yeah. I'll talk to you soon."

Alex closed the lid on the washing machine and set it for a new load. She'd kept Sam home from his day care, hoping to spend some quality time with him on her day off.

She hadn't been there to tuck him into bed the night she'd spent at Brandon's and the guilt still hadn't quite eased.

She was being silly, really. There'd been plenty of times when she hadn't been there for him at night. She couldn't even count the number of night shifts she'd pulled over the years. But somehow, not being there because she was at work was more palatable than missing his bedtime because she was busy making out with someone.

Well, maybe not just *someone*. Brandon was more than just someone. He was her husband. The man she'd pledged her life to—heart and soul, forever. And he was Sam's father.

God, it had felt so good to be back in his arms, to have his mouth on her lips—and other places. She blushed at the thought of what they'd done together.

But it had felt so right, like coming home after a long, long absence. The familiar feel and taste and smell of his body—it had been heaven.

She'd arrived home with only enough time to get dressed and head out the door again to work. Her mother had looked at her with concern, but had remained silent.

Then again, she didn't have to say anything. Alex knew exactly what her mother was thinking. Nothing good would come of re-igniting her relationship with Brandon until she told him about his son.

Alex compressed her lips. Her mother was right. She had to tell him. But how? It wasn't like she could just blurt it out in the tearoom. 'Hey, I had a great time the other night. The sex was mind-blowing. By the way, I forgot to tell you that you have a son.'

Nausea and nerves swirled in the pit of her belly. She knew he wouldn't take it well. She also knew the longer she put it off, the worse it would be, no matter what she tried to tell herself.

Hefting the load of wet laundry onto her hip, she pushed open the back door and headed toward the clothesline. Spying Sam in the sandpit surrounded by Tonka trucks, she smiled. He looked up, grinning and waving.

"Hello, Mommy. I'm taking dirt to the quarry. We're building dungeons today."

The surge of love and protectiveness almost overwhelmed her. There was nothing she wouldn't do for him. She would look after him until her dying breath. Anyone who tried to hurt him would have to answer to her.

But that didn't mean his father didn't have a right to know.

"Mommy, your phone's ringing."

Alex blinked and realized he was right. Setting the basket on the trolley near the clothesline, she jogged back inside and picked up her phone from the kitchen counter. The screen showed a number she didn't recognize.

"Hello?"

"Alex, it's Brandon."

Her heart leaped into her throat and then began to beat a crazy tattoo against her ribcage.

"Brandon. It's great to hear from you. H-how did you get my number?"

"I asked Patrick for it. He was a little reluctant, but I told him I needed to talk to you about the investigation. I hope you don't mind?"

"No, of course not. That's fine. I'm glad you called."

"I'm sorry to do this over the phone, but it's been going around and around in my head. I had to talk to you about it."

Tension gripped her belly. "What is it?" she asked cautiously.

"The other night I...um... I was irresponsible. I'm sorry. I didn't take any precautions. I-I'm sorry, Alex. I should have thought."

Her breath eased, but only slightly. "You're scared I might be pregnant?"

"Yes! No! God, no! Not scared. I couldn't think of anything more wonderful than making a baby with you, but I-I didn't know how you felt about it, about us. This is all so new and I didn't want to rush things and I didn't want to blow it...and then I go and do something stupid like not buying condoms."

Hope began to leak into her heart in tiny, golden droplets. "You want to have a baby? Really? What about what you said, before?"

Brandon exhaled heavily in her ear. "That was four years ago. I know what I said. God, I think back now and I can't believe how hard I fought against the idea. I guess I was so focused on my career I couldn't see past it. You were just as determined to rise to the top. It was why I couldn't see how we could make a baby work. Neither of us were in the same place for very long. We were in and out of undercover operations, international task forces, high-security investigations. It wasn't like we could offer a child a stable environment."

He sighed again. "But now, I can't imagine not wanting to share that kind of love, that kind of joy with you. I-I hope it's not too late."

The hope in Alex's heart blossomed and grew, warming her all over. Was it possible he'd take her news better than she thought? She had to tell him. She'd wanted to give them more time, but she had to do it.

"I've just checked the roster," he added in a rush. "You're off again tomorrow. Can you come over tonight? It's been so long since I've seen you."

Alex smiled. "It's only been a night, Brandon."

"And one day. What can I say? I miss you."

The quiet admission warmed her heart. "I miss you, too."

"Will you come over tonight?"

"I can't tonight. Mom's away at her regular bridge night, but I'll meet you for lunch tomorrow. How about I meet you at the coffee shop around the corner at twelve? There's...something I need to tell you."

There, she'd taken the first step.

"What is it?"

Her breath quickened. It was not something she wanted to do over the phone. "No, not now. It can wait until tomorrow. I-I'd like to tell you in person."

"Should I be worried?"

Alex filled her lungs and let the air out slowly. "Do you love me, Brandon?"

"With my life."

Her eyes closed in relief. "Then you have nothing to worry about."

She prayed she was right.

————————

Cassie ran her finger down the entries on the netball draw and found the listing for the next game. There they were: the Manly Musketeers. They were playing at home on Saturday morning. The game was on Court Four and started at ten.

Excitement coiled tight in her belly. She pushed the piece of paper across her desk and reached for her laptop. Her fingers flew over the keys. She entered the chat room.

He wasn't there.

Her shoulders slumped. She checked the wall clock behind her. Three-fifty. She'd raced out of school and caught an earlier bus home. She didn't normally arrive until a little after four. He probably didn't expect her to be online so early in the afternoon.

She thought about going downstairs for a snack, but then decided against it. Her mom would only start asking her about her day and about her homework and just about anything else she could think of. It was weird. Not that long ago, she used to spend hours talking to her mom. Now, she couldn't wait to escape and head upstairs to her laptop.

An icon flashed on the screen. Her breath caught. *It was him*. He was online. Within seconds, his greeting crawled across the screen.

Hello there gorgeous, what a wonderful surprise to come home from school and find you waiting for me. I hope you're not home sick?

Cassie smiled. He was so thoughtful. More thoughtful than any guy she knew. She hurried off a reply.

No, not sick. Just got out a little early and headed straight home.

She didn't want him to think she was that keen. It was

always good to play things a little cool. That's what her mom had told her, anyway, when they'd had the boy talk.

Well, I'm certainly not complaining you didn't take time to talk to your friends. I've been thinking about you all day. Last period seemed to take FOREVER.

Cassie grinned, warmth spreading through her.

I know exactly what you mean, she typed.

She hit enter and then frowned. That wasn't too forward, was it? Surely it was okay when he'd already told her how much he'd been looking forward to chatting with her?

I can't wait to meet you. Twice I've tried and twice I've failed. Maybe it will be third time lucky? Are you playing this weekend?

Happiness bubbled up inside her. Yes! Yes! Yes! There was a God! He still wanted to meet up with her!

I'm playing at Manly again. I just checked the draw. We're playing at ten o'clock on Court Four. I should be playing in my usual position.

Goal Attack, right?

She grinned. He'd even remembered what position she played. Oh, God, she was *soooo* in love.

That's right. It's nice of you to remember.

I remember everything about you. Now I just have to meet you and my life will be complete.

Cassie shook her head. If she'd heard it on a movie, she would have laughed at its soppiness, but somehow, from him, it sounded perfect.

I can't wait.

Neither can I. Let's hope Dad doesn't have any other plans for me on Saturday.

Fingers and toes crossed.

Hey, how about you give me your phone number just in case something comes up? I can text you and let you know. That way you don't have to wonder if I've forgotten all about you (as if—LOL).

Cassie's fingers stilled. Her parents were forever warning her about giving out personal information online. She'd heard about men who preyed on kids on the Internet.

But this was Justin. Okay, not really Justin, but it was *him*. The hottest boy she'd ever seen. And he was so kind and funny and *nice*.

Sure, there were nasty old men who tried to trick girls into pretending they were their friend, but not him. It could never be someone like him.

She typed a response.

If I give it to you, I'll have to kill you. You know that, right?

His reply brought a smile to her lips.

Then I'll die a very happy boy.

Okay, here it is.

She gave him her number.

Would you like mine?

She breathed a sigh of happiness, knowing that a real predator would never give out their number.

Sure. That would be great.

He gave her a cell phone number. She scribbled it on a piece of paper and then tore it off and folded it into little squares and pressed it against her heart.

I guess I'll see you at the game, then, she wrote.

Can't wait. Saturday is soooo far away.

CHAPTER 19

Patrick strode out of his office, a sheaf of papers in his hand. "All right, everyone. Listen up."

Brandon looked up from his desk. Pushing back his chair, he stood and joined the rest of the squad making their way to where their boss stood.

"What is it, sir?" Ryan asked.

"I've just received a communication from the head of the INTERPOL taskforce. They've been monitoring Janssens' emails. They think they have enough to arrest him but they don't want to do a raid until all the other international taskforces, including ours, are ready."

He looked around at them, his face grim. "Once they take down the ringleader in Belgium, all the other perpetrators around the world will disappear like smoke. Within hours, maybe less, they'll know he's been compromised and they'll do everything they can to get rid of any evidence on their own computers."

"How much time do we have?" Brandon asked.

"Good question," Patrick replied. "I'm not sure. The guys at INTERPOL are calling the shots. We need to get surveillance happening on our list of thirteen and we need to get it happening now. We could have a week, maybe two. They don't want to wait too long, but they appreciate we've had less time to work on our list than they have. They don't want to jeopardize anyone's investigation."

"That's a relief," Brandon muttered and a couple of the men chuckled.

"I know how you feel, Munro, but don't lose sight of the big picture here." Patrick included all of them in his gaze. "There's no room for egos. We're all in this together. INTERPOL knows that. The FBI knows that. Let's do our best to get this right."

"Who's doing the surveillance?" Jack asked, looking eager.

"I've nominated four of you to work with the surveillance team. Ryan, Nick, Sarah and Jack—that'll be you."

Jack grinned and punched the air. Patrick continued, his face somber. "With every minute counting, that's all I can afford. That's why I've enlisted the support of the local police. They've agreed to help and they're supplying enough manpower to watch these men twenty-four seven." He eyed the officers he'd nominated for surveillance. "You'll each work with a group of local coppers. You'll have to take it in turns and spread yourself around so that at least one of you has spent time watching each and every one of our suspects."

"For how long?" Ryan asked.

"For as long as it takes, but hopefully we'll have what we need inside the fortnight. I don't think INTERPOL will wait much longer than that. In the meantime, the rest of you keep monitoring the email accounts and the chat rooms. Let's face it, the majority of these bastards make their moves in the cyber world."

Brandon snuck a look at the clock on the wall in front of him. It was nearly eleven. Only an hour to go before he saw Alex again. Need unfurled in his belly, hot and desperate. The intensity of it scared him a little, but not enough to give up the second chance she'd granted him. Determination tightened his gut. He'd do whatever it took to make this work.

The impromptu meeting came to an end with Patrick urging them on and wishing them all good luck. The squad dispersed and Brandon made his way back to his desk. He checked the clock again. Fifty-five minutes to go.

———————

Alex ran the brush through her hair again and patted a couple of roguish strands back into place. Her hand shook slightly and she silently castigated herself for her nerves. It was only lunch. They'd been rolling around in his bed a couple of nights ago.

But she hadn't been about to confess her deceit about their son a couple of nights ago. Hadn't been ready to admit to a lie so huge she wasn't sure if they'd get through it.

He'd be furious. He'd be hurt. He might even hate her. He'd be all the things she'd be if this had happened to her. Keeping the existence of a child away from his father was mammoth, even if she did feel justified for doing it. Justified at the time of the offence, at least. She'd had moments of doubt many times. It was the last month she felt most badly about. She'd had more than ample opportunity to tell him. It wasn't as if he hadn't asked about Sam's father.

She acknowledged the weight of her guilt with a bowed head. There was nothing to be done about it, now. All she could do was tell him how sorry she was and hope and pray he could find it in his heart to forgive her.

She was pleased her mother had gone out shopping. Alex hadn't found the courage to tell her she was meeting with Brandon again and was grateful she'd avoided another barrage of questions. She had to know how Brandon was going to react before she could bring herself to discuss it with her mother.

Feeling a long way from confident, she chose a deep plum lipstick that always looked good on her and swiped it across her lips. The color went well with her dark red winter dress that wrapped around her curves and ended in a flourish at her hip. The low neckline emphasized her generous cleavage.

She slipped on a pair of black stilettos and gave her hair a final tweak before collecting her handbag from the kitchen table and her keys from the hook near the door.

Her gaze landed on the clock above the sink. Eleven o'clock. An hour and she'd be in the city laying her soul bare to the only man she'd ever loved. Drawing in a deep breath, she exhaled slowly. Sending a silent prayer heavenwards, she opened the door and pulled it shut behind her with a resounding click.

———————

Alex checked her rearview mirror and changed lanes. The traffic was reasonably heavy as people went about their daily business. For once, the sun was shining and the winter warmth of it lifted her spirits. Surely, once she explained why she'd kept Sam from him, Brandon would understand?

He'd be upset. She expected that, even anticipated it and she owed it to him to let him rant and rave and vocalize his hurt. But afterwards, after he'd had time to cool down, surely the love they had for each other, the love they'd always had for each other, would see them through this difficult time, would sustain them. She could only hope.

The sound of her phone ringing inside her handbag momentarily distracted her. Keeping her gaze on the road, she riffled with one hand through her bag. Her hand closed around the phone. She tugged it out and glanced at the Caller ID.

Sam's daycare center.

Her heart jumped and she told herself not to be silly. It could be anything. Perhaps she'd forgotten to pack his hat? Maybe he'd fallen over and skinned his knee? Or it could be he just wasn't feeling well. With a quick look over her shoulder, she changed lanes again and pulled over. Switching off the ignition, she pressed the button and answered the call.

"Alex, it's Julie Wells from the Sunnysmiles Long Daycare

Center. I-I'm afraid there's been an accident."

Her stomach clenched with dread, but she forced herself to remain calm.

"What kind of accident?"

The woman cleared her throat. "There's been a car accident. A truck..." Alex heard the tremor in the woman's voice and her apprehension grew.

"What happened with the truck, Julie? Is Sam all right?"

"The truck... Sam... He..."

Icy fingers tightened around her heart. Blood pounded in her ears. She forced a breath between closed lips and swallowed against the panic.

"Julie, please tell me. Is Sam all right?"

"No, Alex. I'm sorry. He's not."

The pounding in her ears grew louder, blocking out all but snatches of what the woman told her. A truck had run off the road. Plowed into the daycare center. Hit Sam and three other children. Ambulance. Hospital. Critical.

"Where is he?" she screamed. "Where have they taken him?"

"He...he's been taken to the children's hospital at Randwick. Th-that's all I know."

"Oh, God! Oh, God, oh God." Her world spun madly out of control. She turned on the ignition and floored the accelerator. Vaguely, she heard the blast of a horn behind her and pulled the steering wheel hard, wrenching her car back into her lane. More horns blasted beside her, adding to the cacophony of noise in her head. She tried to block it out and focus on the road.

Images of Sam smiling and waving good-bye as she'd dropped him off that morning kept running through her head, faster and faster until they blurred in a kaleidoscope of motion and sound and color. She groaned and pushed a fist against her chest in an effort to stem the pain.

Please, God, please let him be all right. Please, please, please. I'll do anything you want. Please, just keep him alive.

The mantra repeated itself in her head, over and over, until she could think of nothing else. She changed lanes and then changed again so that she could take the exit that led to the hospital. She was still more than half an hour away—maybe more with the thickening traffic.

It was fortunate she'd already been heading more or less in that direction. She suddenly remembered Brandon and swore. The clock on her dashboard read eleven forty-five. In fifteen minutes, he'd be expecting to meet her for lunch. She had to call him.

Working her way through the traffic, she pulled over and reached for her phone. She scrolled through her call bank and found Brandon's number. Pressing the call button, she tried to get her breathing under control. He answered on the first ring.

"Hey there, sweetheart. I was just thinking about you. Are you there already? I hope you managed to find a place to park. The boss has—"

"Brandon." Her voice came out a hoarse whisper. She cleared her throat and tried again. "Brandon, something's happened. There's been an accident. Sam—"

Her voice broke. Tears stung her eyes. She swallowed the lump that had lodged in her throat.

"Christ, Alex. Is he okay?"

She gulped and shook her head. "N-no... I don't know. They've taken him to the children's hospital in Randwick. I'm on my way over there, now."

"I'll meet you there."

She wanted to offer polite refusals, but the truth was, she was desperately grateful for his offer so quickly and so freely given.

"Th-thanks, Brandon. I'd really appreciate that." Fresh tears welled in her eyes. Trying to stay focused on the road in front of her, she sent up desperate pleas in fragmented thoughts and phrases that her little boy would be all right.

She arrived at the hospital in record time and screeched to a halt outside the doors to the Emergency Department. She ignored the signs that advised it was an area for ambulances only. Tow it away; she couldn't care less. She had to find her son.

The doors slid open at her approach and she ran to the triage desk, her heart pounding. A young nurse looked up from where she sat behind a desk.

"Can I help you?"

"Yes, I'm… I'm looking for my son. He was brought in by ambulance from the Sunnysmiles Daycare Center. A truck accident."

The nurse's expression turned grave. Her gaze lowered to the paperwork on her desk. Fear squeezed Alex's heart. Her breathing ceased.

"Please, please. Is he all right? I need to see him."

"There were several children brought in from that Center. What's your son's name?"

"Samuel. Samuel Munro."

The nurse shuffled through the folders on her desk and then chose one of the clipboards. Her expression remained grim. "Here it is. Sam Munro. We were given his name by a staff member at the Center, but we haven't had the opportunity to obtain any other information. Are you able to help me with that?"

Alex frowned, her thoughts in turmoil. "Um… Yes, I suppose. But please, can't I see him? I need to know he's okay."

"Mrs Munro, he's in surgery right now. I'm not sure how it's going." The nurse's voice lowered. "He's in very serious condition. I understand he was trapped under the vehicle for some time. As soon as I know anything else, I'll—"

A loud buzzing noise in Alex's ears blocked out the rest of her words. She was paralyzed with shock. The nurse tried again.

"Mrs Munro, I really need to get some more information from you."

Alex's mouth moved, but no words came out. The nurse looked at her with understanding and then pushed back her chair and walked around to Alex's side. With her arm around her, the nurse guided Alex to a seat and urged her to sit down in one of the hard plastic chairs that lined the waiting room.

"I'll go and fetch you a drink of water. Stay here. I'll be right back."

Alex barely registered the nurse's departure. Staring into space, she tried hard to process what she knew. Sam had been hit by a truck. He'd been pinned beneath it. He was in surgery. No one could tell her if he was dead or alive. No one could tell her anything. She looked around for Brandon, but the entry to the Emergency Department remained agonizingly empty.

The nurse returned with a glass of water. She offered it to Alex.

"Here. Take a sip. I know this is difficult, but we really need to find out as much as we can about your son."

Alex swallowed a mouthful of water, forcing it past the tension that held her throat in a stranglehold. She snatched a breath and took another sip.

"Better?" the nurse asked, her gaze kind.

Nodding, Alex handed the glass back to her and took a steadying breath. She wanted to help. She needed to help. "What do you need to know?"

The nurse stood and went back to the desk to collect Sam's notes. She returned a few minutes later and sat next to Alex, her pen poised.

"Okay, for starters, if you can give me his full name, address and date of birth."

Alex recited the information and was suddenly thankful Brandon hadn't yet arrived. Now wasn't the time to tell him he had a son.

"Is Sam allergic to anything?"

She shook her head. "No, not that I know of."

"Is he on any medication? Has he been ill recently?"

"No. The occasional cold and flu, but overall, he's been so healthy." Her voice caught and she bit back a sob.

"It's okay, Mrs Munro. It's okay."

The reference to Alex's married name jarred her. She vaguely recalled the nurse addressing her that way when she first arrived, but she'd been too focused on Sam and his status to pay much attention. Now it seemed too late to correct the assumption. Besides, it was still her legal title.

The automatic doors to the Emergency Department slid open. Alex looked up and saw Brandon striding toward them, his face pale.

Alex stood and was immediately enveloped in his arms. She leaned against him, grateful for his support. She breathed in deeply of his familiar scent, infusing herself with his solidness, seeking comfort from the warmth and strength of his broad frame.

"Mr Munro?" the nurse ventured.

Brandon's arms loosened around Alex, but he continued to hold her close. "Yes?"

"I've just been speaking with your wife. Your son's been badly injured. He's still in surgery. We'll know more when someone comes out with an update."

"Thanks, but he's not—"

Another door slid open and a tall, young man with short, dark hair and sober eyes strode up to them. He wore blue surgical scrubs. A blue surgical mask hung around his neck.

"Are you Sam Munro's parents?"

Alex's heart skipped a beat. Fear wrapped icy tentacles around her heart. "H-how is he? Please tell me he's going to be all right."

"I'm Mark Davis, one of the surgical registrars." The doctor's gaze settled on Alex, his face grave.

"Professor Shepherd, the head of surgery, is operating on him now. I'm afraid he's in a bad way, Mrs Munro. Apart from several serious fractures, he has a ruptured spleen. We're doing all we can to stem the bleeding, but he's going to need a blood transfusion and fast. Do you know what his blood type is?"

Alex shot a quick look at Brandon, who remained motionless, his expression grim. "He... He's A negative."

"Are you sure?"

She nodded.

The doctor muttered an oath under his breath. "I'll call the blood bank and see what they have in stock. It's an uncommon blood group. If we don't have enough of a supply here, we'll have to contact some of the other hospitals and see what they have. The problem is, it will take time and I'm not sure how much of that we have."

Dread seized Alex's heart and her belly clenched in fear. *Oh, God! Oh, God…this can't be happening.* Not to her son. Not to her baby.

"I don't suppose you're a match?" the doctor asked, a gleam of hope in his eyes.

Alex shook her head. "No."

"But I am."

The doctor turned his attention to Brandon. "You're his father?"

"No."

"Yes."

They spoke simultaneously. Brandon's gaze clashed with Alex's, shock widening his eyes and draining his face of color.

"I'm his—?"

"Oh, God, Brandon. I'm sorry. I'm so sorry."

Fury and pain ignited in his eyes. "Do you mean to tell me he's my son?"

Alex nodded her head, helpless against his anger. This was so far removed from how she'd imagined telling him.

Shock and disbelief ravaged his face. "How could you keep this from me, Alex? How *could* you?" His voice broke on the final word.

She felt every nuance of his pain. "Brandon, I'm so, so sorry. Please, believe me. I was going to tell you."

"*When?* When were you going to tell me?" He bit off the words and hurled them at her. "It's not like you didn't have plenty of opportunity. I even *asked* you about his father, for Christ's sake." He shook his head, his body taut. "You lied to me, Alex. You *lied* to me."

Alex had completely forgotten about the doctor until he stepped forward, his face stern.

"Excuse me. It's obvious there are a few issues you need

to sort out, but if you don't mind, right now, we don't have the time." He turned to Brandon. "You're A negative, is that correct?"

Brandon gave a curt nod, his gaze still lasering Alex's.

"Would you be willing to donate blood? We're going to need more than you can give us, but it's a start."

Brandon's eyes were almost black with suppressed emotion. Devastation and disbelief still mingled with anger. Alex's stomach clenched.

"Of course," Brandon said.

Relief showed in the doctor's face. "Great. Please, if you could come with me. I'll find someone who can help us. Every second could make a difference."

He turned and headed toward the way he'd come. Throwing her one last lingering look that shook her to her core, Brandon followed him.

When they had both disappeared from sight, Alex collapsed into a plastic chair. Her heart thudded against her chest. Her lungs constricted. She was panting like she'd run across the Harbour Bridge and back. The look in Brandon's eyes before he'd left had been one of complete devastation.

She'd always known he'd be upset, angry even, when he found out, but his look of sheer horror and betrayal would haunt her for the rest of her life.

With a groan of agony, she doubled over and let the tears come. She tried to contain the sobs, but they overwhelmed her. Her shoulders shook and her nose filled. Shock and fear took over and she trembled violently.

A firm, warm hand on her back sought to give her comfort. She peered up through the haze of tears and saw the triage nurse looking back at her, compassion and understanding in her clear blue eyes.

"He'll be all right, Mrs Munro. Professor Shepherd is the best there is. You were lucky he was on call."

Alex sniffed and tried to get control of her emotions.

"Don't be afraid to cry, if it makes you feel better. You aren't the first and you certainly won't be the last."

The nurse offered a gentle smile and Alex tried to give it back to her.

"There, that's it. Your little boy will be fine. You'll see. He'll be back bouncing around the house in no time."

Alex shook her head. "You don't know that."

The young nurse squatted until she was eye level with Alex and winked. "I think I do."

Even though Alex knew the woman couldn't possibly know anything for certain, her confidence was contagious and boosted Alex's spirits, if only for a little while.

"Thank you. You're very kind," she whispered, hardly recognizing the scratchy croak that came out of her throat.

The nurse shrugged and smiled. "It comes with the job."

Alex gave her a shaky smile and reached for her phone. She needed to call her mother.

––––––––––––

Alex wasn't sure how long she sat in the Emergency Department, her mother by her side, but it seemed like a lifetime before an older man with wide, white side burns and dressed in surgical scrubs materialized in front of her.

She struggled to sit up and orientate herself, her heart once again back in her throat.

"Mrs Munro?" The fatigue in his eyes told her it hadn't been an easy surgery.

"Yes. I'm...Mrs Munro."

"I'm Professor Shepherd. I've just come from the operating theater. I operated on your son."

"How is he, Doctor?" She grasped his arm with both hands. "Please, is he all right? Please, tell me."

Professor Shepherd knelt down on one knee, bringing himself to her eye level.

"The operation went well. He's a very lucky little boy. We were able to transfuse him with the blood your husband provided and we've obtained a back-up supply from the Prince of Wales Hospital, just up the hill. We've managed to stem the bleeding and right now, he's holding his own. He'll be in Intensive Care for at least the next twenty-four hours so we can monitor him. Once he stabilizes, we'll transfer him to a ward."

"When can I see him?"

"I'll send someone down to get you very shortly. Unfortunately, you'll need to keep your visit brief and limit it to one visitor at a time. I understand your husband's waiting to see him, too."

At the mention of Brandon, Alex's stomach tightened and renewed nerves flooded her throat. She refused to look at her mother.

"I'm... I'm not exactly sure where he is. I haven't seen him since..." Her words petered off. The doctor nodded understandingly and patted her hand.

"Dr Davis told me. I'm sure you'll work things out. For now, what's important is that you both pull together for the sake of your son. He needs your support right now. He's come through the surgery, but he's not out of the woods yet—not by a long shot."

Fear settled viscous and oppressive in her stomach. "When...? When will you know...?"

The professor stood, his expression guarded. "Let's see how he goes over the next twenty-four hours. If his vital signs are good and he continues to hold his own, I think we'll all be breathing a little easier."

Alex let out her breath on a heavy sigh. "Thank you, Doctor. I really appreciate everything you've done."

He offered her a brief smile. "No problem. Glad I could help." With that, he gave her a wave and departed through the doorway from which he'd entered.

Alex took a deep breath and turned to look at her mother. She gasped at the tears in the older woman's eyes. Her chest tightened with emotion and she fell into her mother's arms.

"I'm sorry, Mom. I'm sorry. You were right. I should have told him. I should have told him he was Sam's father."

Her mother stroked her back and murmured whispered

words of comfort against her hair. Alex was reminded of times when she was young and her mother soothed away her hurts with a cuddle and a few reassurances.

"Tell me what happened, Alex."

With her face buried against her mother's shoulder, Alex haltingly told her about Brandon and how he still loved her and how he'd discovered he had a son. Renewed pain wracked Alex's body and tears flowed down her cheeks.

"He hates me, Mom and it's all my fault. You were right; I should have told him sooner. I should have—"

"*Shh*, Alex. It's okay. I'm sure he'll come around. You said he loves you. Give him some time. I'm sure he'll understand."

Love flooded through her for the woman who had always put her daughter's needs before her own. She clung to the hope that her mother was right. There was nothing else she could do.

The doors to the Emergency Department slid open. Alex lifted her head. Brandon walked in, his face haggard. Their eyes met and held. Alex gasped at the desolation that stared back at her.

She looked away, unable to bear it.

He flicked a glance toward her mother, but focused his attention on Alex. "Any news?" His voice was a hoarse whisper.

She swallowed and nodded. "The doctor was just here. He... He said Sam has come through the surgery, but the next twenty-four hours will be critical. They're sending someone down soon to get...me."

Brandon's lips tightened, but the strain around his eyes eased a little.

"I'd like to see him."

"Of course. Professor Shepherd said they'll only let one of us in at a time, but I'm sure you can see him."

Brandon's lips twisted. Palpable anger poured off him in waves. "That's very kind of you."

Alex flushed and dropped her gaze. His sarcasm hurt, but it was nothing less than she expected or deserved.

"Brandon, I don't know what else to say. I'm so sorry. You don't know how sorry I am that you had to find out this way. I never meant for you to find out like this. I was going to—"

He cut her off with a brutal slice of his hand. "Enough. I've heard enough. You're sorry... You never meant... You were going to... Save it for someone who cares."

Desperation clawed at her insides. "No, please, Brandon. Let me explain. I was so scared you wouldn't want to keep him. We'd argued about having a baby for so long. But I was going to tell you the night of our birthday. The night you came home on leave from Jakarta. But then—"

She stopped and could tell from the look on his face that he, too, was recalling the night that had ended them.

His face closed and his gaze turned icy. "Don't you dare make this my fault. This had nothing to do with me. You and you alone chose this path and now you're going to have to live with the consequences. Right now, I don't know if I'll ever want to speak to you again."

His words pierced deep and she almost cried out from the pain of it. Biting her lip, she concentrated on her breathing, trying to slow down the frantic rhythm of her heart.

"Mr and Mrs Munro?"

A young nurse with a bouncy blond ponytail and a warm smile approached them from the corridor that led into the main part of the hospital.

Alex gave a brief nod. Brandon tensed beside her.

"I'm Sally. I'm one of the nurses looking after Sam in the Intensive Care Unit. He's settled and comfortable. I've come down to take you up to ICU to see him." Her gaze moved from Alex to Brandon to Martha and back. "I'm not sure if the professor explained, but just for the next few hours, we're restricting his visitors to one at a time."

Alex nodded. "That's fine."

Sally smiled. "Great. Well, if you'd like to follow me, I'll take you up to see him."

Alex stood, aware of Brandon's heavy gaze. She bent and hugged her mother, taking comfort from Martha's firm embrace. Refusing to look at her husband, she collected her handbag off the chair next to her and followed the girl across the room, with Brandon close on her heels.

––––––––––––

It was the longest twenty-four hours of Alex's life. She sat by the bed, holding her son's hand, so tiny in hers, and prayed that every breath he took would make him that much stronger, would pull him through the ordeal his body had endured.

His left arm was plastered from shoulder to wrist, encasing multiple fractures. Three of his ribs had also been broken and were strapped tightly with thick, white bandages. Another cast encased his left leg from hip to thigh, holding together the compound fracture in his femur. Cuts and scrapes and lacerations marred the soft skin of his face, but bones would heal, scars would fade. It was the damage to his spleen she fretted most about.

Professor Shepherd had told her there was still a chance the wound would rupture and the bleeding would begin again. All through the night, she sat at his bedside and when they'd asked her to leave, she'd paced the corridor outside, ignoring the concerned glances thrown her way by her mother.

When it was his turn, Brandon had gone in without a word or even a glance in her direction. Her heart ached at the sight of his cold, closed face, but she didn't have a clue how to go about fixing it. Besides, she had to devote every ounce of her energy to Sam. Brandon would have to wait.

The morning found her weary and gritty-eyed, but her concern for Sam didn't lessen until Professor Shepherd found her outside the door to the ICU and assured her the worst was over.

"He's a little fighter, that's for sure," the doctor said.

"You mean...? You mean he's going to be okay?"

"He's got a long way to go, but yes, I think he's going to pull through. We'll keep him in here another day or so, but if he continues to improve, we'll move him to another ward."

Relief flooded through her. "Oh, thank God! Thank you, Doctor. Thank you." She turned to her mother who had stayed with her throughout the long difficult night.

A smile lifted the corners of the doctor's lips. "That's okay. That's what we're here for. Why don't you go and say hello to him. He's just woken up."

Later, she'd feel ashamed that she hadn't once asked about the other three children. She'd feel even worse when she discovered one of them hadn't made it.

But none of that mattered when she walked up to Sam's bed and found him looking around in confusion at the tubes and machines and monitors that dominated the small space. His face lit up when he saw her.

"Mommy! Where have you been? Where am I? What happened? It hurts so much."

She blinked away tears of joy and leaned over to hug him. "It's okay, Sam. Mommy's here. Oh, sweetheart, I love you so much. You had me so scared, Sam, but the doctor says you're going to be fine."

"It hurts, Mommy."

"I know, sweetheart. I know. But, it's going to get better. You'll see."

He frowned down at the casts. "What's that thing on my arm? There's one on my leg, too."

"They're plasters," she explained, keeping her voice calm. "You broke a bone in your wrist and two near your elbow and another one above your knee. The plaster helps keep them straight and still, so they can get better."

Sam's eyes widened. "Will I need crunches?"

Alex laughed and her heart lightened. "Yes, sweetheart. You are going to need crutches."

"Was I brave, Mom? When they put the plasters on?"

Alex squeezed his hand. "Yes, honey. You were very brave."

"I wish I saw it. Did you see it, Mom?"

"No, sweetheart. I didn't see it, either. The doctor put the plaster on you while you were in the operating theater."

His eyes opened wider. "Did I go in the operating theater?"

"Yes, honey. You did."

"Why?" he asked, his brow furrowed in thought.

"Because you had a problem with your tummy. The doctor had to fix it."

"Is that why my tummy's sore?"

"Yes, sweetheart. It will be sore for a little while yet, but you're going to be okay, darling. You're going to be okay."

"Can I have a drink, Mommy? I'm really thirsty."

Relief and joy surged through her. "I'll have to ask the nurses first, to make sure it's okay, but I'm sure they'll say it's all right."

While his nurse went in search of a drink, Alex stepped outside the ICU and brought her mother up to speed.

"He's going to be okay, Mom. It looks like he's going to be okay." The relief of it weakened her legs. She half fell into her mother's arms. Martha hugged her close, the two of them crying and smiling through their tears.

"Can I go in and see him?" Martha asked, pulling slightly away.

"Yes, of course. Go right ahead. I'll wait out here."

Once the door to the ICU closed behind her mother, Alex pulled out her phone. With shaking fingers, she dialed Brandon's number. She hadn't seen him since the day before. After the brief visit with Sam, he'd left without a word. She listened as the phone rang out. Eventually, it diverted to voice mail.

Drawing in a deep breath, she cleared her throat. "Um… Hello, Brandon. It's me. I-I thought you might like to know Sam's awake and he's going to be okay. The doctor said he's—he's going to be okay." She gulped and ended the call, swallowing back fresh tears. The stress of the past twenty-four hours had taken its toll. She was exhausted.

A few moments later, Martha exited the ward. Alex straightened from where she'd slumped against the wall.

"How is he?" she asked.

"He's fine. He's great. Full of questions and wondering when he can come home."

Alex breathed a sigh of relief. "I'll go back in and see him."

Martha's face sobered. "Have you called Brandon?" she asked quietly.

Alex compressed her lips and nodded. "I left a message for him a few moments ago. I told him Sam's awake and he's going to pull through." She shrugged. I guess it's up to him whether he wants to come and visit his son."

Martha stepped closer and gave her another quick hug. "There's nothing else you can do, sweetheart. The rest is up to him."

Pain tightened a steel band across Alex's chest and made it difficult to breathe. "What if he doesn't, Mom? What if he never forgives me?"

"Give him time, Alex. He'll come around. He loves you."

Her mother sounded so confident. Alex wished she felt the same.

CHAPTER 20

James glanced around the detritus of his bedroom and checked to see that he had everything he needed. He'd set up the video camera ahead of time and made sure it had plenty of charge.

Unlike the rest of the room, the sheets were clean and the bedspread had been carefully folded back, out of the way.

He picked up the small gym bag off the floor and checked its contents again. He'd already prepared the cocktail of drugs needed to immobilize and disorientate his next victim. It wouldn't render her unconscious, but, like the others before her, it would make her sleepy, distort her thoughts and cloud her memories until she couldn't be certain what was real and what she'd imagined.

The syringe lay in its plastic wrapper in the side of the bag—left unzipped for easy access. He would put it in the pocket of his jacket when he arrived at the netball courts. The hardest part of the whole thing was to convince her to come with him to his car. After that, she was his.

Tugging his phone out of his shirt pocket, he composed a text and sent it to the girl who called herself Lady G. Anticipation surged through him. Tingles shivered up his spine. His cock twitched. In less than an hour, it would begin.

Cassie drew in a lungful of air and did her best to contain the bundle of nerves and excitement that threatened to derail her. No matter how hard she tried, she couldn't keep her attention on the game playing out in front of her. She'd already missed the ball twice and had only scored one goal. It wasn't even halftime.

She risked another glance around the court at the crowd who had gathered to watch the game, her gaze skipping off the faces of the people she knew. He said he'd be here. He *had* to be here.

"Cassie!"

She turned just as the ball landed hard against her chest. Her hands came around it instinctively, clutching it tightly. With a quick look around, she passed it to the Goal Shooter and breathed a sigh of relief when the girl scored.

The whistle blew and Cassie returned to her position, her thoughts still on Justin.

"Hey, Cass, what's the matter?"

Cassie looked around and shrugged as their Center, Marcie Richards, came up to her.

"Nothing. What do you mean?"

Marcie frowned. "You seem a little distracted, like you're here, but you're not."

Cassie shook her head. "I'm fine. I was thinking about something else."

"It must be pretty important. It's not like you to miss so many goals."

"No, no. It's not. I'm... I'm meeting someone after the game, that's all. He's supposed to be here already."

Marcie smiled knowingly and gave Cassie a nudge. "*He*?"

Cassie blushed and averted her face. "Yes, *he*. And it's nothing. Well, not yet, anyway."

"*Ooh*, do tell!"

"Girls! We don't have all day!"

Both girls jumped guiltily as the referee scolded them from the sideline. Marcie took her place in the center of the court. She gave Cassie a quick conspiratorial wink seconds before the whistle blew again.

By halftime, they were leading by two. Cassie jogged over to her gym bag and pulled out her water bottle. Drinking greedily, she re-capped it and tossed it back into her bag. Swiping at the sweat that had gathered on her forehead, she pushed her hair out of her eyes and took a good look around the court.

She still couldn't see him. She grimaced. Disappointment flooded through her and took the edge off her excitement. She hoped he hadn't lied about the photograph he'd posted. She'd have no way of recognizing him, if he did. At least she had his number.

She immediately brightened at the thought. Unzipping her bag, she dug out her phone and noticed she had a new message. Opening it up, her heart leaped in relief. It was from him.

Not feeling too good. Home in bed. Dad has offered to pick you up after the game. He knows how disappointed I was the last time I missed seeing you. Hope you don't mind. I showed him your picture so he knows what you look like. Can't wait to see you.

PS. I'm not infectious...

Happiness surged through her, warming her to her toes. She couldn't contain her smile. It was a shame he was going to miss seeing her play, especially now they were winning, but at least she was going to meet him. Finally. Face to face. With Justin.

Nerves and excitement warred in her belly. The second half was going to drag on forever, especially now that she had something to look forward to. The end of the game couldn't come quickly enough.

James found a spot set a little apart from the rest of the cars that surrounded the playing fields and parked his vehicle. Pulling out a pair of binoculars, he surveyed the netball courts until he found the one he was looking for. His gaze zeroed in on the girl playing Goal Attack and he smiled.

That was more like it. She was tall for her age, her body lithe and athletic. Her blond ponytail bobbed with the movements of her body, teasing him. Desire kindled inside him.

He lifted the binoculars and focused on her face. His breath caught. The photograph she'd posted hadn't done her justice. Even from a distance, she was stunning. Her eyes flashed with excitement and adrenaline, bathing her face in a golden glow. She moved with the grace of a ballerina.

Something nudged at his memory and he spent a few moments trying to work out what it was. He'd learned it was important to listen to the inner workings of his mind. It had saved him from certain disaster on more than one occasion.

Frowning, he lowered the binoculars. It wouldn't do to be caught with them, even if that was unlikely because he was surrounded by empty vehicles. He reached in the gym bag and pulled out the beard that he sometimes wore during a hunt. It was an excellent imitation and had cost him a fortune, but it paid to be careful.

A game had just finished on a court across from hers and people were gathering up folding chairs, picnic blankets and other equipment and heading for the car park. He fixed the beard in place and glanced in the mirror.

His memory continued to prod him, but when a group of girls and a woman came closer, he pushed the thoughts aside and packed the binoculars away. Tugging his baseball cap down lower, he collected the syringe out of the bag and carefully slipped it into his jacket before opening the car door. Keeping his back to the group of women, he headed toward Lady G.

He stood a little apart from the scattered crowd of onlookers and took up a position not far from where she was playing. Up close, she was even more delicious. She turned to smile at a team mate and he froze in shock.

Fuck.

It was Lily's daughter. His stepniece. He hadn't seen her for more than twelve months and he couldn't remember her name, but it was her. She'd grown a few inches and had lost the baby fat that had plagued her earlier, but he was sure it was her.

Fuck. Fuck. Fuck. Of all the rotten luck. He'd spent so much time grooming her. He'd been anticipating tasting her for weeks. Everything was ready. Everything was perfect. She was perfect.

He watched her move back and forth across the court, her short skirt bouncing high, and his cock grew hard. Even knowing she was his stepsister's daughter couldn't stop the rush of blood to his groin.

They were always someone's daughter. Did it really matter that she was Lily's? Besides, it would serve that prick of a husband of hers right. Always looking down on him. The irony would be orgasmic. Tom Munro, hotshot detective, sworn to serve and protect, couldn't even protect his own daughter.

James chuckled and then laughed outright. He glanced around and noticed a few curious stares from some of the onlookers. His laughter faded. Anger ignited. *How could he be so stupid?* It wasn't good to draw attention. Someone might remember.

The final whistle blew and the winning team sent up a cheer of triumph. His gut tightened in anticipation. He stared at his stepniece, willing her to look in his direction.

It didn't take him long to be rewarded. As if sensing his presence, the girl looked up at him and offered a tentative smile. He smiled back, keeping it nice, keeping it friendly. She picked up a gym bag and zipped it closed before tossing it over her shoulder and then took a couple of hesitant steps in his direction.

"Are you...?"

He strode forward, his hand extended. "I'm Frank Baron. David's dad. And you're Lady G, right?"

He grinned and she laughed and looked away, a blush stealing across her cheeks.

Shyly meeting his gaze, she shook his proffered hand and introduced herself.

"It's Cassie, actually. Cassie Munro."

They crossed the playing fields in the direction of the car park. Cassie snuck a sideways peak at Justin's father. No, not Justin. *David*. His name was David. It wasn't hard to see where David got his looks. Mr Baron looked a bit older than her dad, but he dressed with stylish flair and Cassie could tell his leather jacket had cost a ton. He looked vaguely familiar, a bit like the old guy on *ER*. The one her mom was wild about. George someone. Except David's dad had a beard and wore glasses. They were cute round ones, like Harry Potter's, and really suited his face.

"I'm sorry David's not been able to meet you himself. He's so disappointed not to be here." Mr Baron offered her a sheepish grin. "I understand I had a part to play in him missing you the first time. I'm sorry about that."

Cassie smiled and waved off his apology. "It's okay. I'm sorry to hear he's unwell."

"Oh, it's nothing much. Just a virus, I think. He's dosed up on Panadol. I think a visit from you might be just what he needs. Nothing like spending time with a pretty girl to lift your spirits."

He smiled again and Cassie couldn't help but return it, her instinctive unease at being with a stranger dissipating.

"I'm parked over here," he said, indicating a white pickup truck. Pulling a set of keys from his pocket, he pressed the remote and unlocked the car.

"How far away do you live?" she asked, walking around to the passenger side and opening the door.

He flashed another grin. "Hornsby. We'll take the freeway. It won't take us long. David's going to be so excited."

———————

Constable Michael Kennedy took a bite out of his hotdog, mindful of the ketchup that threatened to drip onto his shirt.

"Shit, this is hot," he complained to the AFP officer he'd been partnered with and who now sat beside him in the passenger seat of the unmarked police vehicle.

"Yeah, you'd better wait for it to cool down. I took the roof of my mouth off with the one I just ate."

Michael threw him a grin. "You could have told me that before I took a bite."

Federal Agent Jack Nelson grinned back. "Now why would I do that? It would have spoiled all my fun." He turned his attention back to the drab apartment block they were watching. "How long do we have to be here, anyway?"

Michael took a more cautious bite of his lunch and chewed slowly. He checked his watch. "Mate, it's one o'clock. We've only been here a little over an hour. Quit your complaining. Besides, you guys are calling the shots and it could be worse. You could be sitting at a desk filling in paperwork."

Jack grimaced. "Yeah, you're right, but I don't know why I was so eager to get here. It's nothing like I imagined. Not a sign of action. Nothing's moved since we arrived. I don't think I've even seen a bird fly past."

Wadding up the paper bag and the remnants of his lunch, he tossed the rubbish onto the floor where it joined the other detritus of stale food and empty Coca Cola cans.

Michael shook his head in disgust. "You so didn't just do that, Nelson. Just because you're a hotshot Fed doesn't mean you can treat a State patrol car with such disrespect."

Nelson grinned unapologetically. "Right, I can see how well you take care of it."

Michael turned away and stared out of the window toward the building they had under surveillance. At least they knew their suspect was home. The rear and one side of the white Ford pickup registered to James Gibbons was just visible, poking out of his garage. It had been there when they arrived.

Michael wasn't exactly sure what they were looking for, but Declan Munro had requested the surveillance after speaking with his brother, another hotshot AFP agent. Declan hinted that the man might have ties to a pedophile ring, but nobody had enough to arrest him.

A quiver of excitement ran through him. This could be his lucky break. If he managed to get something on the bloke, something that would stick, he'd be in line for a promotion, for sure. All he had to do was hope the guy was crooked after all, and that he'd do something illegal or worthy of an arrest.

Pushing the half-eaten hotdog to one side, he sat up straighter and reached for his binoculars.

———————

Brandon took another swig from the half-empty bottle of beer and gazed distractedly out at the clear winter afternoon unfolding outside his balcony, suddenly wishing he'd declined Patrick's offer to take a day off. He'd been working his butt off—they all had—but the boss was aware of the additional stress he'd been under ever since Sam's accident and had insisted Brandon take a break.

The sky was crystal blue, so bright it hurt his eyes. Weekend crowds were taking advantage of the fine weather, filling the cafes and shops along the esplanade. A few game souls had even braved the water. The sun that had already passed overhead left a languid warmth in its path.

He shrugged off his jacket and tossed it over one of the deck chairs. Picking up his phone from where he'd left it on the wrought iron table outside, he dialed his voicemail and listened to Alex's message. *Again*. His gut tightened, as it had every time he'd heard her tearful account that his son was going to recover.

His son.

He hadn't seen Sam since the day he'd found out he was his father. Even so, the wonder of it warmed him anew. He was a *father.* He had a *son.* A beautiful son who was the image of his boy's mother.

The only woman he'd ever loved.

But also the woman who had lied to him and kept his son a secret for more than four years. Four whole years of his son's life that he'd missed because she hadn't bothered to tell him.

The pain of it was agonizing, re-igniting his anger. He hadn't been there for his son's birth, his first words, his first steps. So many milestones, so many memories. Stolen. And why? Because she didn't think he had a right to know.

Guilt pricked his conscience. He wasn't being fair. If he took the emotion out of it, the reasons she'd given him made sense, in a weird kind of way. They had fought constantly over her desire to have a baby. Over and over again, he'd argued against it. He'd made it clear a baby was the last thing he wanted. At the time, he hadn't been able to see how one could possibly fit into their lives.

She'd said she was going to tell him the night of their birthday, the night he'd arrived home from Jakarta. But he'd gone and dropped a bombshell of his own and everything else had slid by the wayside.

He drew in a deep breath and blew it out on a sigh. The tightness in his chest eased a little. He knew why she'd done it.

Between the hurt and disbelief that had momentarily immobilized her to the crying and pleading when she'd begged for an explanation while he'd gone methodically around their apartment packing his things, the opportunity to tell him about the baby simply hadn't arisen.

But that didn't excuse the latter. The months and years afterwards when she could have let him know... He accepted, grudgingly, that the longer it went on the harder it would have been to say something, but that didn't excuse her decision. Life was hard. It dealt out knocks—harsh knocks—every day. People dealt with them and moved on. They didn't hide them in the deepest, darkest recess they could find and hope like hell nobody found out.

It had been wrong. Deceitful. And he'd never have believed Alex was capable of this. And what of Sam? For almost four years of his life, he hadn't known his father and somehow she'd decided that was okay.

Her sobs of apology in the message on his phone had torn at his heart, but he was hurting, too. Her deceit had shaken him to the core. Every time he thought about it, fresh waves of hurt and anger threatened to overwhelm him.

Even though he now knew, he hadn't told anyone about Sam. Not even Tom. He still didn't know how he was going to talk about it. What words could he use to explain? There was no way Tom would understand. He'd blame Alex and Tom would be a whole lot less forgiving than Brandon.

Forgiving? Was he already thinking about *forgiving* her?

The phone buzzed in his pocket. He finished off the beer and sat the bottle down on the table. Fishing out his phone, he glanced at the Caller ID.

It was Tom. A reluctant smile lifted one corner of his mouth. His brother had ESP.

"Hey bro, you must be psychic. I was just thinking about you."

"Brandon, it's Cassie. She's missing."

The barely controlled panic in his brother's voice set Brandon's heart racing. "What do you mean, missing?"

"Missing, dammit. We can't find her anywhere."

Brandon drew in a deep breath and forced himself to remain calm. "When did you last see her?"

"This morning. I had an early meeting, but Lily had breakfast with her before Cassie left for netball. She played at ten. We expected her home by twelve. Half past, at the latest. It's now after two."

"Did you call her? Maybe she went to the mall?"

"Of course I fucking called her! She's not answering her phone."

"What about her friends? Have you spoken to any of them?"

"Lily managed to track down a couple of girls she played with this morning. The season's only been going for a few weeks. We don't know everyone on her team, yet."

"What did they say?"

"Neither one of them knew where she was. She played the full game, but they didn't see her leave. The best we got was that one of the girls said she was meeting a boy afterwards, but she only saw her talking with a man straight after the game. The girl didn't know who he was."

"Did she give you a description?"

"Yeah, for what it's worth. I've been to those games. There could have been a hundred people there. Medium height, medium build. Nice jacket. Jeans. Red baseball cap. Oh, and she's not sure, but he could have worn a beard."

Brandon could hear Tom's frustration and his barely controlled fear. He bit his lip.

"Christ, Brandon, it could be anyone. At the moment, it's all we've got."

"Let's not jump to conclusions. We'll try and retrace her steps. Have you called Declan?"

"No, I called Hornsby Station. They told me he's on a couple of days off. I've already called the station at Manly. I got some young constable. He took the details, but since she's been missing less than two hours, they're only going through the motions as a courtesy. They've sent someone down to Manly Oval to ask around, see if anyone else noticed anything. The problem is, Cassie played at ten. Anyone involved with, or watching that game will be long gone by now." He blew out his breath. "I'm heading over there, anyway. I have to do something. Sitting on my hands is driving me crazy."

"Where's Lily?"

She's at home with Joe, waiting by the phone. Hoping like

I am that Cassie's going to walk through the front doorway any minute."

Brandon scratched his forehead. Cassie had always seemed like a sensible girl, mature for her age. Not the typical unreliable, self-absorbed teenager. Still, he had to ask. He kept his voice neutral.

"Has she ever done this kind of thing before?"

"Fuck no! Never! She's such a good girl. It's why we trusted her to catch the bus over to Manly and back every Saturday. When she plays further away, one of us drives her."

"Look, mate, we're going to find her. It's only been two hours. I know it feels like a lifetime to you, but in reality, it's not that long. She can't have gone too far. Someone will have seen her and then we'll find her."

Tom didn't respond. Brandon wished he felt as confident as he sounded, but now wasn't the time to voice any doubts. His brother would already be confronting those in his head. He didn't need Brandon to add to them.

Brandon's phone beeped, signaling an incoming call. He checked the screen and saw it was Alex. He debated about letting it go through to voicemail, but then decided to answer it. Talking to her about Cassie gave him an excuse not to talk to her about Sam.

"Listen, Tom, I have to go, but tell me, what can I do to help? Do you want me to meet you at the netball courts? I could help canvass whoever might still be there."

"Yeah, that sounds good. The more help we have, the better. I'll text you the address."

"I'll track down Declan. He might be able to help, too."

"Thanks, mate. I really appreciate it."

"No worries, bro. We're going to find her."

Ending the call, Brandon answered Alex's beep.

"What is it?" he asked, his tone brusque.

"I-I just called to say hello and…and to see how you're doing. I know you said you didn't want to talk to me, but I thought you might like to know the doctors said they hope to be able to let Sam come home next week. He's been doing so well, getting stronger every day. It'll be another six weeks or so before the fractures heal, but he seems to have pulled through the worst of it; thank God. I was wondering if you wanted to... That is...maybe you could...come over? You know, we could... I don't know...talk...maybe?"

The hope and fear and uncertainty that punctuated her voice almost did him in. Despite everything, he loved her. He'd always loved her. It killed him to hear her sound so despondent. But now wasn't the time to get into it.

"Tom just called. Cassie's missing."

"What do you mean, missing?"

"Just what I said," he snapped. "No one's seen her since her netball game finished earlier this morning."

"Have they—?"

"Before you go asking all those things, I'll tell you, yes. They've called her phone. They've spoken to her team mates. No one knows where she is.

"The local police have gone to the courts to ask some questions. Tom's on his way over there now. I'm going to call Declan and then head over there, too."

"Oh, my God, Lily must be going out of her mind. I'll have to call her. See if there's anything I can do."

"I'm sure she'll appreciate that. I'll... I'll talk to you later." Brandon exhaled on a heavy sigh and ended the call. Dialing Declan's number, he quickly brought his brother up to speed and then stepped back inside and collected his car keys and wallet. Within minutes, he'd swung his Mustang out into the traffic, heading north.

———————

James ran the washcloth over her silken limbs, taking special care to wipe away any trace of him from her skin. She'd tasted even better than he'd imagined. He'd been so enamoured of her youthful beauty, he'd lost track of time and only now did he realize he'd kept her far longer than he had any of the others.

He'd come so close to settling between her spread legs and fucking her like his body begged him to do, but in the end, caution had won out and he'd made do with only the use of his tongue.

She'd stirred a couple of times and once, her eyes had opened and she'd stared at him, only to close a few seconds later. That had unnerved him, but it had also excited him. How he wished he could let her watch him while he loved her.

But he knew it was stupid to even think such thoughts. It was the reason why he'd remained undetected for so long. He never took uncalculated risks. He'd never been one to seek danger for the hell of it and allowing her to remain fully conscious while he carried out his work would be sheer idiocy.

He glanced at his watch and was a little taken aback to realize it was nearly two. He forced himself to remain calm and continued to clean away the evidence of Cassie Munro's time in his bed.

It was a Saturday afternoon. Most teenagers would be shopping at the mall or going to the movies, especially a teenage girl. He only hoped she was no different, and that nobody had noticed her absence.

He'd take her to the mall closest to the netball courts. It was only just up the road from Manly Oval. Close enough that it wouldn't be too much of a stretch for anyone to imagine she'd gone there after her game. She'd probably gone there many times.

The ringing of a phone sounded again and he frowned and now recalled he'd heard it before, while he'd been busy pleasuring himself. He followed the sound to the gym bag she'd carried. It was lying on the floor near his bed where he'd left it.

Tugging open the zip, he pulled out the phone just as it stopped. Fifteen missed calls. His gut tightened. *Fuck.* Someone had noticed.

Scrolling through them, he smiled and then erupted into laughter. Ten of them were from her mother, the other five from her prick of a father.

So, her absence hadn't gone undetected. Too bad. That disappointed him, but wasn't cause for too much concern. A sudden brainwave sent his smile soaring upwards. He opened the phone to the message screen and composed a new text.

———————

Lily Munro's phone beeped and her heart leaped into her throat. Racing across the kitchen, she snatched it up off the counter. There was a new message. It was from Cassie.

Shock and relief caused her legs to fold underneath her. She grabbed for the kitchen counter and steadied herself. With shaking fingers, she opened the message.

Hi Mom so sorry 2 worry u. Went 2 mall after game. Been to movies. Just got out & checked phone. Really sorry. Home soon.

Lily collapsed against the counter and sucked in deep breaths of air while she tried to get her heart rate back under control.

Thank, God.

Cassie was okay. She was going to kill her when she got home, but at least she was okay. She had to call Tom.

The thoughts ricocheted through her head and she breathed sharply, trying to slow them down. Tom. The first thing she had to do was call Tom. With fingers unsteady from relief, she dialed his number.

———————

James secured Cassie's ponytail back in place and straightened her singlet and skirt. She stirred beneath his touch. He'd have to work quickly to get her inside his car and across to the mall before she came to. With a last quick look around his bedroom, he slung her gym bag over his shoulder and hefted her into his arms. Checking through the peephole to the corridor outside, he ensured the way was clear and then opened the door and headed downstairs.

Constable Michael Kennedy smothered a yawn and rubbed at a tight muscle in the small of his back. Another tedious hour had passed and still he'd seen no evidence of anything untoward happening in the apartment across the road. His dreams of cracking a pedophile ring wide open and the glory that would come with that were fading fast. Too bad. He smiled wryly. The thought had been nice while it had lasted.

"Hey, what's happening over there?"

Jack Nelson's question registered about a second after it was uttered. Michael took in the scene across the road and frowned in confusion.

Their suspect was manhandling what appeared to be a young girl into the front of his Ford. He only caught a glimpse of her before she was hidden from sight, but she appeared to be asleep, or at least, very drowsy.

"Do we know whether Gibbons lives alone?" he asked.

Nelson shrugged. "I don't know. But that looked odd. Why would a kid be asleep at two o'clock in the afternoon? Maybe she's sick? Maybe he's taking her to the hospital?"

"Maybe. But wouldn't you call an ambulance if she was that sick? It looked like he was carrying her."

"Yeah."

Michael pursed his lips in thought. "I think I'll call the boss. Better to be safe than sorry." Tugging out his phone, he dialed Declan's number.

Declan returned his phone to his pocket after ending another call from Brandon. At least this time it had been good news. His niece had been found. He'd had a heavy feeling of dread in his gut ever since Brandon had told him Cassie was missing and he was relieved that all the sinister things he'd conjured up between phone calls had come to naught.

He shook his head with a rueful grin. He needed a holiday. No normal person would immediately jump to such evil conclusions. People went missing and turned up found with no ill effects all the time. It didn't mean anything terrible had happened to them.

His phone buzzed again and he pulled it out of his pocket. "Munro."

"Oh, um, Detective Munro. It's Constable Kennedy. I-I just thought I should call you. I'm… We're… That is, Federal Agent Nelson and I have been conducting surveillance at an address in Hornsby. James Gibbons."

"Right. Is there a problem?"

"Yeah, well, we've been here a couple of hours and nothing, but just a minute ago, we saw him leave the building with a young girl. It looked like he was carrying her."

Declan tensed. "Gibbons lives alone. Did you see her go into the apartment with him?"

"No. As I said, we've been here a couple of hours and had seen nothing. She must have been inside with him when we arrived."

"Did you get a good look at her?"

"Kind of. She looked like she was asleep. In fact, we thought she might be sick."

"How old do you think she was?"

"Hard to say. We're parked across the road and we only saw her for an instant, but if I'd have to guess, I'd say about thirteen, fourteen maybe. She had a long blond ponytail and looked like she was wearing a sports skirt and singlet. You know, one of those pleated thingies?"

A buzzing sound in Declan's ears drowned out the rest of what Constable Kennedy said. He frowned and tried to slow the frantic pace of his thoughts.

Brandon had just called him to say Cassie had been found. She'd sent Lily a message. She was at the mall, watching a movie. She couldn't be the girl Kennedy had described. *Could she?*

"Kennedy, have they started moving?"

"Yes, sir. They're in the car now. A white Ford pickup. He's driving. She's in the passenger seat. They've just gone past us, heading south."

"Stay with them. I'm not sure what's going on, but something's not right. I'll get back to you as soon as I can."

Declan ended the call, his heart pounding. A second later, he dialed his brother.

"Tom, is Cassie with you?"

"No, I'm at the mall. I've been up to the movie theaters, checked in all of the toilets, canvassed the food court. I can't find her anywhere. I've sent her another bunch of text messages and called her phone. She's not responding. I don't understand it."

Declan swallowed the dread in his throat. "Tom, I think it may have been a hoax. The message. I think someone's playing with you."

"What the fuck are you talking about?" Tom's voice was full of impatience and laced heavily with fear.

"I don't know anything for sure, but I think someone has Cassie. I think he used her phone to send the message to Lily to put you all off—to buy some time... Who knows? The thing is, I think I know where Cassie is."

"You do? Where? For fuck's sake, Declan, spit it out."

Ignoring Tom's outburst, Declan remained calm. "I have a couple of boys tailing someone who's captured the attention of the Feds. We've had him under suspicion for other reasons. Suffice it to say, the last few months, we've had some weird incidences regarding young girls. We've been involved in a joint operation with the Feds to keep this guy under surveillance." He paused and then decided Tom had a right to know. "Mate, we think he might be a pedophile."

"Christ, you're kidding me? You're fucking kidding me?" Tom shouted, his voice on the verge of panic.

"We don't know anything for sure, but the boys just called. Apparently, this germ has a teenage girl with him. We know he lives alone." He paused and then said it. "She fits Cassie's description."

Tom bellowed with rage. "A fucking pedophile? She's with a fucking *pedophile*? Oh, Christ, she'd better be okay. What am I going to tell Lily? Wait until I get my hands on him! He'd better not have touched her. I'm going to kill him!"

"Tom, I know how you feel, but we need to do this my way. We don't know what's going on. Going after him like a raging bull's not going to help anyone. You need to let me do this. Where's Brandon?"

"How the fuck do I know? I called him right after Lily rang me. As far as he knows, Cassie's back safe and sound. He's probably headed back to Bondi."

"All right, Tom. Call Brandon. Get him to meet you at the mall. I need you to stay where you are. This germ has form. The other girls were both returned to the place where they went missing. Even though Cassie was probably taken from the netball courts, the message Lily received said she was at the mall." He hesitated and then spoke again. "I think that's where he's taking her."

Tom cursed again. Declan felt his brother's anger and unspoken fear through the phone.

"Tom, I need you to calm down and listen to me. I'm going to hang up now and call the guys who are following this creep. See where they are. You need to call Brandon and find out where he is. I'll call you back."

Declan hung up and immediately dialed the number of his constable.

"Boss?"

"Are you still tailing him?"

"Yeah, we're on the freeway, still heading south. Hang on, looks like he's taking the exit to Manly."

Declan tensed. "Stay with him and keep me posted."

"Gotcha."

The traffic lights turned red again and Brandon swore long and loudly, chafing at the delay. He'd barely moved twenty feet since the last time they'd changed. Tom would be going out of his mind.

He couldn't believe what had happened. Tom had called him a few minutes ago and had filled him in. Listening, he'd shaken his head back and forth in disbelief while dread cemented in his gut.

He'd turned the Mustang around and had raced back toward Manly—until he'd hit the traffic gridlock in Mosman. Then he'd hardly moved.

His leg jiggled up and down with impatience. It seemed like the beautiful Saturday afternoon he'd admired from his balcony less than an hour ago had called loudly to each and every Sydneysider in town. Every single one of them seemed to be heading to Manly Beach. The traffic was almost at a standstill. He was just thankful he hadn't been caught with the Spit Bridge open. That would have added another twenty minutes to the trip.

At last the lights changed to green and he floored the accelerator. Fear ate at the edges of his gut and he knew it was nothing compared to what his brother must be feeling.

He drummed his fingers on the soft leather of the steering wheel and tried to concentrate on a game plan. There was no point in calling for backup. Between the three of them and Declan's men, they'd have enough to take the bastard down.

Calling in the cavalry might only scare Gibbons off. It was imperative the scumbag think he'd gotten away with it. If he panicked and took off without releasing her, they might never see Cassie again.

As much as he didn't want to think about it, he knew better than most how horrific, unspeakable things happened to good people every day. He'd witnessed it on more occasions than he cared to remember.

Brandon pushed the grim thoughts aside. Dwelling on all the awful possibilities would help no one, least of all, Tom or Cassie. But it brought it home in one god-awful way how precarious life could be.

He thought of Alex and of Sam and of all the pain he'd experienced over the last four years. The pain of loss—the loss of his marriage, the loss of his wife, the loss of his best friend. It had been a grief so deep it had been like mourning a death.

He thought about how he'd feel if something happened to Alex. Or Sam. He shuddered. He couldn't imagine being in Tom's shoes. The fear, the anger, the absolute helplessness.

With a quick glance in his side mirror, he floored the Mustang again. The car surged forward and he whipped past three vehicles on the inside lane. The road signs that indicated the exit to Manly loomed up ahead of him.

He reached for the phone and dialed Declan's number. He had to find out what was happening. His brother answered halfway through the first ring.

"Brandon."

"Talk to me."

"Kennedy just called. He's with one of your guys and they're tailing our man. They've just taken the exit to Manly. They're about five minutes from the mall."

"Who are we chasing? Do we have a name?"

Declan's voice turned grimmer. "Yeah. He's one of the guys you mentioned last week. We've been watching him and a couple of the others in relation to our own investigation. His name's James Gibbons."

"Christ, Gibbons. The one with no record."

Frustration surged through him and he thumped his fist on the steering wheel. "It's always the way."

"It's no point thinking that way now, bro. We need to take this bastard down. Where are you?"

He glanced out the window. "About five or six minutes away from the mall, if the traffic doesn't get any heavier."

"Good. We should arrive about the same time."

"Where's Tom?"

"He's still at the mall, waiting for an update. I'm thinking our man might do the drop-off near the eastern end of the complex. It's not his closest entry point, but it's mainly loading docks at that end. Much less traffic and fewer curious onlookers. I'll call Tom and tell him to make his way down there and wait."

"What's our guy traveling in?"

"A white Ford F250. Licence plate AB ZT 177." Declan paused. "I haven't called for backup. I didn't want to scare the bastard off by having too many police vehicles around. I hope I've made the right decision."

"I agree, mate. It's a tough call, but the last thing you want is for the perp to panic."

"Yeah, let's hope it works out and that between us we can keep Tom away from him."

CHAPTER 21

Tom stared at the faces in the crowd of shoppers moving around him, their features blurring into a frenzy of color and movement and sound. He paced and stopped and paced again and tried to stem his rising panic. The smells from the food court, normally alluring, turned his stomach.

Music from invisible speakers, meant to be calming, reverberated inside his head, adding to the tumult of noise and confusion. He had to get outside. Cassie was outside. Declan had said she was. *Outside. Outside. Outside.*

He shook his head, wishing he could end the noise. He couldn't hear. He couldn't hear Cassie. She needed him. *Cassie. His baby girl.*

He barely managed to hear the sound of his phone over the cacophony surrounding him and snatched it out of his pocket.

Declan. Relief surged through him.

"Dec, thank God. What the hell's happening? Where is she? Where's my daughter?" Finding an exit at last, he shouldered his way out of the shopping center.

"Tom, calm down. Please, mate. I need you to stay calm. Where are you?"

"Outside. I'm outside, like you told me."

"Good. He's heading toward the eastern entry. Brandon and I are not far away. The boys are still tailing him. They're under strict instructions not to let him out of their sight."

"Who else is covering us?"

"I'm trying to keep it low key. I don't want him to panic and take off without releasing Cassie. Get over to the eastern end, down near the loading docks. We'll meet you there."

Tom shoved the phone back in his pocket. Adrenaline surged through him, helping to dilute the fear. He took off at a run.

Cassie stirred in the seat beside him. James glanced across at her. Relief flooded through him. He was beginning to think she wouldn't wake in time. They were almost at the mall. He could hardly dump her while she was still unconscious. That was just asking for trouble.

No, his plan was simple, like it always was. He wouldn't return her to the netball courts. The games were probably over and anyone still there would definitely notice them.

If she found herself at the mall, she might be confused about how she got there, but it wouldn't be that out of the ordinary that it would cause any major anxiety. With a bit of luck, she wouldn't have any memory of their time together and he could go back to his apartment and get on with editing her video.

The thought sent a surge of excitement through his body, centering in his groin. His hand drifted to his cock and he rubbed it through his jeans, relishing the thought of what was to come.

Cassie's eyelids fluttered and then opened. She looked at him and blinked. "Uncle Jim?" She blinked again. "What...? What are you doing?"

James cursed under his breath. He'd forgotten to replace the beard before leaving the unit. He hadn't even thought about it. Having kept her in his apartment longer than he'd planned, he'd been in a rush to leave. He hadn't bargained on the fact that she'd recognize him. He should have anticipated such a complication, but the simple fact was, he hadn't.

The first strains of panic infiltrated his gut. How was he going to explain to her why she was in his car? He hadn't seen her for more than twelve months. It wasn't like he could pretend her parents had asked him to collect her after the game.

Now he was going to have to change his plan. He couldn't simply drop her off at the mall and go on his merry way like he had with all the others. She knew who he was. Who he *really* was.

He bit his lip and sifted through his increasingly frantic thoughts, trying to come up with a valid excuse.

"What are we doing? Where are we going? What...? What's happening?" Cassie's gaze darted frantically between him and the windscreen, confusion clouding the cobalt blue of her eyes.

"Where's...David? You said... That is... I thought..."

A feeling of peace swept over him and he knew what he had to do. For the first time in his life, he'd tell the truth. He owed it to her. She was family, after all.

"Cassie, Cassie, Cassie," he crooned. She looked so bewildered. Fear had crept into her face. It wouldn't take her long to realize something was dreadfully wrong. It was such a shame she'd recognized him, but it was probably for the best.

"What are you doing, Uncle Jim? Why...? Why am I in your car? I thought you were..."

He smiled, feeling empowered as the moment came upon him. "I know what I told you, Cassie and I'm sorry. I really, truly am. But I couldn't help it. I'd spent so long chatting to you, building your trust. I didn't know it was you, that *you* were Lady G. You were just another beautiful, innocent girl hanging out in chat rooms. When I saw you at the netball courts, I recognized you, but I couldn't help myself. I just had to have you."

Realization dawned. Cassie's mouth gaped wide and her face filled with horror.

"You... You're...*Justin?*" Her voice was hoarse with disbelief. Her head swung from side to side in increasing panic. *"Nooooo! Nooooo!"*

James glanced at the gym bag he'd left on the back seat, grateful he still had another loaded syringe in the side pocket. He always kept one ready, just in case. 'Til now, he hadn't needed it.

"Shh," he murmured soothingly. "It's okay, sweetie. I'm not going to hurt you. I'm your uncle. I'd never hurt you."

The exit to the mall loomed up in front of him, but he knew what he had to do. With seconds to spare, he wrenched the steering wheel and crossed over two lanes of traffic. Horns blasted behind him, but he didn't pause. With his foot down hard on the accelerator, he took the exit that would lead him back to the freeway. He left the mall behind them in a cloud of exhaust fumes.

"I'm sorry, boss. We've lost him."

Declan cursed long and loudly into the phone. "What the fuck do you mean, you lost him? You were right on his tail. He was turning into the mall."

"Yeah, he was. But at the last minute, he changed his mind and pulled across the traffic. We couldn't change our course without causing an accident. We had to make the turn."

Declan bit down on his anger. It wouldn't do any good to give vent to his grievances now. He had to get things back on track. "Where are you?"

"In the car park."

"Where's Gibbons?"

"Back on the freeway, I think. That's the way he was headed."

"Fuck. Fuck. *Fuck.*" Declan scrubbed at his hair with both hands, the frustration nearly killing him. Dragging air into his lungs, he made an attempt to regain control.

Dread settled in his gut. He had to tell Tom. He had to tell Tom they'd fucked up. But first, he'd call Brandon. Brandon hadn't yet arrived at the mall. There was a chance he was still on the main road. He could be their only hope.

The traffic in front of Brandon once again came to a standstill and he cursed aloud. He was less than two hundred feet from the exit. His phone buzzed. *Declan.*

Brandon grimaced and answered it. "I know what you're going to say, but I can't get there any quicker. The traffic's piled up just before the turnoff. I can't see what's happening, but we're barely moving. I swear to God, every man and his dog is trying to get to the beach today."

"Brandon, we've lost him. For some reason, he changed his mind. The boys were committed to taking the exit. We think he's back on the freeway. Can you get out of where you are and try and find him? If he is on the freeway, he'll be on it for at least five or six minutes before he can exit again. You might be able to catch up with him—"

"Christ, Dec. Tom must be ready to rip you to shreds."

"Yeah, no doubt he will when I tell him."

"Shit. I don't envy you that job." Brandon cleared his throat and checked his rearview mirror. "Anyway, leave this to me. If I spot the bastard, I'll call you."

With a squeal of tyres Brandon pulled across a double lane of traffic, narrowly missing a bus. No longer mindful of damaging his car, he wove in and out of the traffic, forcing his way through. Family was more important than *things,* even something as precious as his Mustang.

He accelerated again and cut in front of another car. The driver hurled abuse at him and demonstrated his anger with rude hand gestures, but Brandon paid it no heed. His niece's life was at stake. Nothing else mattered.

Freeing himself from the tangle of traffic at last, he sped toward the freeway. Less than a minute later, he was on it and immediately began scanning the vehicles in front of him for a white Ford F250.

A vehicle matching the description changed lanes ahead of him. His gut clenched. The pickup was about five hundred feet in front of him, too far away to read the license plate. He sifted through the traffic again and cursed when he spotted another white F250.

Fuck. It was also too far ahead to make out the plate. He bit his lip in consternation. Which one to follow? The one closest to him had its blinker on, indicating it would take the next exit. The one further ahead remained in the middle lane. The odds were fifty-fifty. Good, if you were a gambling man. But he wasn't and even if he were, he'd never gamble with the safety of his brother's daughter.

Indecision gnawed at his gut. If he chose the wrong one, it could be fatal. Increasing the pressure on the accelerator, he gained on the vehicles in front of him. Squinting through the traffic, he made out part of the license plate on the closest vehicle. A... It was all he could see. Adrenaline surged through him. It had to be it. Flicking on his indicator, he moved to the left and followed the Ford off the freeway.

Not wanting to alert the other driver, Brandon stayed well back. The car turned right and then left and then right again. A set of traffic lights loomed up ahead, turning red on their approach. Brandon accelerated and then changed lanes. He came up beside the pickup, his nerves taut.

Glancing across to the driver's side, he gasped in disbelief. An Asian woman of about thirty stared back at him, her face expressionless. In the backseat, he spied a couple of kids smiling and waving at him through the window.

He drove his fist against the steering wheel. Hard.

Fuck, fuck, fuck.

It wasn't him.

The AFP squad room was a hive of activity, at odds with the late hour. The sun had long since set, but the day shift had stayed on to provide additional manpower and had been joined by the night shift.

It was more than eight hours since Cassie went missing and the tension in the room remained high. A search by air had failed to locate James Gibbons' vehicle. Another surveillance team had also been dispatched to his apartment, but so far, nothing. If he was aware they were onto him, it was unlikely he'd return to his abode, but it was a possibility they would be prepared for, no matter how slim. The apartment would be watched 24/7 until they had him under arrest. A joint taskforce made up of AFP officers and State police was being hastily put together by the superintendent.

A low-level feeling of dread in the pit of Alex's belly had been a constant presence ever since Brandon had told her about Cassie's disappearance and she ached with the strain. She wanted her niece safe and sound. She couldn't even begin to imagine how Lily was feeling.

Wanting to do whatever she could to help, she'd left Sam in the care of her mother and the hospital staff and had come into work. She glanced across at Brandon where he paced the length of the squad room, a frown darkening his features. Gripped tightly in his hand was the list of thirteen suspects they'd narrowed down from the original one hundred and sixty-five. Gibbons was on it.

Patrick had urged them to remain calm. Gibbons was part of a much larger investigation and the super wasn't going to jeopardize an international investigation by moving too quickly.

"Okay, everyone, listen up."

She looked up when Patrick spoke. Making her way around the clutter of desks, she joined the other officers as they gathered around their boss. The grim expression and white lines of tension around his mouth did nothing to allay her nerves.

Brandon stilled, his gaze sharpening on Patrick's face.

Alex tried to slow her racing heart, a reaction as much to the tension in the room as her nearness to her husband. She hadn't spoken to him since the telephone call when he'd alerted her to Cassie's disappearance.

"All right, just so you know where we're at..." Patrick said. "I've contacted the other agencies involved. I'm still waiting to hear from INTERPOL and the FBI. The time difference is causing us some problems. Some of the powers that be are asleep."

A couple of eye rolls and quiet chuckling broke the tension. Alex noticed Brandon didn't laugh, didn't move. She knew how he felt. Every minute Cassie remained unfound increased the odds she would be hurt—if she hadn't been already.

The evidence seemed to indicate she'd been taken straight after the game. She'd been with Gibbons, a suspected pedophile, for hours.

Alex's mind shied away from the implications. There was no point in thinking along those lines. It would only drive her crazy and would make the inaction even more impossible to accept.

Patrick eyed the team of State and AFP officers surrounding him, his gaze landing on Brandon.

"Make no mistake, we all want to find this girl, but we need to put it in perspective, no matter how hard that is to do. If we can help it, I'd rather not jeopardize months of work involving hundreds of suspects and thousands of investigation hours for the sake of one girl. I hope everyone understands that."

Brandon flinched and his hands clenched into fists, but he remained silent and Alex felt a wave of admiration for his courage and professionalism. She didn't think she'd be able to remain so calm in his situation. He had to be straining at the bit to get out there and do something, anything. Whatever it took to find Cassie and bring her home.

"We can't afford to jump the gun on this," Patrick continued. The plan is to conduct simultaneous raids across all thirteen of our suspect's premises. INTERPOL and the FBI and every other law enforcement agency involved in this investigation will be conducting similar raids around the world. It's imperative that none of these persons receive a tip-off that anything's amiss. That's why it's so important we all act together, and at the same time."

He looked around, meeting the gaze of each one of them. "Unfortunately, this Gibbons character has forced our hand. It appears he has a young girl in his custody. For a man who has no children and who has an extensive history of visiting online child pornography sites, that's of grave concern."

Brandon's lips turned white. Alex's heart clenched.

"But we're going to do this right. I've been liaising with Detective Senior Sergeant Declan Munro of the Hornsby Local Area Command. For those of you who don't know, they've been working in conjunction with us, running surveillance on Gibbons. Fortunately for us, one of the local boys and Jack Nelson were watching this bloke's apartment and saw him carry a young girl to his car and leave with her."

His gaze flicked to Brandon. "According to Detective Munro, the girl matched the description of Cassie Munro, the niece of both Declan and Brandon Munro." There was a general murmur of surprise amongst the group of officers and a few surreptitious glances thrown in Brandon's direction. Most of them had been unaware of his personal connection to the case.

"Jack and the constable from Hornsby tailed the vehicle, a white Ford F250, to the Warringah Mall, but then lost him. They've been watching his apartment ever since, but so far, he hasn't returned. We're thinking he may have taken her somewhere else."

"What do we know about this Gibbons character?" Ryan asked.

"Not much, unfortunately," Patrick replied with a grimace. "He's one of those smart enough to fly under the radar. No previous charges, or arrests—not even an outstanding parking ticket. Works in IT as some sort of sales rep. Travels a fair bit up and down the coast." His expression turned grim. "Really, he could be anywhere."

"Does he have any property registered in his name?" Alex asked.

Patrick turned to her. "Nope. We've checked with the Land and Property Information Office. Nothing at all in his name, not even the unit in Hornsby."

Alex spoke again. "What about any family members? You said he had no children, but what about parents, brothers and sisters?"

Acknowledging her question with a nod, Patrick answered. "We're still looking into that. He came from a dysfunctional family."

"Don't they all?" Brandon murmured, his voice icy steel.

Patrick ignored him and went on. "Gibbons' parents divorced when he was young. Five or six, I think. We haven't been able to find out what happened to his mother. His father re-married when Gibbons was about sixteen or seventeen to a woman who had a young child. He was largely living on his own by then and it appears he had very little contact with his new stepmother and stepsister."

Brandon frowned. Something niggled at the edge of Alex's memory. Brandon turned to her, his eyes dark with turmoil.

"Lily?" he mouthed, his expression uncertain.

Alex shrugged, her mind racing. Lily had a stepbrother. He worked in IT. He'd told Alex he traveled a lot.

Her heart pounded. Could it be Jim? Could he have targeted his *niece*? The horror of it was almost too much to imagine. She looked back at Brandon and nodded slowly.

"In an awful, awful way, I think it makes sense," she whispered.

Brandon's eyes gleamed with feral anticipation. "Sir," he interrupted Patrick. "Does anyone have a picture of James Gibbons?"

Patrick frowned and looked toward a couple of the detectives from the Hornsby Local Area Command who had joined the taskforce. "I'm not sure. Do you guys have any images of Gibbons?"

They looked at each other and shrugged. "Not that I know of," one of them volunteered, "but I can call the boss and find out. Perhaps someone on the surveillance team got photos."

"Get onto him and if he has any, tell him to email them to us right away."

"Yes, sir."

The two State officers moved away, one of them pulling out his phone. Alex sidled up to Brandon, hardly daring to voice the question.

She kept her voice low, not wanting to be overheard. "You think it might be Lily's stepbrother?"

Brandon's expression was grim. "Let's hope not, for her sake. But there's always been something odd about that loser."

Alex felt the instinctive need to defend him. "That doesn't make him a pedophile."

"No, but the similarities are too many to ignore. James and Jim. Works in IT. Lives in Hornsby. We can't sit on this. If we can find a picture of James, we'll know for sure."

Alex frowned. "You don't know Jim's last name?"

He shook his head. "I never bothered to find out. He wasn't at their wedding. I don't think they were talking back then. Lily only reached out when she started having children. I think she felt sorry for him because of the way his own childhood had been disrupted."

"So was hers," Alex pointed out.

"Yeah, it's not like he was the only kid in the world to go through a divorce."

"Superintendent Manahan?" One of the Hornsby detectives called out from across the room. Alex and Brandon came to attention.

"Boys, how did it go? Has Detective Munro got any pictures?" Patrick asked.

"You're in luck. He's going to email them right away."

"That's excellent news." Patrick turned to Brandon. "Do

you think you might know this Gibbons chap?"

"Yes, sir. Maybe. I'm not sure, but if I can see what Gibbons looks like, I'll be able to tell you."

"Good, well get on with it, then. Hopefully that brother of yours has sent them through by now. Let me know what you find out."

Brandon looked at Alex, his face grim. She nodded and followed him as he strode back to his desk, her heart beginning a slow, steady thump inside her chest.

———————

Brandon's fingers weren't quite steady when he tapped on the keyboard and accessed his email. His gut clenched when he spied the new message from Declan. It had been sent thirty seconds ago.

Alex stood near his shoulder. He heard the quick intake of her breath and knew she felt like he did. If Gibbons was Lily's stepbrother, his sister-in-law's world would never be the same—whether they brought Cassie home, or not. Tom had been going out of his mind during the hours since Cassie's disappearance. If he discovered that the man who was suspected of taking her was his wife's stepbrother... Brandon shuddered to think what his brother would do.

He could barely bring himself to open the message, but he had no choice. They had to know. One way or the other.

His fingers were leaden. His gut churned. With dread weighing him down, he clicked on the attachment.

It was him.

The images had been taken from a distance somewhere outside his apartment, but there was no doubt about it. James Gibbons was Lily's stepbrother.

Over the pounding of his heart, he heard Alex's sharp intake of breath. Tension came off her in waves. The normal buzz of the squad room diminished to a dull roar. He heard nothing but his harsh breathing.

Alex's fingers squeezed hard around his arm. He turned to

her. He was as shell-shocked as she looked. Her face was pale and the tension around her mouth had bleached the color from her lips.

He shook his head in disbelief. Leaning his elbows on the desk, he supported his head in his hands and scrubbed at his gritty eyes. Although he'd started to suspect as much, to have the harsh reality that Gibbons was related to him, if only by marriage, was beyond difficult to absorb.

But now wasn't the time. They'd identified him. Now they had a chance of finding him. And Cassie.

Adrenaline surged through him. He pushed away from the desk and stood.

"I'll tell Patrick. We need to call Lily and find out if she has any idea where her stepbrother might be. He's not at his apartment, but maybe there's some other place she knows about that we don't."

Alex nodded, still looking dazed. "Yes. Yes, you're right. We need to call her."

Brandon heard the reluctance in her voice and knew where it stemmed from.

"I wish as much as you do that we could do this in person, but time is of the essence. Driving over to the house would cost us at least an hour. Who knows what we could accomplish in that time?"

Alex bit her lip. "Yes, you're right. Of course."

Brandon hated to walk away from her when she was still so obviously in shock, but what he'd said was true. Every minute counted. With one last look in her direction, he turned away and strode toward Patrick's office, his mind in turmoil.

———————

It was one of the hardest things Alex had ever had to do. Although Brandon had offered, she'd insisted that he let her be the one to call Lily. She didn't know why she'd insisted on being so heroic, but all she could remember was the friendship she'd had with Lily in the years before Sam and then later, after years of silence, the way she'd welcomed her with open arms and without a word of recrimination.

Lily was a friend in so many ways, far better than she deserved. She owed her this. Alex swallowed the lump in her throat and listened to the phone dial out. It rang only once before it was answered.

"Hello, this is Lily."

———————

Alex ended the call with a sigh that was tinged with excitement. Swiping at tears with the back of her hand, she jumped up, almost knocking her chair over in her haste to stand.

Lily had been shocked and overwrought, but after a tense silence and many open-ended questions that Alex had no answers for, Lily had eventually recalled an old fishing cabin owned by her stepbrother's father along the banks of the Hawkesbury River. The cabin was about thirty-three miles north of the city, near Brooklyn.

Lily had only been there a couple of times, the last time when she was a teenager, but she was able to give Alex an address and it was this that fluttered in her fingers as she made a beeline for Patrick's office.

Brandon saw her coming and his gaze searched hers, the warmth and understanding in his eyes almost bringing her to tears again.

"I'm okay," she mouthed and then focused her attention on Patrick. "I think I have something."

After explaining how she'd come about it, she gave Patrick the piece of paper on which she'd scrawled the address in Brooklyn and then stood back and waited. Patrick scrutinized the details. A few moments later, he looked at her and then his gaze shifted to Brandon.

"All right, let's see if this pans out. Now that we know Gibbons doesn't own that dump in Hornsby, it makes sense he might have gone here, particularly if it's isolated." He lifted a questioning eyebrow in Alex's direction.

She shrugged. "I'm not sure, sir. Lily didn't say, but she did tell me Jim—James—used to love to go there and hang out although she doesn't know how long it's been since he was last there."

Patrick nodded brusquely. "I'll call Declan and give him the address. We'll need the extra manpower. He can have his men meet us there." He eyed Brandon solemnly. "Given your connection to our victim and her abductor, I'd like to take you off this altogether, but we're short staffed and you've had more field experience than anyone here. Do you think you're up for this?"

Brandon's jaw clenched. Alex knew there was no way in the world he would sit in the office while a manhunt involving his niece was underway. He stared at Patrick unflinchingly.

"Yes, sir."

Patrick compressed his lips and nodded. "Very well. I assume your brother will feel the same way. Fortunately, he answers to someone else. I'll give you fifteen minutes to get ready. Go and tell the others."

Brandon made to leave. Patrick called out to his back. "Weapons, Kevlars, the lot. I'm not going to take any chances and we don't know how well armed this character is. If he does have your niece, he's going to be feeling pretty desperate when he realizes he's surrounded by law enforcement."

Brandon half turned and his lips tightened. Alex longed to take his hand and squeeze it, but she didn't know if he'd welcome her show of support. So, she hung back and remained silent and wished things were different.

As if sensing her desolation, Brandon shifted his gaze to hers. She tensed.

"How did Lily take the news?" he murmured.

"About as well as we expected."

Brandon's gaze intensified. "You did a very difficult thing, Alex. I'm proud of you."

Love swelled up inside her and she had to pin her arms to her sides to prevent them from reaching out for him. His eyes darkened and he closed the tiny gap between them by pulling her hard against him and giving her a brief, fierce hug.

"We can do this," he whispered against her hair seconds before he released her.

Slightly disorientated by his nearness and the spicy scent of his cologne that filled her nostrils, Alex blinked at his abrupt departure. On her way out of Patrick's office, she couldn't help but wonder whether it was Cassie he was talking about or them.

Chapter 22

Cassie stared at the stained, fibro walls of the fishing cabin and tried to stifle a sob. She'd been unconscious for most of the journey and had only stirred when her uncle had lifted her out of the car. She had no idea where they were, but he'd had to wade through a thick jungle of undergrowth and scrubby bushes to get there.

The occasional sound of a motorboat told her the river was not far away, but which river, she couldn't even begin to guess. She didn't even know which direction they'd traveled. The last thing she'd seen were the signs to Brooklyn before a jabbing pain in her thigh had stolen her attention. It was only when he'd withdrawn his hand that she'd caught sight of the needle and then she had only enough time to process the knowledge that he'd used it on her before reality had faded and darkness set in.

If he'd taken her to Brooklyn, then they were a long way from home. She didn't know what time it was, but judging from the shadows that fell in weird, dark shapes across the dusty floorboards, the day was nearly done.

Another sob tightened her throat and she choked on a breath of moldy, rank mattress that lay rough and scratchy on an old wire bedframe beneath her cheek. Her head hurt. Her mouth was parched. Everything looked fuzzy.

Tears welled up in her eyes and ran in slow rivulets down her cheeks. She wanted her mom. She wanted her dad.

She'd even be happy to see her bothersome brother, Joe. She'd been missing for hours. Surely they'd noticed by now?

It wasn't like her to go anywhere after a game without telling them first. Surely, they knew that? *Please, please God, please let them notice and wonder and worry.* She didn't think she'd ever find herself praying for her parents to worry about her, but right now, as she swallowed down her panic, she prayed with all her might for just that.

Tied spread-eagled to the bed, she bit down on the pain and tugged once again on the ties that bound her wrists and ankles. Her arms and legs ached from being stretched out so wide. She couldn't see if she was making any progress, but the bindings remained stubbornly tight. She blinked back more tears.

She couldn't believe how stupid she'd been. She'd lost count of the number of times her parents had lectured her on cyber safety—even Aunty Alex had weighed in on it when she'd come over—and yet, Cassie had ignored all of it and had become a victim of something she had never imagined.

Since she'd discovered Justin was her uncle, she hadn't been able to look at him. He'd come into the cabin from outside a short while ago with an armful of sticks and had set about making a fire. The cool, night air had settled in and she was grateful for the warmth. It had helped still her trembling limbs, but still she couldn't bring herself to look at him.

At least she was still clothed. Her singlet top and sports skirt weren't much, but they were better than nothing. Now that she knew what he was, fear that she'd refused to acknowledge nearly overwhelmed her. She wasn't exactly sure what pedophiles did, but from the way her parents had always spoken about them, she knew it wasn't good.

Caught up in her tumultuous thoughts, it was a moment before she realized he'd moved closer. The bed she lay on gave way under his weight. He sat down beside her, a menacing knife in his hand.

She froze. Despite the heat from the fire, she shook

violently. Her teeth chattered. Her body turned leaden. Forcing her limbs to move, she pulled hard against her bindings. They didn't budge.

He leaned forward and she whimpered.

"Cassie, Cassie, Cassie," he crooned. "Don't be scared. You and I have become such good friends."

He reached out and pushed a lock of hair out of her eyes. She bit back a scream. He smiled in amusement and tenderly ran a finger down her cheek. Icy tentacles of terror clutched at her belly. She stared at him in horror, unable to look away. He slid the knife under her netball shirt and sliced at the fabric, working slowly, methodically, from her belly up.

"Sweet, little Cassie. How beautiful you've become. Like a beautiful, beautiful swan." He frowned. "Not that you were ever an ugly duckling, but so far puberty has been kind to you. So, so kind." He peeled the shredded shirt open and exposed her tiny, pink buds to his heated gaze.

Squeezing her eyes shut, she turned her head away from him. His fingers gripped her chin and forced her to look at him. "You were always so special. I remember years ago your mom would parade you around the house in those cute little dresses with the matching frilly panties and I'd watch you and want you. For so, so long, I've wanted you, but you were just a baby. I had to wait for you to grow up." He trailed his fingers across her chest. She moaned in terror. Tears ran freely down her cheeks.

He shook his head and chuckled. "Who would have thought you'd drop into my lap like a ripe, red cherry just waiting to be plucked?"

Nausea churned in her stomach. "Wh-what are you doing?"

He stroked her hair with a gentle hand and smiled. "We're going to have so much fun. I've never let my little girls watch me play, but now that you know who I am, everything's different. There's no need for secrecy between us. It's going to be so much fun." He smiled widely.

Cassie stared at him uncomprehendingly and shuddered. Instinct warned her that whatever he had in mind would be terrifying. She struggled again with the ties that bound her hands and feet. It didn't feel like rope, more like plastic or tape. Whatever it was, it might as well have been welded on for all the give in it. Fear rose to the surface again. She swallowed a sob of desperation.

Her uncle leaned over and pressed a kiss to her cheek and then stood. "I need to find the old kerosene lamp. It's going to be dark soon and it's so much more fun playing games with the light on."

He walked away and Cassie sucked in some air. She had to get a grip on herself. If there was any chance of surviving this nightmare, she had to keep him talking, keep him busy, keep him thinking of other things and not the things he wanted to do to her...

"Ah, here it is." His voice came to her from the other side of the room. From what she could tell, the cabin was made up of a single room about three times the size of her bedroom. An old wood stove sat against one wall and inside it, the fire her uncle had lit earlier still blazed. An old wooden table, scarred and dusty, took up half the floor space between the stove and the bed. A couple of rickety chairs stood close by.

A cupboard was against the wall to the left of her and to the right, what she imagined was the back door. She'd seen her uncle leave through it and a short time later, he'd returned. She guessed it led to some kind of outhouse because it was obvious the cabin didn't house a bathroom.

A wan light flickered, catching her attention. Her uncle held an old-fashioned lantern in his hand. The smell of kerosene singed her nostrils. Panic flared in her belly. She cleared her throat and tried to speak normally.

"W-where are we? This place looks old."

The distraction seemed to work. Her uncle acknowledged her question with a brief smile and placed the lamp on the table. "This cabin's been here for more than seventy years. It belongs to my father and I think it was his father's before that.

"I come here when I need time to think and to get away

from everything. Not many people even know it exists. No one bothers me here."

Something inside of Cassie told her she had to keep him talking. She offered him a shaky smile. "It must be nice to have somewhere special to go, away from everyone."

James smiled. "Oh, yes, although I don't come here as often as I wish. Work and...other things have a way of interfering." He spread his arms wide. "As you can see, it's been awhile since I was here last."

"Have you ever brought anyone else here?" She bit her lip the moment the words left her mouth.

His expression turned sly. He walked toward her.

"Why, are you jealous? I brought you here." He crouched beside the bed and ran his hand along the length of her ribcage, spreading the torn singlet as he did so. "Sweet, sweet, little Cassie. You belong here."

Terror paralyzed her limbs. Panic began to choke her. "P-please, Uncle J-Jim. P-please don't hurt me. P-please let me go. I p-promise I won't tell anyone. M-mom and Dad p-probably don't even know I've g-gone. I p-promise I won't say anything. P-please, please..."

She hated the whimpering fear in her voice, but was powerless to stop it.

He stood and leaned over her, his lips inches from hers.

"I can't," he whispered, "even if I wanted to. It's too late." His hand reached out and cupped her breast.

Cassie screamed.

A high-pitched scream rent the quiet stillness of the bush. Alex froze. A startled cockatoo took flight, screeching its own protest. Her gaze flew to Brandon. He stared back at her, his face pale.

Declan's head whipped around. Beside him, the handful of State police officers stared at the ground.

Alex glanced around at the members of the taskforce, all

dressed in camouflage fatigues. They were heavily armed, including the men led by Declan. His face was tense in the early evening dimness, but he kept still, his gaze focused on the rundown cabin perched on the edge of the woods about fifty yards away.

Alex thought of Tom and Lily, waiting helplessly at home for news. Alex knew how hard it had been for them to remain behind and let the police do their job. Both of them had wanted nothing more than to leave for the cabin and find their daughter. Alex wasn't the only one grateful that they'd seen sense.

Upon the team's arrival at the fishing cabin, they'd spied the white Ford pickup parked a few feet from the dilapidated building and their suspicions of Gibbons' whereabouts had been confirmed. They'd had the cabin under surveillance for the past ten minutes while Ryan Boland and Jack Nelson, both armed with Glock 19 semi-automatic pistols, carried out a reconnaissance. They were on their way back to the group when the scream tore through the night.

The noise unnerved all of them, even as it justified their presence. Gibbons was not alone. The officers reappeared and headed straight to Brandon.

"You're right, mate. He's in there. And so is the girl. He's got her tied up on the bed against the back wall. She looks unharmed, although it's hard to tell. We only caught a quick glimpse through the front window. The place is so full of dust and grime, it's difficult to see anything."

Brandon nodded, his face tense. "Thanks, fellas. You've done well." With his voice pitched low, he called for them to gather around.

"All right, this is how it's going to happen. I'm going to call Patrick and tell him we've found them. There's no signal here, so I'll have to go back up the hill a bit. It's a good thing. It means Gibbons won't have any means of communicating, either. We won't have to wait for INTERPOL or the FBI to give us the go ahead. We'll have him in handcuffs before he has an inkling what's happening."

He drew in a deep breath and continued. "After I bring Patrick up to date, we're going in. I'll lead the assault from the front. Alex, Ryan and Jack will come with me. Declan, you and your men will take the back. You'll need to stay low in case he looks out the window. Dirty or not, we can't take the risk that he sees us."

His gaze traveled around the group. "Any questions?"

Alex drew in a deep breath. "Let me talk to him."

Brandon swung around to face her. He was shaking his head back and forth even before he uttered a word.

"Please, Brandon. It makes sense. I know him, but not like Tom and Lily know him. Or you. I only met him once. He may not even remember me, but then again, maybe he will. He doesn't know I'm in law enforcement. He knows nothing about me, other than I'm a friend of Lily's."

She pleaded with her eyes. "It might be all we need. If I can put him off balance for even a few moments, one of us might be able to get to Cassie and free her. If we can prevent having to draw our weapons, we have a much better hope of avoiding bloodshed."

Declan nodded thoughtfully. "Alex is right. Her presence on his doorstep might confuse him. He won't immediately connect her to law enforcement. It might give us the chance we need."

Brandon's lips compressed in an agony of indecision. He stared at Declan and then back to Alex. His frown was fierce. She reached out with a hand that was not quite steady and laid her palm over his heart, feeling the strong, steady beat of it through the layers of his clothing.

"It's okay, Brandon. I've trained for this. We both have. I've worked beside you, remember? Nothing's changed. I'm as sharp as I ever was."

Ryan stepped forward. "She's right, mate. She's the best shot we've got. Of course, we hope it doesn't come to that..." He looked down at his feet, shifting uncomfortably.

Brandon's expression turned grimmer. He looked at Alex, his eyes boring into hers. He squeezed his eyes shut and took a deep breath. Then nodded.

"Okay."

She sagged in relief, even as adrenaline surged through her. Fear edged her consciousness. Fear was good. She was about to go into what could explode into a lethal situation. Fear kept her sharper, more wary. Fear could save her life. Brandon spun on his heel and headed up the hill with his cell phone in his hand. Less than five minutes later, he returned.

"We're good to go," he said, his gaze encompassing the assembled group of law enforcement. "Patrick hasn't yet received the nod from INTERPOL, but with Gibbons out of communication range, he's given us the green light."

Alex drew in a deep breath and let it out slowly, willing her heartbeat to steady. Brandon turned to her, his expression somber.

"You ready?"

"She nodded grimly. A moment passed. Without thinking, she pulled Brandon's head down to hers and pressed her lips against his. She felt his momentary surprise, but then his arms came around her and he squeezed her tight. There was desperation in his hard embrace.

"I love you," he murmured against her ear and then set her away from him. "Be careful."

Alex pulled out of his arms and stumbled away. She tried desperately to concentrate on the cabin that loomed up in front of her. Brandon's parting words reverberated inside her head. Joy warred with disappointment as she realized she hadn't had the wherewithal to respond to him. But now wasn't the time to dwell on it. Lives were at stake. Cassie's, definitely, and maybe even hers.

No one knew if Gibbons was armed, but they had to assume he was. What they did know was that when he realized they'd found him and that he was cornered, he'd likely become desperate and desperate men were dangerous.

Dread weighed like concrete in her belly. She crouched low in the undergrowth and crept forward one step at a time. She was now close enough to see a faint light visible through the front window.

Glancing behind her, she was reassured by the darker shadows of Brandon and his team. They'd agreed she would approach the cabin on her own and try to draw Gibbons out. At the same time, Declan would approach from the rear and attempt to rescue Cassie.

The plan was sound, but anything could go wrong.

She sucked in a breath and counted slowly to ten. She was less than five feet from the door. The low hum of voices reached out to her. Night had fully descended, but the moon was with them, glowing golden from a perfect, round orb. It was enough to illuminate the ground in front of her and the crumbling concrete steps that led to the front door.

Taking another breath, she stood and trod carefully up the stairs. With a fist that was not quite steady, she knocked on the door.

"Jim, it's Alex. Alex Cavanaugh. We met at Lily's barbeque."

———————

Cassie's heart leaped with gladness at the sound of her aunt's voice. Aunty Alex was outside! Oh, please, please God. Please, let it be all right. Let her uncle speak with her aunt and let her go. Let her leave this place of horror and never come back.

She still lay spread-eagled on the musty mattress. Seconds earlier, her uncle had used the knife on her skirt, leaving her sick with terror.

Her uncle was as surprised as she was to hear Aunty Alex's voice. The wildness in his eyes momentarily subsided. He stopped pulling at her gym pants and rose from the bed. His body stilled. She couldn't tell if he was poised for fight or flight. She watched it all as if in slow motion.

"Alex? Alex from the barbeque?"

The confusion in his voice was reflected on his face. He turned and walked toward the front door then halted abruptly and did an about-face. Cassie shrank back against the mattress, the ties at her wrists and ankles protesting against the movement. She bit her lip against the pain.

"Jim, please open the door. I know Cassie's in there. Please let me see her."

His body jerked and Cassie tensed, hardly daring to breathe. He clutched his head in his hands and turned it from side to side. He turned and paced the length of the cabin.

"No, *no, no!* Alex, you can't come in. I'm here with Cassie. We're here together. Sweet, sweet Cassie. Go away, Alex. You shouldn't be here."

"Please, Jim. At the barbeque, you seemed like such a nice man. Not the kind of person to do something terrible. I'm sure you love Cassie as much as I do. You don't want to hurt her."

Cassie's heart thumped hard against her chest. The front door cracked open and slowly widened.

Aunty Alex appeared in the doorway, looking strange in camouflage clothing. She had one hand extended toward her uncle in a gesture of peace. Cassie held her breath.

"Hello, Jim. Remember me? We met at the barbeque. You told me about your job and all the traveling you do. We had a lovely chat."

Her uncle cocked his head, as if he was listening and weighing up her aunt's words. Frantic prayers chased themselves around inside Cassie's head. She tried to slow her breathing, forcing tiny quiet breaths through her parched lips.

She caught movement out of the corner of her eye and watched as the back door she'd spied earlier eased open. The tiniest crack of moonlight landed amongst the dirt, sending the dust mites dancing.

Another thought struck her. If her aunt was here, then her parents might also be outside. Someone had told Aunty Alex about the cabin. She only prayed it had been her mom. That meant she knew. She knew about Uncle Jim. She knew about Cassie. Her mom could be trying to come through the back doorway right now.

She risked another glance in her uncle's direction. He was still focused on her aunt who had now made it all the way inside. Aunty Alex caught her eye and nodded in her direction—the tiniest of movements, but Cassie took it as a sign of encouragement. Hope flared in her chest.

Brandon watched Alex disappear into the gloom of the cabin and hoped he'd made the right decision. Tension knotted his gut. *Why the hell had he agreed to let her go?* Gibbons could have any number of weapons and no one had any clue how he'd react when he realized he'd been discovered. Brandon would never get to her in time if Gibbons decided to hurt her.

Anxiety gnawed at him and he resisted the urge to check the safety on his gun. The heavy weight of the Glock was reassuring against his palm, but he'd be a hell of a lot calmer when Alex reappeared safe and sound. Now that she was out of sight, the tension was driving him mad. Not knowing what was happening in there was almost more than he could bear.

As if he could read his mind, Ryan moved up beside him and gave him a nudge. Brandon offered him a grim smile, acknowledging the other man's attempt at reassurance. Brandon had initially been suspicious and probably even a little jealous of Alex's closeness to her partner, but right now he was glad to have the support of someone who cared about her.

"What do you think's going on?" Ryan asked, his voice low.

"No idea, but at least it's quiet. That has to be a good thing."

Alex tried to breathe through the nerves that churned inside her. She had to keep him calm, keep him talking. Keep him thinking about normal everyday things and not what he was doing in an old fishing cabin in the middle of nowhere with his teenage niece.

She caught movement out of the corner of her eye and watched the back door ease open. In silence, she let the first feelings of relief slide through her and sent a desperate plea heavenwards. With her gaze trained on Jim, she tried once again to distract him.

"This is a pretty cool place, Jim. I bet you love coming here."

He frowned and looked as though he was struggling to follow the thread of her conversation. It took him a moment to respond.

"Yeah, it's my father's. He used to bring me here all the time when I was a kid, when he wanted to get away from my mother. She did nothing but yell and swear all the time. It was an escape for both of us."

"This close to the river, I bet you did a lot of fishing."

He nodded and a smile lifted the corners of his lips. "Yeah, we caught a lot of fish here, Dad and I."

Alex moved further inside the cabin and came to a stop right in front of him. With his back turned toward the rear door, she hoped it would give Declan and his men the chance they needed. Trying to hold his attention, she inclined her head. "Does he still come here?"

"Not that I know of. It's been a good while since I was here." His gaze darted around the room and Alex froze, praying he wouldn't turn around, but he looked back at her and smiled again. "The place doesn't exactly look lived in."

Forcing a chuckle, she nodded. "Yeah, I think your housekeeper could do with a demonstration."

"Or a raise," he added.

This time, her grin was almost genuine and she marveled at the quirky sense of humor that disguised a monster.

The back door creaked. The noise seemed magnified in the small room. Alex's heart stopped beating.

Jim's head snapped around. He caught sight of Declan near the half-open door and he roared, "Stop! Stop right now or I'll shoot."

Alex glimpsed a flash of steel in the dimness. Her throat went dry and dread turned her legs to concrete. Without thinking, she grabbed Jim by the arm that held the gun.

"Jim, please. Don't do this."

He shook his head back and forth, the wildness back in his eyes. "I can't go to jail, Alex. I can't. Do you know what they do to people like me in places like that?"

Cassie lay frozen on the bed. Alex tried to catch her eye, but the girl seemed to have lost the ability to move.

Keeping her gaze fixed on the man in front of her, Alex spoke again. "Jim, give me the gun. Please. There's nothing to gain by hurting anyone. It's all been a bit of a misunderstanding," she lied. "You wanted to spend some time with your niece." She shrugged and forced the words past her lips. "There's no harm in that. But if you shoot someone, Jim, nothing good is going to come of it. It will be very hard to explain that away."

Hoping her words were enough to give him pause, Alex looked toward Declan and shouted, "*Now!*"

The words catapulted Declan and the men behind him into action. All of a sudden, the room was full of men in fatigues, shouting and pointing weapons at the man beside her.

Jim wrenched his arm away from Alex. In slow motion, she watched him aim the gun at her head.

Smoke rose from the tip of the gun. Microseconds later, white-hot pain exploded in her head and the world receded around her. Gibbons diminished into a blur. With her last remaining strength, Alex drew her gun and fired.

The front door smashed against the wall of the cabin. Brandon filled the space, his expression thunderous and ravaged by fear.

Darkness descended and she collapsed onto the floor amongst the dust and debris of another lifetime.

———————

Brandon scrubbed at the whiskers on his chin and rubbed at the grit in his eyes. The lights and beeps of the various machines that surrounded Alex's hospital bed had become a familiar symphony and one that was now almost lulling him to sleep. He couldn't remember when he'd last closed his eyes. It felt like weeks.

He reached for her hand, pale and soft, where it rested with an innocent vulnerability against the white sheet. The warmth of her skin gave him comfort, something the doctors so far had not.

Guilt weighed him down, adding to his pain. Why, oh why had he agreed to let her go in there alone? It was his fault. She was lying in a coma, prognosis uncertain, and he was the one who'd put her there.

A nurse approached on noiseless rubber-soled feet and checked the bag of fluid that dripped silently into Alex's arm. Next, she kneeled and recorded the contents of the bag that hung off the side rail of the bed.

He looked away and heard the nurse scratching with her pen on the folder of notes she held in her hand. He couldn't bear to see his wife reduced to such anonymity—no longer a person, but a medical specimen to be poked and prodded and recorded.

He was being unfair. The care and attention she'd received from both the medical and nursing staff had been exceptional, but he didn't care. None of them, for all their kind efficiency, could tell him when she'd wake up, when she'd smile, when she'd open her mouth and say hello. Tell him she loved him.

Agony tore through him again and his eyes burned with tears that pushed ever harder to fall. He gritted his teeth, clenched his jaw and sucked air into his nostrils. He didn't deserve the release tears would bring.

How could he have been so stupid, so selfish to let her think he'd never forgive her? Oh, he'd told her he loved her just before she'd headed into the lair of an unpredictable criminal, but how original was that? They were throwaway words from throwaway movies that had been done a hundred times before.

How was she to know he'd meant them? *Really* meant them? Now, he might never get the chance to explain, to make her see how much he meant them and how sorry he was for making her doubt his love.

The longer she remained in a coma, the more pessimistic her prognosis became. It hadn't even been a full week, but the grim faces of the medical staff as they drifted in and out of her allotted bed space in the ICU told him more than he wanted to know.

There was no reason for her to still be unconscious, they told him. No medical reason that they could ascertain. The bullet had barely grazed her temple. The fall she'd taken afterwards had bruised her brain, but the swelling had now receded and the damage hadn't been severe enough to warrant a coma. And yet, here she was. It baffled them and made them even more cautious when he demanded to know what was happening.

A movement on the bed caught his eye. He blinked and sat forward, then blinked again. Alex's eyelids fluttered. He rubbed his eyes and looked again. There it was. They were *fluttering*.

Joy and overwhelming relief surged through him. It was the first time she'd moved since she'd been brought in. He stood and scrambled for the buzzer and then reached for Alex's hand and squeezed it. Bringing it to his lips, he pressed desperate kisses across her palm, willing her to give him another sign that she was waking.

The same nurse who'd attended earlier approached the bed.

"Can I help you, Mr Munro?"

Brandon squeezed Alex's hand tighter. "My wife. I think she's waking up. She moved her eyelids. I'm sure of it. I think she's waking up!"

The nurse nodded cautiously and leaned over Alex.

Taking a small flashlight out of her pocket, she gently lifted one of Alex's eyelids and shone the light into her eye.

Alex turned her head away. Brandon yelped loudly with excitement. "See, I told you! She moved! She responded to your flashlight."

The nurse offered a slight smile. "Yes, she did. It's a good sign, a really good sign. Let me page the doctor."

Brandon tried to contain his excitement. One small response didn't mean they were out of the woods. He regained his seat beside her bed, but then stood again, unable to sit still. Pacing within the tight confines of the space allotted to her bed, he kept his gaze pinned to her pale form.

She had to wake up. She had to. He'd only just found her again. He couldn't lose her for a second time. That would kill him.

"Bran...?"

Brandon came to an abrupt halt and stared at the woman in the bed. Her voice was hoarse and barely audible, but her head moved and then her lips and then her voice came again.

"Bran...don?"

He rushed over, mindful of the tubes and bags and other medical paraphernalia that crowded her bedside.

"Oh, God! Oh, Alex! Oh, sweetheart. I thought I'd lost you! I love you! I love you so much. Please, please forgive me!" The tears he'd refused to shed until that moment, poured from his eyes and ran down his cheeks. He didn't care. She was awake. Awake and lucid. Watching him with a frown, as if trying to work out how she'd gotten there.

Her hand moved to the IV tube. He put his hand over hers and gently pulled it back. "It's okay, sweetheart. You've been unconscious since they brought you in. They'll take it out when they're sure you're okay without it."

He moved to the end of the bed and called out. "Nurse, nurse! Please, come and see. She's awake! You need to come and see."

Hurrying back to Alex's side, he took her hand again and

held it tight. "It's going to be all right. Oh, darling, it's going to be all right." He pressed a kiss to the back of her hand and then held it to his heart.

The nurse arrived, a wide smile creasing her face when she saw Alex was awake. "Welcome back, Mrs Munro. I don't know whether your husband told you, but you've given us all a little scare. We weren't sure what was going on with you."

She patted the blanket that covered Alex's legs. "I've called the doctor. We'll wait for him to arrive and see you for himself before we do anything, but I'm sure he'll be as pleased as I am to see you awake."

"Drink?" Alex croaked.

"Of course." The nurse brought a cup of water with a straw in it to Alex's mouth. "Easy does it," she advised.

Alex took a few sips and then turned her head in Brandon's direction. "How's Cassie?"

"She's fine," he reassured her. "We found her in time. She was admitted overnight for observation and she was seen by a counselor. Tom and Lily took her home a few days ago. They're arranging for her to meet with a child psychiatrist, someone who's dealt with this kind of thing before. Alex nodded, her face filled with relief. As if in sudden recollection, she frowned. "How is Sam?"

Brandon squeezed her hand. "He's fine. Your mom came by a little while ago. They were ready to discharge him, but when the doctors found out you were here, they decided to keep him in." He looked away, feeling uncertain. "I-I've been visiting with him every day. He-he's a great kid."

Emotion welled up in her eyes. Brandon swallowed a lump that had lodged in his throat. Leaning over the bed rails, he kissed her.

"I'm so glad to see you awake."

She blinked away tears. He could tell by the look in her eyes that she was his and always had been. He didn't know how long they stared at each other, but it wasn't until he became aware of the doctor approaching the hospital bed that he broke the connection and acknowledged the other man with a nod.

"Well, Mrs Munro, it's nice to finally meet you. I'm Dr Matthew Reeves. I've been overseeing your treatment."

Alex smiled. "Thank you."

"You had us all perplexed. We weren't sure what was going on with you."

Alex shrugged and smiled again. The doctor moved over to the monitor that displayed her vital signs and took note of the data and then lifted the stethoscope from around his neck and listened to her chest. After repeating the check of her pupils, he stood back and pronounced that the worst was over.

"Everything looks good. We'll keep you under observation for the next day or so, but you might be able to be moved out of the ICU and into another ward tomorrow."

Relief weakened Brandon's knees. He leaned one hand on the mattress for support and turned to the doctor with a heart full of gratitude.

"I can't thank you enough, Doctor. I-I don't know what I would have done if I'd lost her." He thrust out his hand.

The doctor returned his handshake and made a promise to check on Alex again in an hour. When he took his leave, the nurse followed him.

"What happened to Jim?" Alex asked quietly.

Brandon bit his lip and shook his head. "I'm sorry, sweetheart. He didn't make it."

Her face filled with regret. "How...?"

"It doesn't matter now. What matters is that you rest so you can get better and get out of here."

"How long have I been here?"

"It's Friday morning. You've been here six days."

Her face registered her surprise. She shook her head. "No wonder you look..."

He grimaced and ran a hand through his hair. "Like shit?"

She smiled and nodded.

"I had more important things on my mind than showers and shaving."

"I see that." Her eyes darkened with emotion. "Thank you for visiting Sam. Does... Does he know you're his dad?"

Brandon shook his head. "I wanted to wait until we could tell him together."

Alex stared at him, her expression filled with love and gratitude.

"Thank you," she said simply.

Brandon found her hand and took it in his. He drew in a deep breath and released it slowly. Cassie had been found. Sam was healing. Alex loved him as much as he loved her. Everything was going to be fine.

CHAPTER 23

One month later

Brandon pulled into the driveway of Tom and Lily's grand old Chatswood home and shut off the ignition. Nerves danced around inside Alex's stomach and she did her best to chase them away by giving her husband a wide smile.

He leaned across the gear stick and pressed a soft kiss to her mouth. "Have I told you lately how much I love you?" he murmured, his lips sliding across her cheek to nuzzle at her ear.

She grinned and tried to balance the pan of potato bake on her lap. "It has been awhile. At least an hour or two. You'd better tell me again in case I forget."

He smiled and pinched her lightly on the arm. "Minx."

She opened her eyes wide, a picture of innocence. "You told me you like it when I'm feisty."

His eyes darkened. His hand slid down to cup her breast, unerringly finding her nipple through the light fabric of her cotton blouse.

"Careful, or I might unleash my wild side." He growled low in his throat.

Desire sprang instantly to life. Her gaze held his.

"Dad, can we go in now?"

Sam's gentle whine from the back seat penetrated the haze of need. Brandon removed his hand with reluctance, but he winked and mouthed "later." She squeezed her legs closed against another surge of longing.

Her nerves returned to the surface. Apart from Lily's brief visit while Alex had been in hospital and a couple of quick phone calls that had been limited to questions about her recovery, they hadn't given themselves the opportunity to talk. Really talk. About Brandon. About Sam. About Cassie. Even about Jim.

When he'd deemed her strong enough, Brandon told her what had unfolded in the cabin outside Brooklyn. He'd explained in a gentle tone how it had been her bullet that had found its mark. James had died instantly from a single bullet to his heart.

Although she'd been overwhelmed with guilt, Brandon had reassured her that her quick thinking actions had saved her life. He'd crashed through the door in time to see James take aim at her and if it hadn't been for her sharp aim, she and Cassie could have died.

She'd killed Lily's stepbrother…

Brandon's reassurances and his love had helped eradicate some of the guilt, but every time she thought of Lily, the guilt resurfaced. James had been her stepbrother, after all. And Alex had killed him.

Brandon gazed at her, his eyes filled with understanding.

"Ready?" he asked softly.

She drew in a deep breath and nodded. "I guess so."

"You'll be fine. Let's go."

The yard already overflowed with people when they made their way through the French doors that led out the back. Sam immediately took off running in the direction of a group of children that included his cousin, Joe. Alex felt a surge of gratitude that Sam's injuries had healed so well.

She looked around and nodded greetings to several of her colleagues, including the superintendent, Ryan and

Declan and some of the men she recognized from the Hornsby LAC.

Her stomach clenched when she saw Lily across the lawn. Catching her eye, she lifted the pan of potato bake in a questioning gesture. Lily headed toward her. Alex tensed in anticipation. The smell of Lily's perfume surrounded her as her sister-in-law engulfed her in an awkward hug.

"Hi, Alex. Thank you for coming. It's so great to see you up and about."

Alex nodded and adjusted the pan in her hands. "I made some potato bake."

Lily glanced down and smiled. "Thank you; that was very kind of you. Let's put it inside for now."

She turned and walked in the direction of the house. Alex hesitated and then took another deep breath and followed her. It was now or never.

Depositing the still-warm pan on the granite counter top, Alex nervously wiped her hands on the back of her jeans.

"Lily... Um, I just wanted to say sorry for...everything. We haven't had a chance to talk about what happened. I feel so..."

God, this was harder than she thought. She cleared her throat and tried again, not daring to look at the woman who stood across from her.

"I feel so responsible. I'm sorry."

"What do you have to be sorry about? I would have done exactly the same thing. If you hadn't shot him, he would have shot you *and* Cassie."

Alex peeked at her in surprise. Lily's expression was fierce.

"The bastard shot you. He *shot* you! I'm so lucky to have you and Cassie alive, still here. I'm thankful every single day that you did what you did. You had no choice, Alex. Please don't feel responsible for his death."

Alex shrugged helplessly. "He was your brother."

"My *step*brother," she clarified, her face grim. "You don't know how hard I tried over the years to make him feel part of the family, but he was never interested. He'd show up every now and then and pretend to make an effort, but now I wonder if he only did it so that he could be around Cassie."

Her voice broke on the last word and her shoulders shook. Alex stepped forward and put her arms around her friend.

Lily cried quietly against her shoulder. Her voice was muffled when she spoke again.

"I can't believe how stupid I was. I never even guessed. Tom didn't like him from the start and Brandon felt much the same. I guess I felt like I had to defend him. He was my stepbrother, after all."

She sniffed and Alex reached for a tissue. Lily accepted it gratefully and pulled away to wipe her eyes. With a wobbly smile, she continued her explanation.

"Jim had a rough childhood. His mother was an alcoholic and a drug addict who spent more time in jail than out and his father had no idea how to raise a son. It was only after Jim's father married my mother that Jim had a semblance of stability in his life. By that time, he was nearly an adult and the damage had already been done."

She shook her head slowly. "My mother did her best, but Jim had already left home and we only saw him on rare occasions. None of us had any idea what he'd become."

Lily closed her eyes. Alex felt her pain and wished there was some way she could alleviate it.

"It wasn't your fault, Lily. It was nobody's fault. Jim made his own choices. Nobody forced him into that lifestyle. You have to believe that."

Lily nodded and sniffed again. "I do, but it's not easy." She turned and met Alex's gaze. "Do you know what the hardest part is?"

Alex shook her head.

"That it was me who invited him into our home, into our lives. Into Cassie's life."

"You can't think like that, Lily. I won't let you. He met Cassie online. She'd been chatting to him for weeks. It had nothing to do with you or him or your family. It was one of those freak things. It could have happened to anyone."

"Tom told me Jim was involved in something much nastier, some international pedophile ring?"

Alex nodded. "Yes, we'd been working on the investigation for months. INTERPOL, the FBI and a handful of other international law enforcement agencies had been tracking suspected online predators for some time. James was one of them. We didn't know for sure it was Jim until after he kidnapped Cassie.

Lily shook her head, her eyes wide. "I had no idea. Not the slightest, foggiest idea, all that was unfolding right under my nose."

"That's the danger of it. That's why so many of them get away with it. To most of us, they are ordinary, everyday people."

"But he was my stepbrother," Lily protested. "I should have suspected *something*."

Alex patted her shoulder. "Don't beat yourself up about it. These men don't exactly go around wearing signs around their necks."

"Yes, but *you* guys suspected. He was on your list."

Alex shrugged. "That's what we're trained to do. It took a lot of man hours to get to that point; believe me. Cassie told Brandon she'd been chatting online with James who went by the chat room name of Justin. Only then did I realize I'd chatted to him, too, as I worked the case. That really freaked me out."

"What happened with the investigation? Did you identify any of the others?"

With a nod, Alex answered. "The operation went well. There were another four raids in Sydney, two on the south coast, a couple in north Queensland, two in Perth and two on the outskirts of Melbourne." Her voice turned grim. "We have strong evidence against ten of the twelve and will prosecute for child sex-related offences, including hours of video footage taken by James. We're still trying to identify his victims." She paused. There was no way she was going to tell Lily about the footage they'd found of Cassie. The thought of it made her sick to her stomach, even now. Forcing it aside, she continued.

"We also pulled apart his hard drive. It contained evidence of numerous sales of child pornography. With a bit of luck, we'll put even more of them away."

Silence fell between them. Alex was the first to break it.

"How's Cassie bearing up?" she asked quietly.

"She's going well, considering. Kids seem to be able to bounce back so much quicker than we do. She's been seeing a counselor every week and appears to be making a lot of progress. In fact, most days, she's almost like her old self. She went back to school not long after she was discharged from hospital. She's even back playing netball."

Alex felt relieved. "I'm so glad to hear that."

A flash of movement caught her eye. Sam rushed past, nothing more than a flash of bright color through the clear glass of the French doors. He saw Alex and waved, a huge grin splitting his face.

Gratitude and love flooded through her. Lily noticed her smile and followed her gaze.

"It's good to see Sam's recovered. I was so concerned when Brandon called us. He was almost out of his mind with worry. I called the hospital, but they said they were restricting Sam's visitors. We were waiting for him to come out of Intensive Care before we visited." She shook her head. "That seems like a lifetime ago now."

Alex's eyes filled with tears. Why had she ever stayed away so long? Over the years, she could have done with the support of a good friend. Guilt and regret flooded through her, scorching her face. She could barely bring herself to look at the woman who stood across from her.

"You knew Brandon was his father, didn't you?" she said quietly.

Lily moved away and pulled out a barstool. "Not at first," she replied, taking a seat. "But when he told us you said Sam was two, I knew something wasn't right." The hurt in her eyes pierced Alex's heart.

"Lily, I'm so, so sorry. I-I—"

"Brandon told us why you separated. I understand why you didn't tell him about Sam. I-I only wish you had told me. I could have been there for you. That's what friends are for."

Guilt and shame almost overwhelmed Alex. She shook her head. "It's easy to look back now and know what I should have done. At the time, it seemed like the only option was to keep it to myself. Brandon was always so close to his family. I-I didn't want to give you a reason to have to choose."

She looked away. "I can't tell you how much I wanted to, Lily, how I wished things had been different...but at the time, I didn't feel I had any other choice. Brandon never wanted a baby. By that time, he was back working overseas. I couldn't call him. All we had was email."

She shook her head as the memories resurfaced. "It was too much. I-I guess I just wanted to run and hide and deal with it on my own. Sam was a reality I had to quickly come to terms with. So was raising him on my own. It was..." She shook her head helplessly.

Lily's face filled with compassion. "I wish you hadn't faced all of that on your own."

Alex sniffed. "I had Mom. She was a rock. Dad had died just before Sam was born and she had every reason to wallow in her own self-pity." Alex offered a wobbly smile. "But she didn't. She sold her house and bought another right down the road from us. She's been there for Sam and me from the very beginning. I couldn't have done it without her."

Without a word, Lily stood and put her arms around her. It was the catalyst Alex needed to finally let go—of her anger, her grief, the strain of maintaining her deception, her stress over the shooting.

A sob escaped and then another. She cried quietly while Lily rubbed her back with comforting strokes and said nothing. When it was over, Alex grappled for another tissue and swiped at her eyes before turning with gratitude toward her friend.

"I'm sorry. I'm sorry for everything. And I'm sorry for

blubbering all over you like that. I'm supposed to be comforting *you*."

Lily smiled gently. "I know, and I love you for it. "I'm glad. I'm so glad you had someone. That you didn't have to do it all on your own."

Alex nodded and squeezed Lily's hand. "Thank you for being so understanding. I didn't think you would take it like this. It's one of the reasons why I never told you." She flushed. "I'm so sorry I misjudged you. I should have known better."

Lily returned the pressure and smiled. "None of that matters, now. I'm just glad everything's turned out okay. With you and Brandon. With the shooting."

Tears formed again in Alex's eyes. "Thank you, Lily. Thank you for being so understanding. I don't know if I would be as strong as you in the same circumstances."

Lily offered a sad smile. "We do what we have to do, Alex. None of us knows what we're capable of until our hands are forced. That's just the way it is."

The French doors slid open and Brandon's head appeared in the opening. Spying the women, his expression grew somber. "Hey there," he said, his voice neutral. "I was wondering where you got to."

Alex pushed her stool away from the counter and stood. Meeting him halfway, she put her arms around his waist and hugged him tight.

"We're fine," she whispered. "Just fine."

Hours later, she lay snuggled against Brandon's side, relaxed and content after a slow and sweet session of lovemaking. A balmy breeze drifted across the balcony of Brandon's apartment—*their* apartment—and in through the open window.

It had taken her less than thirty seconds to agree to Brandon's suggestion that she and Sam move in with him.

Sam had taken the news that Brandon was his father with remarkable aplomb. After some initial confusion and a handful of blunt questions, he'd seemed to accept it and now appeared pleased to have a father in his life.

Her mother, of course, had been overjoyed.

Brandon's arm snaked out and drew Alex in close against him. She lay her ear against the warm, naked skin of his chest and listened to the strong, sure sound of his heartbeat. This was how it was meant to be. Brandon was her husband. The father of her child...

He was her heart.

They were home.

NOTE TO READERS

I do hope you have enjoyed reading Brandon and Alex's story. It was a difficult and challenging topic, but as a mother of five pre-teens, the issue of online safety is very much at the forefront of my mind. I love that neither Brandon nor Alex are without flaws. I love to think they could be any one of us, doing their best to live their lives in a good and honest way. Some days that's harder to do than others.

In Book Four of the Munro Family Series, you will meet another Munro brother. **The Betrayal** is Declan Munro's story. You first met Declan in *The Predator* and yes, he's every bit as gorgeous as his brothers. Here's a sneak peek:

When much-decorated Australian Federal Police officer Declan Munro is accused of illegally accessing confidential police files containing child pornography, his world is turned upside down. Fronting the investigation into his alleged criminal behaviour is Senior Internal Affairs Investigator Chloe Sabattini.

A veteran investigator, Chloe is taken aback to discover that not only is Declan likeable, his protestations of innocence are also believable. But the evidence can't be ignored and she vows to investigate the matter with all of the resources available to her.

But the more she delves, the more she's convinced of Declan's innocence. Someone is framing him. But who? And why?

An innocent man's life hangs on the line. Will she discover the truth before it's too late?

The Betrayal will be available in May, 2014. If you would like to receive news on upcoming Munro Family stories, release dates, book launches and other snippets, please sign up for my newsletter at www.christaylorauthor.com.au.

I love to hear from my readers. Please feel free to email me at christaylor@antmail.com.au Let me know who your favorite Munro family member is.

THE MUNRO FAMILY SERIES

THE PROFILER
(Book One – Clayton and Ellie)

THE INVESTIGATOR
(Book Two – Riley and Kate)

THE PREDATOR
(Book Three – Brandon and Alex)

THE BETRAYAL
(Book Four – Declan and Chloe)

THE DECEPTION
(Book Five – Will and Savannah)

THE NEGOTIATOR
(Book Six – Andy and Cally)

THE RANSOM
(Book Seven – Lane and Zara)

THE DEFENDANT
(Book Eight – Chase and Josie)

THE SHOOTING
(Book Nine – Tom and Lily)

THE MAKER
(Book Ten – Bryce and Chanel)

About the Author

Chris Taylor grew up on a farm in north-west New South Wales, Australia. She always had a thirst for stories and recalls writing her first book at the ripe old age of eight. Always a lover of romance and happily-ever-afters, a career in criminal law sparked her interest in intrigue and suspense. For Chris to be able to combine romance with suspense in her books is a dream come true.

Chris is married to Linden and is the mother of five children. If not behind her computer, you can find her doing the school run, taxiing children to swimming lessons, football, ballet and cricket. In her spare time, Chris loves to read her favorite authors who include Richard North Patterson, Sandra Brown, Kathleen E Woodiwiss and Jude Devereaux.